YOU
WON'T
KNOW
I'M
GONE

YOU WON'T KNOW I'M GONE

KRISTEN ORLANDO

Swoon **READS**

Swoon Reads | NEW YORK

A Swoon Reads Book
An imprint of Feiwel and Friends and Macmillan Publishing Group, LLC
175 Fifth Avenue, New York, NY 10010

Our books may be purchased in bulk for promotional, educational, or business use.
Please contact your local bookseller or the Macmillan Corporate
and Premium Sales Department at (800) 221-7945 ext. 5442 or by e-mail
at MacmillanSpecialMarkets@macmillan.com.

Library of Congress Control Number: 2017944699

ISBN 978-1-250-12361-9 (hardcover) / ISBN 978-1-250-12362-6 (ebook)

Book design by Vikki Sheatsley and Eileen Savage

First edition, 2018

1 3 5 7 9 10 8 6 4 2

swoonreads.com

To Samantha:
Little one, you've stolen my heart. I love you so.

ONE

MY EYES FLIP OPEN AND MEET THE BLACK. THERE'S not a trace of pale light in this windowless room. The first two seconds are bliss. With my first conscious breath, I forget. But the next breath comes, tighter this time; that feeling of dread, a dark cloud, a shade deeper than this room, coils its way around my lungs. And I remember where I am. Why I'm here. What I've done.

I was a sound sleeper as a child. Mom said I wet my bed until the age of five, not because I didn't know how to use the bathroom, but because I slept so hard, even that urgent pulse in my bladder couldn't stir me awake. I haven't had a restful night of sleep since I was eight. Not since my parents sat me down over a scalding plate of chicken pot pie and told me what they really did for a living. Those long, dense stretches of shadowy sleep vaporized like the steam off my plate. Even as a kid, I think I was waiting for something bad to happen. I'd startle awake in the middle of the night, listening. Waiting. Watching. My fingers would search for the knife behind my headboard, and only until I felt its cool blade on my skin could I fall back asleep. The pluck and buzz of its steel was my screwed-up lullaby.

For the last six months, there's been no getting me back to sleep. Sam has tried with her tiny blue pills. I let them knock me out night after night because without them I'd never sleep. But once I'm awake, I'm up. There's no lulling me back into the misty gray of drug-induced rest.

I can hear Sam breathing somewhere in the darkness. I shift my weight, searching for her clock, and the military-style bunk bed creaks beneath me. The bright red digital numbers read 4:00 on the dot. It's the first time I've woken up on such a clean number. Last night it was 3:24. The night before: 4:51. The night before that: 5:42. I've been making mental notes of those times, memorizing the numbers, like they're going to mean something or decode some important secret. I know they won't. But locking in those numbers, tracking the time my body jolts me awake, feels like the only thing I've had control of since the fall.

My body slowly rises, my muscles rigid as I try not to make a sound. If Sam wakes up, she'll tell me I need more sleep before the Tribunal. She'll place another blue pill into my palm and stand over me while I choke it down. My feet leave the warm cocoon of blankets and find the icy, concrete floor. Goose bumps rise on my skin as my toes search for my slippers. My hands feel for the sweatshirt at the bottom of the bed, on loan from one of the Black Angel operatives. When the watchers transported me from the safe house yesterday, it was an unseasonably warm April day. Eighty degrees by noon. But several stories belowground, I've lost all sense of warmth. Of time, too.

I carefully pull on the door, cracking it just enough to slip my body through without letting too much hallway light spill into our cavernous, nearly empty dorm. The dorm is where all the female Black Angel trainees sleep when they're stationed at CORE. But their year in the Black Angel Qualifiers is nearly up and most have either been cut or are stationed all over the world, fighting for those last spots in the Black Angel Training Academy.

The sight of the empty hallway forces a cold and steady breath through my pursed lips. When I'm at CORE, all I get are questions in the form of words or looks. The concerned queries may be even worse than the debriefing questions from senior leaders, judgment and anger wrapped like barbed wire around every word. Those, I can handle. The "how are yous" I cannot. It's not even what they say or how they say it. It's the expectant body language that makes the tide of bile rise in my stomach. Head lowered and cocked to one side. Watery eyes. Lips creased into a sympathetic frown. A hand that carefully reaches for my shoulder. Most of the time I pull away. But if I'm feeling compassionate, I let them touch me. I remind myself they've lost her too.

My fingers brush alongside the cinder block walls in the tunnel beneath Langley. Thousands of the world's best spies track terrorists or intercept threats against the United States several stories above my head, having no idea this tunnel, these Black Angel situation rooms and training facilities even exist.

Six months ago, I never thought I'd see the inside of CORE. I was ready to turn my back on the Black Angels, escape into the warmth of a normal life. But now I'm back in the shadows, desperate to reclaim my place here. The people who once applied the most pressure to get me into the training academy are the ones pushing me out. It's been a long fall off the precarious pedestal they forced me upon. And I don't even know if I've hit bottom yet.

"What are you doing up?" a voice says from behind me. I turn around to see Sam mid-yawn, her hands fumbling through her sleep-matted blond hair.

"Can't sleep," I answer quietly. Sam walks toward me in plaid pajama bottoms and an oversized Georgetown sweatshirt.

"You really need your rest," Sam answers, looking toward the digital clock stationed at the end of the hallway. "You've got a long day ahead of you. I could give you half a—"

"No," I answer and shake my head slowly. "I'm fine. No more pills tonight."

Sam's eyes scan my face, her eyebrows raised, not believing me. The crescent gray moons that cradle my dark eyes give away my exhaustion. I lower my eyelids and dig my teeth into my sore, in-flamed lips. I've been picking them again, an anxious tic my mother broke me of years ago. It's like my nerves know she's not here to gently grab my hand, pull it to my side. Without her, I've been pull-ing at long strips of dry skin until my lips are either completely smooth or red with metallic blood. Each tear is a risk with conflict-ing outcomes. There is no in between.

"Well, I guess we're both up for the day," Sam says, taking a seat on the steel bench outside one of the situation rooms. "Breakfast doesn't start for two hours. So come sit with me."

She pats the space next to her. I don't answer. Just stare at the cement floor, my legs pulling me toward her. I grasp the cold, smooth surface and lower myself down. The hallway's fluorescent lights' incessant buzzing burrows into my ear canals, sending a shiver down my body. I pull the collar of my borrowed sweatshirt toward my face and get a whiff of something floral. I breathe it in again, trying to decode the scent of a stranger. Lavender? Or maybe jasmine?

I wait for Sam to speak. She waits for me to do the same. My eyes stare forward at the white cinder block. I count the number of paint globs that hug the curve of each stone. One, two, three, four.

"They're going to tear me apart, aren't they?" I finally ask. In my peripheral vision, I can see Sam's face turn toward mine, but my eyes stare straight ahead, fixed on those tiny white globs.

Sam breathes in a heavy sigh. "I can't lie to you, Reagan. I can't tell you about the questions they asked me either. But my testimony yesterday was . . ."

"Brutal," I answer and suck in a painful breath. She doesn't need to answer. I know it was. I saw it all over her face when she hugged me hello in the dorm after I arrived. She smiled, her voice brimming with forced cheerfulness. But fear lingered in her two pools of blue and no matter how many times her eyes fluttered, she couldn't blink her worry for me away. "It's okay. I already know what will happen. I know they're going to question every single move I made. Pick apart every little choice until they can prove I got her killed."

"Don't say that, Reagan," Sam says and grabs for my wrist. "You did everything you could. You were willing to trade your life for hers. You have to fight to stay here or you're as good as gone. They want you out. You couldn't save her, but you can still save yourself."

"I know," I reply as an icy breath filters through my raw lips. Jagged pieces hit me all at once. That flash of light. That waterfall of blood. Mom's eyes, pleading and afraid. I put my free hand to my face and furiously shake my head, trying to erase the memory before I hear the echo of my own screams.

"But maybe they're right," I continue as the memory breaks apart. "Maybe if I had done one thing differently she'd still be alive. Maybe if I hadn't gotten in a fight with her, they'd have pulled me out of New Albany earlier and Torres would never have found them. Or maybe if I hadn't gone to Colombia at all or stayed on the truck or . . ."

"Stop," Sam says, her warm hands tightening around my freezing skin. "If you hadn't made those choices, they'd *both* be dead."

"Yeah, but maybe if I had let Laz go after her or shot Torres when I had the chance . . ."

"Reagan, no," Sam says, her gentle voice giving way to the beginnings of exasperation. "You can't do this to yourself. You can't or you'll go insane."

"Then I guess I'm insane," I say, my voice monotone. My breath becomes slower, shallower. Soon, the only sound I hear is the *tick, tick, tick* of Mom's favorite watch, which I've kept permanently on my wrist since Colombia; a present from her parents after medical school that she always kept in her go-bag.

Sam's fingers slowly slide off my wrist. She leans her back against the cold, cinder block walls and we settle into a heavy silence.

"I can't believe I'm even here," I say softly, searching up and down the deserted hallway.

"In this position or in this building?" she asks.

"Both, I guess. After all my training. After all the bullshit they've pumped into my head, trying to make me believe I'm special or something. The training camps and pep talks and money they've invested. I can't . . ."

A toxic mix of anger and sadness bubbles up my throat, stealing my voice. I face Sam; her kind eyes urge me to continue.

"I can't believe how fast they've turned on me. You should have seen the look on their faces when I said I still wanted into the academy. You'd have thought I told them I put my own gun to my mother's head."

After days of debriefing post-Colombia, Thomas Crane, my parents' main contact at CORE, and the other senior leaders were ready to hand me my new life, confined to a single manila envelope. New name, new passport, new driver's license, new cover story. Reagan Olson. Seventeen-year-old high school senior with a dead mother and government official father. They had secured a spot for me in a foreign boarding school. Said they'd get me into the University of Oxford or the Sorbonne, far out of the reach of Torres. Provide me with my own security detail. I told them that wouldn't be necessary. That I'd be attending the training academy with the new recruits this summer. With that, every eyebrow in the room rose in unison. Their mouths unhinged. I don't know if they were surprised I still wanted to be a Black Angel after everything that had happened or if they were just stunned by my nerve. I can only imagine what they're saying about me behind closed doors. The girl who breaks every rule, defies orders, gets her mother killed, and still thinks she belongs. Ballsy move, chick.

Thomas had put his hands in his pockets, his eyes fixed on the ground. Seconds ticked by. Perhaps he was waiting for me to say I was joking. How could I imagine I'd still be allowed in? After what I just did?

"That decision is no longer yours to make, Reagan," Thomas

finally said. "You have lost your automatic bid into the training academy. You'll have to plead your case before the Black Angel Tribunal and see if they'll even allow you into the Black Angel Qualifiers. If they let you in, you'll have to try out like everyone else."

And that was that. Only two spots in the training academy are offered to Black Angel children right out of high school, and the female spot that had been promised to me now belonged to someone else. And there was nothing I could do or say to get it back.

After my debriefing, I was shipped off to a farmhouse in rural Virginia. With Torres off the grid and promising revenge, I've spent the last several months cut off from the world, surrounded by security cameras and guards but no real people. Just online high school courses and Netflix to occupy the endless hours alone. Dad and Sam made the two-hour trip to check on me when they could. But my body still ached with loneliness for my mother, for my friends. Luke was whisked off the plane after we landed from South America and transported who knows where. I haven't been allowed to talk to him or Harper or Malika. We are ghosts to one another. Half memories and unanswered questions. It's hard to even think about them. But I'd do it all over again; I'd alienate myself from the world for twice the time for the chance to become a Black Angel. Because it's the only way I will find him. And kill him.

My fate now lies in the hands of five senior leaders. Five votes determine if I'll ever be able to snuff out the rage that flickers at my core. It's a slow-burning ember now, but its smoke has begun to fill my body, choke my lungs. This fire will soon engulf me and won't stop until I put a gun to the head of Santino Torres and watch his crimson blood pool from his brain.

TWO

WHAT IS HE SAYING IN THERE?

My nerves are on fire, heating my body in the chilly underground bunker. The heels of my black, unpolished boots clack against the acid-stained concrete floors, echoing down the East Hall, which is lined with a dozen high-tech situation rooms, several boardrooms, one large lecture hall, and the Tribunal chamber.

I slow my cadence as I walk past the heavy chamber doors. But I hear nothing. Not even muffled debate. It's completely soundproof. Dad has been in there for hours. Over forty minutes longer than they had expected. I glance down at Mom's watch ticking steadily on my wrist. My testimony was supposed to have begun at eleven o'clock. It's nearly noon. What is taking so long? What is he saying about me?

Sweat gathers beneath my armpits and rises to the curve of my neck, and even though it's freezing down here, I wish it was ten degrees cooler. I run my fingers along the front of my carelessly pressed black button-down shirt, silently scolding myself for not taking more time to iron it this morning like Sam insisted.

"So, what are you in for?" a voice says behind me. I turn around to see a boy about my age leaning against the cinder block wall. Well over six feet tall, with dark skin and teddy-bear brown eyes, he's dressed in a crisp, white button-down shirt, navy slacks, and a matching jacket. He catches me eyeing his outfit and smiles. "My mother told me I needed to wear a tie if I wanted to be taken seriously, but I just can't stand those things. Feels like being slowly choked to death."

The skin of my neck singes with a sense memory, panic quickening my pulse. I close my eyes and try to stop it. But it comes anyway. Heavy hands on my neck. The hot spray of spit on my skin. Metallic, bitter blood in my mouth. I see his face, the silvery specks outlining his body and beyond that, black. Death. I bring a hand to my forehead, shielding the terror that must be written on my face, and shake my brain until the memory from Colombia breaks apart.

When I open my eyes, the boy's smile has fallen into a crooked line. I force the corners of my mouth to rise into an I'm-okay-and-not-going-mad smile.

"Yeah, I can see that," I answer, the words louder than I meant them to be. The sound of my own voice catches me off guard because I'm not used to hearing it. At the safe house, I could go days without speaking a single word.

"I'm Cam Conley," he says, walking toward me. "Fellow in-trouble trainee. And you are?"

"I'm Reagan ... Hillis," I say, my voice hesitant, realizing it's the first time I've ever introduced myself using my real name.

"Oh, so you're Reagan Hillis," Cam says, his eyes widening. He offers me his hand, which I quickly shake. His skin is warm.

"You know who I am?" I ask, raising my eyebrows.

"Of course," he answers, pushing his smudged black-rimmed glasses farther up the bridge of his nose. "Everyone knows who you are."

"And why do I feel like that's a bad thing?"

"It's not," Cam replies and shakes his head. "If you're a trainee, you know who the elites are. You're one of the elites. For those of us lower on the totem pole, present company included, we've been compared to you our whole lives."

"By who?" I reply.

"Our parents, leaders at CORE," Cam answers, shrugging his shoulders. "They dangle your names and accolades out in front of us to try and make us better."

"Really?"

"Oh yeah. There's a whole Black Angel hierarchy, but I guess if you're at the top, you don't really need to know that."

"Oh," I reply, my stomach pulling into an unsettling series of knots, my mind suddenly less preoccupied by the Tribunal.

Wonderful. Everyone hates a teacher's pet.

"So," Cam says, leaning casually against the wall again, as if we're just stopping to chat in between classes at school. "What did you do to get in trouble?"

"How do you know I'm in trouble?" I answer and look over at the chamber doors, willing them to swing open so I'll have an excuse to cut this conversation short.

"Anyone who is standing outside the Tribunal chamber is in

11

trouble," Cam says, tilting his chin toward the imposing double doors. "Me? I don't know ten different ways to break a man's neck like you probably do, but I can hack into pretty much any system in the world. I got curious about some files. Swiped my dad's computer, broke into some highly confidential databases one too many times, got caught. And here I am."

"Are you at risk of not making the Black Angel Qualifiers too?" I ask.

"Yeah," Cam answers, nodding. After a moment, his eyes brighten with recognition. "Wait. Are you?"

My head slowly bobs up and down as my teeth dig into my sore bottom lip.

"Holy . . . wow," Cam replies, placing his hands on top of his head. "Reagan Hillis out of the academy and maybe out of Qualifiers. That's hard to believe. So seriously, what did you do?"

A knot of inconsolable sorrow, burrowed beneath my sternum, breaks free and rises up my throat. I expect my mind to float back to that night, but it flips through its mental scrapbook instead, stopping on a page of Mom.

I see her, a shadowy lump on my bed as she tapped, tapped, tapped my favorite doll's arm on my stomach, begging in her silly, high-pitched Mimi voice for breakfast or cartoons. Our special morning ritual when I was particularly grumpy. When I wouldn't move, she'd up her game, cry out, "Mommy, wake up, I've got to go to the bathroom. Mommy, I've really got to go! Mom . . . hurry!" When I still wouldn't stir, she'd plop Mimi's bottom down on my nightgown, make a fake pee sound, and say, "Too late. Sorry, Mom."

It never failed to make me giggle. The thought of it now makes me want to smile. And cry. And scream.

Stop, stop, stop. I slam my mental memory box shut and my face goes numb. *Stupid, stupid, girl*, my mind scolds. My hands cling to the cool surface of the cinder block wall as my entire body inflames. Every inch of me knows. *She's gone, she's gone, she's gone*; my skin pulses with the truth. But my mind refuses to listen. Those words whisper past its edges, never settling, never staying. They can't. Especially not now. I welcome the armor around my brain. I swallow the key to my memory box. Because if I don't, I'll wade into the black until it reaches my knees, my torso, my neck. I've refused to be pulled in by the undertow of grief because I know I'll dive in search of the bottom. I'll want to touch its deepest parts, an ocean under an ocean, and never, ever come back.

"Reagan?" Cam says, his voice soft. I turn my face back toward him and his eyes shift from curious to concern. "I'm sorry. I thought maybe you did something careless like me. I didn't mean to upset you."

"I did something careless too," I reply, the words ragged as they leave my tongue. "And it cost me a lot."

Cam opens his mouth, but before the words can tumble out, the chamber door opens and I can hear my father's angry voice echoing inside. Goose bumps prick and prick and prick. The heat of my blood, the chill of my skin crash and tangle. If my body was a storm front, I'd be a tornado.

He turns and his brown eyes meet mine. The dark, purple bruises that covered his face after Colombia are gone, but the deep cut on his cheek, sewn together in a crisscross of black stitches our first day here, has left a thick, pink scar.

My furious heart still throbs when I see the evidence of his Torres-induced beatings. The corners of my mouth rise with love and concern. I wait for my father to return even the smallest of smiles. He doesn't. His eyes don't warm, his mouth stays frozen in a perfectly straight line, unmoved by my presence.

Those first couple of weeks, I collected about three dozen words between us. A few partial sentences. A couple "I'm sorrys." One mumbled "We'll be okay." He was a mess. He barely spoke to anyone in the safe house in Ecuador. Those first forty-eight hours after Mom died, he sat in the corner, his back against the wall, head in his hands. Cried. Then stared. He left me to be comforted by Luke and Sam and Laz.

These last few months, I've only seen him a handful of times. Too broken to go back on Rescue/Take-down missions without Mom, he's become a senior director at CORE, overseeing special ops missions in the field, traveling God knows where for weeks at a time. When he comes back to DC, he'll show up at the farmhouse unannounced to check on me. He brings me treats I devoured as a kid like Hostess Zingers and Swedish Fish. Sometimes he'll leave magazines on my bed that are a few years too old or a few years too young for me. He asks how I'm doing without really asking because he doesn't want to hear the real answer. And he refuses to talk about Mom.

I thought his coldness, his distance, was because he was shattered. Torn apart without his wife. But looking at his face through the chamber doors, he doesn't look lost or hurt or sad. He looks livid.

At me.

THREE

MY THROAT IS DRY. I TRY TO SWALLOW BUT ALMOST choke, the pain knife-sharp. Saliva won't come quickly enough. I could reach across my table for the pitcher of cold water, its condensation clinging to the curve of the glass. But my hands stay at my sides. I'm afraid they'll pick up on my nerves. Pull at my exposed threads. Unravel me.

The white wooden chair I'm seated in is not meant to hold a body longer than five minutes. I've been inside the Tribunal chamber for half that time and already my tailbone and spine are radiating. The five Tribunal members seated at the long white table in front of me, elevated two imposing steps up, have much softer seats. Modern and sleek, but cushioned and comfortable with high backs and padded armrests. I look around the stark white room and realize I'm the only one in a wooden chair. I wonder if that's part of their strategy. Make her as uncomfortable as possible so she'll give up. Ask to go home. Wherever the hell home is.

"Miss Hillis, as one of the elites, we know you had an invitation to skip Qualifiers and join the training academy right out of high school, but in light of your conduct this past fall, the Tribunal and several senior leaders are questioning whether you are a right fit for the Black Angels after all," says a man with muddy brown eyes and a full head of jet-black hair. His face is chiseled, dimensions perfect, like they were carved out of stone. Stony Face leans forward in his chair, the jacket of his crisp dark suit flapping open. Beneath his tailored shirt is the body of a twenty-five-year-old, but the deep lines around his mouth and the sporadic sparks of gray in his hair give him away. He's in his late forties. Maybe even early fifties. His imposing stature reads Rescue/Take-down team. A seasoned Black Angel. All of them are vets. I'd expect nothing less from something called a "Tribunal."

Two men in suits flank his left, two women to his right. The women are in dresses, one black, one gray, each with matching blazers. The brunette with large gray eyes, one shade lighter than her dress, has a colorful scarf draped around her neck. As my eyes scan the small, cinder-block-enclosed space, I realize that cerulean-blue scarf is the only hue in this room that's not some shade of black, white, or gray.

"There are very serious allegations against you, Miss Hillis," says the woman with the scarf. "Allegations of deceit, of blind insubordination. During our days of testimony, several people said your conduct jeopardized the entire mission—"

"Yes, but if I hadn't been involved—" I begin to speak, to the surprise of the entire Tribunal. A quick rise of Blue Scarf's hand tells me I'm only hurting myself, confirming the damning testimony. Defiant. Rebellious. Rule breaker.

"You will have your turn to plead your case, Miss Hillis," she continues, her voice rising with annoyance. "Now, under normal circumstances, if these allegations were made against a trainee, much less someone who is not even in the program yet, they'd be grounds for immediate dismissal. But you . . . you are Reagan Hillis. I'd be lying if I said that we haven't been watching your progress for years. You've shown immense promise. But talent without respect for authority is fruitless. You've gravely disappointed this Tribunal and all Black Angel agents. We expected much more from you."

"I'm sorry," I whisper, more to myself than to them. Irritation flashes in her icy eyes and silences me again. I lower my head, press my raw lips together, and that hollow cave inside me begins to throb. The moment Torres put a bullet through my mother's skull, it's like I was cut open, a vital organ ripped from my body. My flesh carelessly stitched back together with rusted staples. Now that empty space involuntarily screams with pain. I suck in a full breath, trying to fill the ache with new air, but it whistles through.

"Miss Hillis, the testimony against you has been quite mixed," Blue Scarf says, her hands neatly folded with self-satisfied authority on her table. "We've had to ask a series of tough questions to all of those involved in the mission, including your father. Some say you defied every order given to you and behaved recklessly. Some have defended you and said you were able to see things others couldn't. That if it hadn't been for your actions, others would have died in that field in Colombia. You've had several months to think about your actions. Do you still believe we should consider you for the Black Angel Qualifiers?"

"I wouldn't be here if I didn't," I reply, my voice controlled, strong. "I had a long-standing invitation into the academy. This is where I belong."

"Do you understand why that invitation has been revoked?" Blue Scarf asks, pushing a pair of tortoiseshell glasses farther up her nose.

My teeth chew at the inside of my lip as I scold myself for not coming up with a stronger strategy before walking into the chamber.

"Yes and no," I finally answer. "I went against Black Angel Directives. I knew it then and I know it now. But I broke those rules to save lives. My intention was not to be combative. After what I saw with the blown mission in Kentucky, my instincts just took over. I thought my parents would die without me there to fight for them. So, I did what I thought needed to be done to bring them home alive. My thought process didn't go any further than that."

"See, that's part of your problem," Blue Scarf interjects, her bony finger cutting back and forth through the air, pointing at me. "You don't consider beyond the 'right now.' From the testimony I've heard this week, it seems you only think about yourself."

Selfish girl, my mind whispers. Those words and their synonyms have been used to describe me so many times over the last several months that I have to wonder if they're true. First by my mother back in New Albany. Then on the mission. During my debriefings. Now the Tribunal. Maybe I *am* selfish. For wanting a different life. For fighting so viciously with my parents. For breaking every rule to save them. After the kidnapping, the muscles in my body, primed from years of practice, just took over. I didn't think. Didn't analyze or try to stop myself. Not once. But was it all instincts? Out of love? Or selfishness? To loosen the heavy chains of guilt that would paralyze me if I never got to say I was sorry?

Blue Scarf and the other woman share a glance, pulling me back from my daze.

"I don't really see it that way," I reply and push away the toxic thoughts gnawing at my resolve. "I was thinking about the potential victims in this mission: my parents. I knew my actions could put my status at this agency at risk. But I also knew that I had the skills and the strategic mind to be out there. I knew they needed me. So I went."

"You think very highly of yourself, don't you?" Blue Scarf says, her gray eyes narrowing. "You've been treated for years like you're God's gift so I guess it's only natural."

Sweat pricks once again at the glands underneath my arms, my black shirt clinging tighter to my moist skin. I dig my fingers into my hip bones to stop from exploding. I know that's what she wants. Give them one more reason to throw me out of the Black Angels for good.

"I certainly do not," I reply, trying to keep my voice calm. "I'm not going to lie. I was told growing up that I was born to do this. But I also worked tirelessly to learn every skill. I am a product of the two best trainers in the world. But I still have a lot to learn. I've always felt that way. I'm not God's gift. I'd rather be in the Qualifiers than have that automatic invitation into the academy, if you must know. I want to prove that I deserve to be here."

Blue Scarf looks down at the papers in front of her, scanning through debriefings, testimony notes, her own scribbles. She strikes me as the type of woman who doodles. I can picture her on the phone or in a meeting, clouds and stick figures filling the margins of her notebooks.

"Your combative behavior really started the Saturday your parents got home from their hostage rescue mission in Colombia," she says, looking up at me. "According to your father's testimony, you left the house without the guard and gun they demanded you have, got drunk, stayed out until four in the morning. Came home and got into a screaming fight with them. That doesn't sound like Black Angel material to me. That sounds like the lashing out of a temper-tantrum-prone child."

"Is there a question in there?" I ask, my mouth speaking before my brain can stop it.

"Miss Hillis," Stony Face interjects before Blue Scarf can speak, assault missiles ready to fire behind her sullen lips. He gently touches her arm, a signal to stand down. "We need to understand your mind-set leading up to the mission. We feel that your actions that night were out of character. I think we just want to know why there was a shift?"

My mind circles around that night. Little pieces flicker. The foul taste of Mad Dog. My panic over leaving. My mother's angry eyes. Their disappointment. My disgust.

"I was tired of being kept in the dark. I was sick of my life not being my own. I was done being perfect, because what did I have to show for it? A go-bag full of half memories and places I can never return to. Of friends who don't really know me. I was just pissed off."

The anger. It was always there, silently waiting. I never showed it. I had muzzled it, even when it was pounding at my door. The bitterness ate away at me, like a slow-burning acid. So that night, when the anger knocked for what felt like the thousandth time, I opened the door. I welcomed it in.

"I was foolish. I was defiant," I continue. "I got drunk for the first and last time in my life. I said terrible, terrible things. And I'll have to live with that now."

The back of my skull radiates pain, like being struck from behind by a two-by-four, as I think about some of the last words I said to my mother, so thick with hate. Her eyes, polished emeralds, slick with tears. Her voice whispering guilt and regret. And me, refusing her apology.

"Is that why you want to be a Black Angel now?" Blue Scarf asks, her voice softer, manipulatively leading. "That fight was about you not wanting to do this. So do you want to earn back a spot in the academy to pay your penance?"

"Of course not," I reply quickly, even though I wonder if there are several grains, maybe bushelfuls, of truth in her words. "That mission opened my eyes. It made me realize this is the life I'm meant to lead. I had my doubts. I had anger because it never felt like my choice. But now it is, and I see things so clearly. I don't want to do this to right wrongs or for my mother. I want to be a part of this agency for the thousands of people I know I could help or save. The world will never stop being a dark and horrible place. But maybe I can help provide that sliver of light. Of good."

The words slip out of my mouth with such ease, I cannot separate the truth from the pretender; the calculating liar they've trained me to be. I've been able to talk my way into and out of any situation for years. So how much of what I say is real? And how much is just to get to Torres?

For the next two hours, they grill me about my actions in the Ohio safe house, in Colombia. And I tell the truth. I defied my superiors. I manipulated my way across the border. I let my emotions carry me out of that truck and across that field.

"Why did you put down your gun in the storage room?" Blue Scarf asks, her eyes heavy, as if she's having difficulty computing what I've done.

The energy it takes for me to not think about Torres's cold, damp basement could power CORE's entire compound. If I didn't tether my mind, those moments would play on repeat forever. But with each question, the shattered pieces rise, sliding back into place.

"They were so close together, I couldn't get a clean shot on him," I reply and clear my stinging throat. "There was no way he was going to let her go. But I thought perhaps he'd be willing to trade. He wanted me. He came for me first. His revenge killing. He wanted to see them suffer so I gave him what he wanted. I put down my gun and offered myself up in exchange for her life."

My mother, with all her bravery and talent and kindness, could do so much more in the world than I ever could. She should have lived. I should have died. The world is a much scarier place without her here to protect it. Protect me.

"But he killed her anyway," Blue Scarf says, as if I didn't know.

"Yes. He did."

My nose wrinkles, filling with a rancid sense memory. I take in another breath, but there it is again, gunpowder and wet metal.

Blood. The scent will hit me out of nowhere. Making coffee. Brushing my teeth. The smell even wakes me, from one nightmare and into another. It's like those molecules burrowed themselves deep into my nasal passage that night.

I can't stand this pain in my throat any longer. I reach across the table, trying to steady my hand as it pours a glass of water. I wonder if Blue Scarf can see my controlled tremble. I bring the liquid to my lips, open my throat, and down it in one gulp.

When I look up, Blue Scarf is leaning back in her chair. Her arms are crossed, examining me.

"I am sorry, you know," she says and my body freezes. She registers the shock on my face, the right side of her mouth rising with a sympathy I had yet to see. "We have to ask you tough questions here, Reagan. But I'm sorry for what you've had to go through."

"Thank you, ma'am," I reply, my voice even scratchier than before. Her gray eyes hold mine, a sudden sadness passing between us. And I wonder how well she knew my mother. If they were friends. If they talked about me. If she knew my chubby five-year-old face from the crinkled photo my mother always carried with her.

Blue Scarf leans forward, breaking our connection, snapping back into her role of senior leader. She looks down at her notes and then back up at me. "Do you consider your actions reckless?"

My lips purse and push to one side as I think about my answer. I knew this would be a question they would ask me. You'd think I'd have a clear idea about what I want to say. I don't. So I try the truth again.

"Well, I only wanted to do good," I answer. "I know my actions might look out of control or reckless. But I thought I was doing the right thing. I didn't care if I died that night. I only cared about them living. So if I was reckless, then I am sorry. I just wanted to save my father. Save my mother. And I failed."

The last words ripple as they hit the air. My aching throat burns with unwelcomed tears. My fingers search for the double heart pendant on my wrist, Mom's bracelet hidden beneath my shirt. *I will not cry. I will not cry.*

Blue Scarf's face has changed again. Her eyes flick up at me, sorrowful. She takes off her glasses, pinching the bridge of her nose. She asks her question with a tentative voice. "One last thing. Do you think your actions contributed to the death of Agent Hillis?"

"What?" my thin voice squeezes out before her question steals the rest of my breath. A shiver stabs at my skin and I struggle for new air. It enters my lungs in panicked gulps and I'm back in Torres's basement. I see his manic eyes. The way her body fell, almost in slow motion, onto the dirty mattress. I feel her blood on my hands, sticky and still warm.

Did you kill her? Did you kill her? Did you kill her?

"I'm sorry," she finally says, looking down at the table and breaking our stare. "It's a question we've had to ask every person that has testified."

"And have people actually said I did? Have they said my actions got my mother killed?"

"The truth?" Blue Scarf asks, her eyebrows rising like two question marks over her glasses. I nod. "Some said absolutely not. But a few others believe had it not been for your conduct, your mother would still be alive today."

My lips release a quivering breath. My throat convulses,

choking down tears. The grays and blacks and whites in this room swirl until I can't distinguish one contrasting color from the next. That question follows my every waking moment. But it's the first time someone said out loud what my heart already knew.

"Can I ask one thing?" My thin voice rattles, trying to swallow back the sobs threatening at the base of my throat. "What did my father say? Did he say yes? Did he say I got my mother killed?"

Blue Scarf turns toward Stony Face, pressing her slender lips together until they all but disappear. The look my father gave me in the hallway is the only answer I should need. But their loaded silence puts a period at the end of that painful declaration.

Finally, Blue Scarf turns back to face me. "You know we cannot reveal the answers to top secret testimony, Miss Hillis," she answers, cocking her head to one side. "I'm sorry, but I still need an answer. Do you think your actions contributed to the death of your mother?"

Your mother. Not Agent Hillis. Not Elizabeth. Perhaps Blue Scarf meant the term to be less harsh. But the question pierces, the word *mother* thrusting the knife deeper. And that hollow spot begins to shriek. I scan their faces. Ten anxious eyes stare back at me, awaiting my answer.

"I ask myself that question pretty much once every sixty seconds." I bite my lip, push my hand into the flesh of my stomach, trying to redirect the agony so I can get through this. "And still, I can't give you a straight answer. Maybe. Maybe if I hadn't gone after her alone, we could have freed her. Maybe if I'd done just one thing differently, she'd be alive. Even after this investigation, after you make your decision, I'll still be asking myself that question. Perhaps not every sixty seconds, but at least every day."

I pause, trying to imagine a life where that question doesn't slip into my thoughts every minute, every hour. I wonder if that will ever happen. Or if I'm just kidding myself.

"I do know one thing," I continue, my hands digging deeper into my stomach, fingering organs and stealing my breath. "If I hadn't run into that field, if I hadn't disobeyed orders and gone down to Colombia, she'd still be dead. And my father would be dead too. I ran toward the gunfire when everyone else was ready to run away. And it wasn't just because those were my parents tied up in that barn. It's because I was taught you don't leave people behind. I jumped out of that truck, I ran into that house, even though I knew I could die. So if that doesn't make me Black Angel material, I don't really know what you're looking for. A perfect person who makes no mistakes but also takes no risks? Who cares more about Directives and procedures than the lives of their targets? If those are the type of people you want in this agency, then you're right. Maybe I don't belong here after all."

Blue Scarf holds my eyes for a few silent seconds, then nods dismissively. My signal to leave.

"We'll have a decision for you later today," she says as I stand up. "Good day, Miss Hillis."

As I walk toward the door, all I can see is my father's face, standing in this exact spot after his own damaging testimony. I should have seen his betrayal then. I may be his daughter. But I killed his wife. Didn't I?

Before I can reach the door, the quiver starts at my breath, then my lips, spreading until every part of me is pulsing and shaking. I want Luke. I want Sam. But most of all, I want my mother.

Don't do this here. Don't do this here.

My body carries me out the door to the hallway. I get about ten steps before my shaking legs give out and I collapse onto the steel bench outside the chamber.

How could he? How could he?

Pain radiates through every part of me. My hands ball into tight fists and curl into my heaving stomach. And for the first time in months, I feel the crushing weight of my mother's death. With one more breath, that hollow spot inside me rattles, then explodes, its black poison spreading, its tormenting burn searing me from the inside out, until all I want is to follow her into the darkness.

"Reagan," a voice says, my hands suddenly enveloped into a pair of warm palms. I look up and Cam is seated at my side, my own face reflected back in his concerned eyes. And what he must see cannot be good. "Are you okay? What can I do? Who should I call?"

"No one," I reply quickly, shaking out my head and sucking down the emotions I so foolishly let out of their little box. I sniff back the tears that scratch against my throat and stand up quickly, pulling my hands from his grasp. "There's no one to call."

No one. I have no one.

As I turn down the hall, I can feel my chance of making the Qualifiers slipping away, and with it, Torres's heartbeat grows stronger in my ear. I can see his face. Laughing, drinking, killing. Living, as my mother's body grays with decay. I close my eyes, take in an unsteady breath, and embrace that black cloud of dread, that whisper of certain doom.

FOUR

STEAM RISES FROM MY COFFEE CUP, LICKING MY FACE.
I lean closer, trying to feel its heat, but my nerves have shut down. My
entire body, numb. Feeling nothing is the only way I can survive.

I stare into the black and blow, rippling the liquid, before adding
my milk. The white hits the dark center, exploding into a delicate,
creamy cloud. CORE doesn't have my beloved Splendas. Just sugar.
I drop in three cubes. They enter the scalding drink with a trio of
plops.

A hand touches my right shoulder and I immediately tense. I've
been waiting for a member of the Tribunal to come and get me for
hours. Summon me to the chamber to hear their final decision.

"Why so jumpy?" a rich, honeyed voice asks. I turn around. Laz.

"I thought you were Thomas or one of the senior leaders," I
reply and my tense shoulders fall. Laz has such a calming presence.
On the mission in Colombia, he was the only one who believed I
belonged there. The only one who put my worried and racing mind
at ease.

"I was hoping I'd see you before I left," he says, his eyes smiling even though his lips do not.

"You're leaving?" I reply, and reach up to touch his large hand, his long fingers straddling my collarbone and shoulder blade. "But I haven't gotten to see you at all."

"I know," he says with a nod. "Duty calls. Taking one of the agency's jets back down to Colombia. I just wanted to say good-bye. I hope they let you in, Reagan. I fought hard for you. You deserve to be here. Don't let them make you think anything less."

"I don't know, Laz," I say and shake my head. "Maybe they're right. Maybe I was reckless. Maybe I did get my mother killed."

"*Niña*," Laz answers with a gasp. "No. How can you believe that?"

"My own father said I did," I reply, my tongue growing thick with the heavy truth.

"I don't believe it," Laz says. "You are one of the most fearless people I know. You *are* a Black Angel. And if they don't let you in, they are fools."

The corners of my mouth involuntarily curl. I stand, rise on my tippy toes, and wrap my arms around his thick neck.

"Thank you for fighting for me," I say into his shoulder as his arms tighten around my rib cage.

"You're someone worth fighting for." He pulls out of our hug and pats my cheek. Fatherly. Way more fatherly than my own has been. "I spoke nothing but the truth."

"I hope they let me in so I get to see you again," I say and grab at his wrist. "I don't want this to be good-bye."

"It would be an honor to serve with you," Laz says and slides his hand into mine. "You're a strong, special girl. You'll be okay. I'll continue to pray for you."

He leans in and presses his warm lips to the apple of my cold cheek, leaving behind a kiss.

"I'll take all the prayers I can get right now," I reply as he pulls away.

"*Dios te escucha*," Laz says, his index finger pointing up toward the heavens, then back down to his ear. And the déjà vu of that moment knocks me backward. Laz tightens his grip on me as my body momentarily bows.

"You said that to me in Colombia," I reply, regaining my balance. Three Spanish words burned on my brain. He said them just moments before the team jumped from the back of the truck and into the Colombian night. He was whispering, praying. Inviting me to pray with him.

"I know. And it's still true," he answers. He looks me up and down, making sure I'm steady, before letting go of my hand to pick up the black bag at his feet. "It's okay to pray, Reagan. God hears you."

I wanted to believe him then. And I want to believe him now. But I don't. God didn't hear my prayers in Colombia. He didn't save my mother. He didn't take me with her. I doubt he'll hear me now.

Laz walks toward the exit, weaving his way through the tightly packed round Formica tables of the cafeteria. There's only two other agents in the cafeteria, lingering over an early dinner together. They're young, maybe mid-twenties. I've seen the woman before. Once in the hallway and once in the bathroom. She's given me a polite smile, an awkward nod, but that's been the extent of it. People don't know what to say to me. So they don't say anything at all.

When he reaches the door, Laz turns and looks back at me, his hand raised in a silent good-bye. I take him in. His weathered skin. The slick braid that swings between his shoulder blades. The wrinkles that explode like fireworks around the corners of his dark eyes when he smiles. I file those pieces of him away in case this really is good-bye. I hold up my hand one second too late. His head is already down. He slips through the door and is gone.

I stand, my hand frozen in the air, waving to no one. I'm finally around people and they're leaving me one by one. Laz, soon Sam. She'll be shipped out on a mission before week's end. Life keeps moving while mine feels like it's been permanently stamped with a red and blotchy TBA. Undetermined and undefined.

The uneasy knot pulls tighter in my stomach as I sit back down. I bring my coffee to my lips. It's barely lukewarm. I gulp the tepid liquid, anxious for another hot cup. As I stare back down into the swirls of caramel, I think of Luke, wishing he was sitting next to me. When I'm alone at the farmhouse, sometimes I pretend he's there. I'll hear the creak of the old wood floors and tell myself it's him in the other room. When I can't sleep, I imagine the weight of his arms around my body. And when I'm feeling particularly lonely, I set out an extra coffee cup at breakfast. I pretend I see him out of my peripheral vision eating toast at the kitchen counter while I watch the morning news.

The watchers had rushed Luke off the plane in Virginia with such aggression, my body seized with dread. I jumped out of my seat, trying to follow them, but Laz held my arm, forcing me still.

"Where are you taking him?" I yelled, my eyes filling with fresh tears. But no one answered me. The jet fell silent. Luke looked over his shoulder as he reached the doorway and my heart pounded as I took in his final fragments, memorized his whole. As my eyes traced the long lashes that surrounded his pools of cornflower blue, all I could think about was the golden hour; those fleeting minutes before a summer sunset, when the world is warm and everything the light touches turns to magic. That's the way Luke always made me feel. And as he was led by the arm out that jet door, they took away my spot of golden sun, my trace of magic. And the world never felt so cold.

I ask, but they won't tell me where he is or what's happened to him. His whereabouts are classified. I wonder if he's still in New Albany with his family or if they've all been moved to a safe house, hidden away from Torres and his army of assassins. I wonder if he's lonely. If he misses me. If he's safe.

"Reagan." I hear my name from behind me. I turn to see Thomas standing a few feet away. "They're ready for you."

The tiny trace of warmth the thought of Luke brings to my body disappears. I try to jump up, but that agonizing knot in my stomach loops and loops and loops until it's so large, it crushes my lungs, anchors me down.

"Okay," I finally reply, my voice thin from lack of oxygen.

Move, Reagan. Move. My nerves fire and my body finally reacts. I stand and follow Thomas. My legs add ten pounds with every step, wobbling my limbs as we walk around the high-security intel center at the heart of the compound and turn down the East Hall. I try to keep up with Thomas's brisk pace, but my feet feel like they're melting into sticky puddles on the concrete. As we get to the steel, soundproofed doors, the thick barrier doesn't even matter. My heart is beating so loudly in my ears, I can't even hear Thomas say, "Go on in." I only know because I can read his lips.

My hand reaches for the icy handle. I pull down and walk inside.

"Good evening, Miss Hillis," Blue Scarf says as soon as I enter the room. Her eyes dart toward my horrible wood chair. "Please take a seat."

The word *please* comes out gravelly. A command rather than an invitation. I quickly pull out the chair and settle in. As she rifles through her papers, my fingers grab at Mom's double heart charm beneath my shirt, my hurried heart beating a staccato prayer. *Please God. Please God. Please God.*

"Miss Hillis, we've had a very long, very heated debate about your conduct. Both before your parents' kidnapping and your questionable actions in Colombia," Blue Scarf begins. "Now, we are not happy with what you've done. Nor will we ever fully understand your actions. But we can sympathize with them. We think . . . well, some of us think . . . that you were acting on the instincts taught to you by your parents and that, with proper training, you could become the agent we had all hoped for. That being said, this Tribunal has accepted you into the Black Angel Qualifiers."

My hands involuntarily rise to my face and cover my smiling mouth; a rush of heat streaks across my chilled cheeks and my cramping shoulders sink with relief. *Oh my God. I'm in.*

"We need you to understand, this was a very close vote. We have reaccepted you but with some very big caveats," Blue Scarf

33

continues and my hands and smile fall. "Once you enter the Qualifiers in June, you will have to try out just like everyone else. And the senior leaders will be watching your every move."

Great. I bite down on my lip to stop my chest from ballooning with a sigh.

"You'll be admitted into the Qualifiers on probation," Blue Scarf continues, fiddling with the fabric tied in a loose bow around her neck. "Most trainees get two warnings and a term of probation before being kicked out. But not you. *This* is your second chance. Do you understand?"

"Yes, ma'am," I reply with a robotic nod, my body already flinching back into old Reagan mode: obedient, respectful—a rule follower, not breaker. If I want to make it through my year in the Qualifiers and gain access to the intel I'll need to hunt down Torres, a life of numbness, of feeling half dead, is the price I'll gladly pay for revenge.

"We need you to move into CORE immediately," she says, looking me up and down the way Sam does during her monthly visits to the safe house, her eyes far more judgmental than Sam's. I've caught flashes of my reflection in passing mirrors but haven't wanted to study myself. I've seen enough to know I don't look good. My skin is gray. My cheeks are gaunt. You could create a birdbath out of my hollowed collarbones. I haven't weighed myself, but I wouldn't be surprised if I've lost at least fifteen pounds. I'm a waify shell of my former self.

"You haven't trained properly in months," Stony Face asserts, his eyes studying me. "We know this has been a difficult time for you with the loss of your mother, but you are in no shape to be a

Black Angel. You've clearly lost muscle mass. You've lost significant strength. If you even want to compete, you better get your butt in gear and fast. Everyone who comes into Qualifiers is in peak condition. And the way you look now, you wouldn't even make it through a day."

He's right. I don't even know if I'd make it through a workout. I've been so consumed with just getting through each day, I haven't thought about actually making it through Qualifiers. The competition will be fierce. And if I don't get in shape, I'll be laughed out the door before lunch.

"Okay. I'll pack my gear and be back here tomorrow. Thank you for this opportunity," I continue with a small, respectful smile. "I will not disappoint you. I promise."

"Here's hoping," Blue Scarf replies flippantly, her body settling into a deep, vexing sigh.

Yes. Here's hoping.

FIVE

TAP. TAP. TAP.

The sound of tree branches scratching at my bedroom window pulls my body away from the neatly folded stacks of T-shirts, yoga pants, and workout bras on my bed. I wander over to the pane of glass that separates me from the swirling wind and impending spring storm. I instinctively pull the open flaps of my zip-up hoodie tighter around my body as lightning brightens the dreary night sky.

One Mississippi. Two Mississippi. Three Mississippi.

The thunder rumbles, three seconds and three miles away. Or at least that's what my father taught me when I was little. I always find myself counting the seconds between that crack of light and boom of thrashing clouds.

Lightning flashes in the distance again, illuminating the acres of farmland behind the safe house as rain begins to fall. The temperature has fallen nearly twenty degrees since I left DC after the Tribunal. I guess that's April weather for you.

When I arrived back, I built my last fire in the wood-burning fireplace. I've never lived in a house with a real fireplace before. I know I'll find it difficult now to return to the hiss of gas and frozen, fake logs. I've grown to love the crack and pop of the wood. The sparks. Even the smell. I'll miss that fireplace most of all when I leave home.

Home, my mind repeats as I pull myself away from the window. I trace the corners of my impeccably decorated room. Mercury glass nightstands bookend my queen-sized bed. A small, gray linen chair with silver studs sits beneath a wide-framed window; a tiny metal table, artfully stacked with books I've never read at its side. It's a beautiful room. A stunning house. But it's constantly cold. Unfailingly impersonal. I've touched everything with care. Like I'm a permanent guest in someone else's home, someone else's life. I've moved around so much, I've never attached the idea of "home" to a residence. But it never felt quite like this before. As I sit down on my bedspread, I look over at the sterling silver picture frame of my mother and me on my nightstand and realize that she was more than a person. She was a place. A feeling. *She* was home.

I tear my eyes away from her wide smile, that hollow spot inside me pounding back to life. I dig my fingers into my jagged hip bones, redirecting the pain. Lightning pulses outside, but before I can count the seconds for the thunder, I hear the front door open downstairs. My body flinches into a standing position, my eyes quickly scan the room, making mental notes of all my weapon hiding places. *Gun beneath the wardrobe. Knife behind the headboard.* Even with two watchers guarding the house 24/7, I can't stop my muscles from tensing with every new sound, never knowing who is on the other side of the disturbance in this constantly silent space.

I hear the sound of keys being thrown in the bowl at the center foyer table, which means it's one of two people: Sam. Or my father.

Shit.

"Sam?" I call out my bedroom door, my fingers crossed behind my back with childlike delusion. As if that could change the fate of who is really in the hallway.

"No, it's me." My father's gruff voice carries up the stairs.

"Double shit," I say under my breath, anxiety piercing my lungs. The delicate lining of my throat swells as I think about his face from earlier today, the anger in his eyes. The furious accusations on his lips inside that chamber. He's about the last person in the world I want to see.

"Will you come downstairs, please?" he calls.

"Just a minute," I yell back and turn toward my transparent reflection against the darkened window. Lightning flashes against the dark sky.

One Mississippi. Two Mississippi.

Thunder rattles the window frame. The storm is getting closer.

As I tiptoe toward the door, I can hear Dad opening and closing plastic bins in the living room. By the time I returned after the Tribunal, the safe house was in the midst of being packed up. I can hear the clanking of glass and porcelain, like he's looking for something.

Just go. Just go, my mind encourages me as I force my body to move.

My legs carry me out of my room, down the creaky, steep staircase and into the cozy foyer. I cross the front hall and poke my head through the threshold that leads into the tastefully decorated living room. Dad is sitting on the royal blue sofa, still dressed in his CORE leadership attire (a button-down shirt and tie), rummaging through a bin marked "kitchen." It's packed with much-too-fancy stemware and flamboyant polka-dotted coffee cups. Mom would have hated this collection of dishes. She'd have declared their splashes of color "tacky." She'd have them sent back. The ornate crystal wine and champagne glasses too. Mom liked understated. Classic. Timeless.

"What are you looking for?" I ask coolly as I step into the room. A log shifts in the fireplace and a cluster of sparks float toward the chimney.

"Just looking for my college coffee mug," Dad replies without bothering to turn around. "These things belong to CORE. I don't want it shipped off to the next safe house."

I cross the room and delicately lower myself onto a white driftwood wingback chair near the fireplace as Dad pushes aside clumps of beige wrapping paper and colorful mugs. Finally, he pulls out his Air Force Academy mug and holds it up with a self-satisfied smile.

"Got it," he announces, placing it on the marble coffee table in front of him.

"They certainly don't waste any time getting everything packed up," I declare as I peer into an open box marked "holiday," filled with colorful bulbs. CORE decorated the house for Christmas with fresh greenery, bowls of cinnamon-scented pinecones, and an eight-foot tree artfully decorated with gold ribbons and glittering bulbs. Our family decorations never made it on the branches. I never asked what happened to my favorite ballerina ornament or the sequined Styrofoam cup I made in first grade. I was too afraid of the answer. Even without our family decorations, someone at CORE went to a lot of trouble to make the safe house feel homey. They even hung stockings on the mantel. But this year, they only hung two. A needless reminder of who was missing. I took them down and threw them in the back of the hall closet, wishing they hadn't hung them at all.

"So, did you come all this way for a thirty-year-old mug?" I ask as Dad busies himself with refastening the bin lids at his feet. He has yet to look at me. Which is nothing new. He probably thinks he earns fatherly points by checking in on me, but most of the time, it's like we're not even in the same room. His body language, bull-shit excuse for father-daughter chats (always surface-level topics like school and the weather), and the way he rarely looks at me, let alone touches me, shows me in no uncertain terms "I'd rather be anywhere but here." Sometimes, I wish he'd do us both a favor and just stay away.

"It's a nice mug," Dad replies, finally glancing up at me, his eyes a bit kinder than this morning. "But I didn't drive two hours for a mug. I'm leaving in the morning to head up a Black Angel terror-ism task force in Europe."

"Do you know how long you'll be gone this time?"

Dad shrugs and scans the coffee table's choice of magazines. "Three months? Six months? I'm not really sure. That's why I came out. I wanted to say good-bye. And, well . . . and I guess wish you good luck at Qualifiers."

Dad settles into his spot on the couch, mindlessly thumbing through a month-old copy of *Time* magazine. One I know he's al-ready read. Fury eats away at my center. *How could he? How could he?* My mind repeats today's broken record. My lungs swell, heavy and tender with thin air. It's hard to breathe near him. It's hard to *be* near him.

"So is this the way we're going to do this?" I finally ask after what feels like hours of sitting across from each other, and worlds apart.

Dad clears his throat and loudly turns the page of his magazine before grumbling, "Is this the way we're going to do what?"

"I don't know, live," I answer quickly, my voice teetering on annoyance.

"I don't know what you're talking about," he answers, his voice almost sleepy, his continued indifference singeing my flesh.

My heart pumps my blood faster and faster, angry and hot. Of course he'd say that. Act confused despite his Mensa genius level IQ. Sit on the couch like everything is fine. That's the Hillis way.

"How can we just sit here and pretend like today never happened?"

"I'm not pretending anything, Reagan," he replies, shaking his head and pulling his magazine closer to his face.

"Bullshit," I declare, and before I can stop myself, I've leapt off the chair and pulled the magazine out of his hands, ripping it at each corner. Dad doesn't move; his eyes stare down, stunned. And as I throw the magazine back on the coffee table, I'm a little stunned myself.

"Jesus Christ, Reagan," Dad finally replies, his hands smoothing the wrinkled pages, handling last month's news with more care than me. "What has gotten into you?"

"Don't play dumb," I reply, anger bubbling up my throat,

altering my voice. "Are we seriously going to sit here and pretend like what you said in the Tribunal today didn't happen?"

"What exactly do you want from me?" Dad asks, closing the magazine, still not looking at me. "It's over. You're in. What more is there to talk about?"

"Oh, I don't know. How about the fact that you almost damned me to a life outside the Black Angels? Or that you didn't defend me when they asked if I got Mom killed?"

"I did defend you," he starts and I cut him off.

"Not according to the Tribunal," I reply. "They told me some people testified that they believed my actions got Mom killed. And when I asked them if one of the people was you, they didn't deny it. And it was written all over their faces. You said yes. How could you say that about me?"

"I didn't say that you got your mother killed." My father's voice rises.

"Then what did you say?"

"I said I didn't know."

"A passive-aggressive, noncommittal answer like that is just as bad as you saying yes. In fact, I'd rather you had just said yes. Then at least I'd know for sure where you stood."

"How can you be so selfish?" Dad's voice soars as he stands up from the couch and begins gathering up his coat. "How dare you fight with me? You know I'm still grieving your mother."

"Well, so am I!" I yell and point to the center of my chest. "This didn't just happen to you, you know."

"Reagan, what is your problem?" Dad is now screaming back at me.

"Are you serious, Dad?" I yell again, my hands shaking and thrown over my head. "Mom is dead and the last person I have left can't even look at me. You can barely stand to be around me. So what was the plan? Get me kicked out of the Black Angels and shipped off to some foreign college where you'll only have to see me once or twice a year? Is that why you betrayed me? To get rid of me?"

"Don't you dare use that tone with me, young lady," he yells, his trembling index finger pointed at me. "I am still your father. And more importantly, now I'm your superior. I'm your boss."

"Fine. That's how I'll think of you from now on," I reply, my voice settling into an indifferent calmness. "Why are you even here? Shouldn't you be at CORE? Boss?"

"I thought my daughter would like to say good-bye to me before I leave for God knows how long," he replies, throwing his jacket over his wrinkled button-down shirt and loose tie. "Look, you want the truth? You want to know what I really said in there?"

"Yes," I answer, my arms crossing over my chest as I settle back down in my chair.

"When they asked me if I thought your actions killed Mom, I didn't know what to say," Dad says, his hands held out in the air. "I know you loved your mother. I know you were only trying to help her. But I don't know because I wasn't there. I didn't see it happen. I gave a nonanswer. Sue me. But when they asked me if you should still be allowed to try out for the Black Angels, you know what I said to them? I said no. Because truthfully, Reagan, I don't know if you're the right fit for the team anymore. I don't know if you belong there. You defied orders. You were combative and reckless and

43

went against everything we taught you. I didn't betray you by saying you got your mother killed. I would never say that. But I did testify that I no longer believed you deserved the right to call yourself a Black Angel. So if that's betrayal, then I betrayed you. But you're right about one thing. Sometimes, I can't stand to look at you. You remind me of her. And that hurts too much."

My breath catches in my chest as the truth slides from his body, foul and obese with despair. My eyes sting as I tear myself away from his broken face.

I swallow hard at the rigid, thickening lump in my throat; sobs rattle the center of my chest. *I will not cry. I will not cry.*

"It may not even matter," Dad says, pushing aside the boxes at his feet as he clears a path toward the door. "From the looks of you these days, I don't even know if you'll make it past the first round. The Tribunal may be playing politics right now. Letting you in to save face even though they know . . . you'll be cut before the first week is over. So good luck. You just might need it."

Screw you, my mind screams, and it takes every ounce of energy not to shove him out of the room or burst into tears. My lower jaw trembles as he grabs his coffee mug and heads for the door. My teeth sink into my quivering lip as I hear him walk across the foyer, grab his keys, and open the front door. He slams the heavy wood door behind him, its crack echoing throughout the empty house.

One Mississippi. Two Mississippi.

It's only when I hear his key turn and lock me inside that the tears start to fall. They come fast and hot, my lungs gasping for new air that won't come quickly enough. My stomach throbs; my body doubles over and falls to the floor. I want to be as low to the ground as possible. I fear if I stand up, I'll fall farther and farther toward the center of the earth.

My sweatshirt has opened up and these old wood floors are freezing. I army-crawl closer to the fireplace, my tears turning into loud, full-body sobs. The kind of heaving cries you have as a little kid when you fall and hurt yourself and nothing can make you feel better. My lips and chest convulse. I cannot breathe. And all I want is my mother.

She dies over and over again. Every hour of every day. And I just want this torment to stop, this grief, this life to be over. I feel like I'm walking around, grasping at the fractured pieces of myself that keep falling from my body. I try to put myself back together, but I can't. Nothing seems to fit or wants to stay. So I just keep picking up the slivers, hugging them to my chest, the splinters of my former self glittering in my hands. But my father cannot see them. He doesn't see that I'm falling apart. On the outside, I look whole. And I just want him to see me. I want him to understand how messed up I am. Just care. Just give a shit.

My shaking fingers reach for a gold bulb inside the holiday box. I pluck it from its pile and hold it in my hands, staring at my mutated reflection in the painted glass. And before my overanalytical brain can stop me, I hurl it into the fireplace. It shatters into a million pieces, the glass popping and sputtering in the heat. I pick up a green bulb and throw. Then a red bulb, a purple bulb, a blue bulb, a silver bulb. I throw and throw and throw. They shatter against the painted brick inside the fireplace; the broken pieces ignite and scatter like New Year's Eve confetti. I cry and scream and throw until I cannot reach any more bulbs from my crumpled spot on the ground.

When there are no more bulbs, I look down at my body. Tiny, colorful shards of glass prick at my legs. But I don't feel them. All I feel is the searing ache at the hollow spot inside me, tripling in size.

Lightning flashes outside. I take in a breath with each new count.

One Mississippi. Two Mississippi. Three Mississippi... Four... Five.

The thunder never answers. The storm, swift and fierce, is gone.

SIX

MY SHOULDERS SCREAM WITH EQUAL PARTS PAIN AND desperation as I drag my feet through CORE's labyrinth they call a compound and toward the girls' dormitory. Two Black Angel–sanctioned duffel bags pull at my collarbones, each shoved full of clothing. The zipper's teeth strain against the bulge of jeans, yoga pants, T-shirts, sports bras, and underwear. The over-packing is not due to vanity. I think I have one cute outfit in my whole trainee wardrobe, rolled up into a ball somewhere at the bottom. But when I don't know what to expect, my type-A side plans for every scenario. Will I need a bathing suit at Qualifiers? A baseball cap? A pair of running spikes? I don't know. But they're in there just in case.

I make my way around the intel center and turn down the South Hall, home to over twenty-five permanent residents and dozens of visiting or displaced agents. CORE's underground acres are divided up into four very long hallways with the highly guarded and top secret intel mission control room at its center. Just being an agent won't get you inside. You must have the highest level security clearance. I imagine it's wall-to-wall screens with satellite images, video surveillance teams, and intercepted messages, each screen picked apart and analyzed by a talented, diverse team of agents whose median IQ has to be over 170.

The East Hall is lined with a situation rooms, boardrooms, lecture halls, and the Tribunal chamber. The North Hall is where they house all the training facilities: several martial arts rooms, a state-of-the-art gym, a twenty-person shooting range, a weapons room stacked with thousands of weapons (from M4 carbines and Beretta M9 pistols to MK19 grenade machine guns and XM2010 sniper rifles. Not to mention enough ammunition for a small army), and an enormous panic room with steel-and-concrete walls ten feet deep (as if this bunker wasn't enough). Down the West Hall are tiny pockets that make CORE feel a little bit like home. A hundred-seat cafeteria where a small team of chefs prepare high-protein meals, a library full of books and magazines, a tiny bar with low lighting and high-end liquor, and a rec room with plush couches, a large-screen TV, Ping-Pong, and pool table.

My legs carry me past the closed doors of the boys-only dorm room, the tiny single bedrooms of high-ranking CORE officers, and the gender-divided bathrooms. The communal bathrooms at CORE look exactly like the ones I saw during my college tour at Templeton except for one luxury. Next to the row of shower stalls is a large sauna. After hours in the compound's martial arts studios, weight rooms, and training circles, a sore body needs some heat and steam.

When I reach the girls' dorm at the end of the hallway, it's dark and empty. My hand feels along the cinder block wall for the light switch and flips it on. Twelve neatly made beds are lined up, ready for the influx of trainees for Qualifiers in June. As I scan the room, I'm surprised to see two duffel bags at the bottom of one of the bunk beds. *Hmm. Who else is here?*

I cross over to the bottom bunk bed in the corner where I slept next to Sam before the Tribunal. My heavy bags fall to the floor with a duo of loud thumps as I collapse onto the mattress. The bed whines beneath my weight and the sense memory of that sound brings me back to my testimony in that chamber, the fight with my father. All the emotions I've clubbed and dragged and buried seep from that hollow spot in my stomach, and my head pounds as I push away the sorrow tickling at the back of my throat.

"Well, hi there, roomie," a voice greets me from the doorway. I look up to see a girl wrapped in a thick white bathrobe, her wet black ringlets cascading down both of her shoulders. I clear my throat and sit up on my bed as she crosses the room, holding out her hand to greet me. "I'm Anusha Venkataraman. I wasn't expecting to see another trainee for at least a month."

"Hi, I'm Reagan Hillis," I reply, sitting up straighter on the bed and shaking her hand. Her grip is firm, her palm calloused, but as she pulls away, I'm surprised by the elegant shape of her hands. Long fingers, short, smooth, manicured nails. My hands are nothing to write home about. Enormous palms and tiny, short, wrinkly fingers with cracking skin and jagged, picked fingernails. I instinctively pull them into the sleeves of my sweatshirt.

Anusha sits down on the bed across from me, bringing a white towel up to her long hair. "So, what's your story? I thought I'd have the room all to myself until June."

"Sorry to intrude on your seclusion," I reply.

"Oh no, I'm happy you're here," Anusha answers, rubbing her hair in between the terry cloth. "I got here late last night and was already a little afraid of being lonely. I got used to sharing a room in the air force."

"Air force?" I ask, raising my eyebrows.

"Oh," Anusha says, pointing her chin toward me. "You must be a Black Angel Legacy, right?"

"Yes," I reply. "My parents are . . . were . . . they're on the Rescue/Take-down team. So, you're not a legacy?"

"I'm an EOP," Anusha replies, switching the towel to the other shoulder of raven hair. A small smile parts her lips as my brows cinch together with continued confusion. "I can tell by your face you haven't been briefed yet on the program."

My head nods in agreement and Anusha fills me in on a program I didn't know existed. One the Black Angels started after 9/11. The trainee classes were dwindling as Black Angel couples (along with the rest of the nation) had fewer children. And with the rising tension and possibility of more terrorist attacks on US soil, the Black Angels instituted the EOP; the Exemplary Outsider Program. The leaders at CORE track the progress of cadets in each of the top military academies: the Air Force Academy, the United States Naval Academy, and, of course, West Point. Every year, CORE selects at least one promising student from each top school to join the Black Angel Qualifiers and try out for a spot in the training academy.

"You must have been top of your class in the air force," I reply.

"I was doing pretty well," Anusha says with a shrug. "Scored really high on all the exams. Beat out the rest of the cadets across all our skills testing. My dream has always been to be in the CIA. The EOP lets me bypass all of those steps, so the offer was hard to resist. Still, I had to think about it. Took me a few days to process it all."

"It's a lot to give up," I reply.

"Yeah, it is," Anusha says, throwing her towel over the side of the bed. "My mom and dad were both in the air force. That's where they met. I always thought I'd follow in their footsteps, you know?"

Anusha pulls herself off the bed and crosses the room toward a wall of dressers to get changed. I stare down at my duffels at the edge of the bed, my life now confined to this bunker and whatever fit inside those black bags. The center of my chest expands as I think about Harper and Malika. I wonder what they're doing, what I'd be doing, in my former life. Dress shopping for the prom. Stressing over graduation parties. Getting excited for college. I lean my cheek up against the cool cinder block as my skin ignites, aching with memories I know I'll never have.

"So, you never told me why you're here early," Anusha says, pulling on a pair of yoga pants and a sweatshirt. She turns back toward me as she knots her wet hair into a messy bun. "I thought legacies don't arrive until June."

"Anusha, am I kicking your ass in pool or what?" a familiar voice calls from the doorway. I look up and see Cam leaning against the threshold. His face turns and finds my own, my body tucked away in the dorm's farthest corner. "Oh, hey, Reagan. You're back."

"You two know each other?" Anusha says, pointing back and forth between us.

51

"We go way back," Cam replies, giving me a wink. "Been in the trenches together, so to speak. Glad to see we both made it."

I nod, a silent understanding passing between us. Cam saw me at the edge of my most broken. A small, sad smile separates his lips and I know he won't ask me again why I'm here or what I've done. Not until I'm ready.

"Reagan, want to join us for a game of pool?" Cam says, shoving his hands into the pockets of his dark jeans. "I hear you're good with a gun, but what can you do with a pool cue?"

"I should probably get unpacked," I reply, leaning forward to unzip one of my bulging duffel bags.

"You sure?" Anusha asks, crossing the room and hanging her bathrobe on a wall hook between our beds. "I hear the chefs whip up some mean late-night snacks."

"No. I'm good." I busy myself with pulling out sports bras, pajamas, and training gear. "Thanks. You guys have fun."

"Okay, but don't fall asleep," Anusha says, pointing toward me, her lips parting into a wide, easy smile. "We need to stay up and exchange life stories when I get back. I want to hear all about you."

"Sure," I lie, wishing I had one of Sam's hexagon sleeping pills to cast its thick fog over my bed before Anusha returns.

"See you later, Hillis," Anusha calls over her shoulder as she and Cam head down the hall.

I stare at the empty doorway as I realize that's the first time anyone has called me by my real last name. The first time someone has asked to get to know me. The real me. Easy lies no longer need to be prepared on the tip of my tongue. I don't have to stare up at my bedroom ceiling on sleepless nights, imagining scenarios, planning out the falsehood I'd spin and story I'd create.

Unexpected panic balloons first in my chest, then crawls up the back of my throat until its long, dark fingers rattle against my brain. The lies, the cover stories, the manufactured version of me is all I've ever known. The pretender was my shield, my security blanket. Without her, I'm just Reagan Hillis. And I have no idea who the hell that girl is.

SEVEN

STRONG FINGERS GRIP AT MY NECK. I ATTEMPT TO suck in a breath but they clamp down harder, digging into my flesh. I try to pull away, but they claw into my skin, leaving behind flames in the form of fingerprints.

A sense memory flashes. Black room. Angry eyes. Blood and death.

Stop. Stop. Stop. I close my eyes and stifle the panic attack that haunts the hollow of my chest. My eyes flick open. Several faces stare back, waiting for me to make a move.

Anusha's fingers tighten and I don't resist. I let gravity pull us closer together. It's been months since I trained properly, but the robotic Reagan knows what to do. With one hand I punch her in the groin. With the other, I pull her head backward. Under normal circumstances, I should easily be able to slam her body onto the mat. But instead, it's my back that echoes against the plastic, the contact forcing out every last pocket of air. My eyes widen and my mouth gapes open as I gulp a noisy breath into my burning lungs.

"I'm so sorry, Reagan," Anusha declares, rushing to my side and extending a hand down to me. I can feel my eyes narrowing, flashing frustration and annoyance, far more at myself than the air force cadet who laid me flat on my back in a room full of Black Angel operatives. My hand falls to my stomach instead of reaching for Anusha's as I take in another desperate breath. I roll away from the disappointed faces, wishing I could curl up into the fetal position, go to sleep, disappear. After a moment and another breath, I pick myself up off the floor.

"It's okay," I finally answer, my voice shaky and at half strength. Anusha touches me on my exposed shoulder and I have to fight the urge to roll it off. She's been excessively kind to me over the last week since we both arrived for pre-training, while I've kept our conversations sparse and to the point. She must think I'm a total bitch, but she doesn't show it. Maybe she's been filled in on my mother, on the Tribunal. Perhaps her kindness is out of pity. Either way, she doesn't deserve me pulling away, closing her out. But after living alone for six months, I'm not quite sure how to function. How to be human. Let alone be the real Reagan I so desperately wanted to be. For years, all I wanted was to stop hiding, to come out of the shadows. But now, I wear that darkness like a cloak. I wish for invisibility.

Five foot eight and solid muscle, Anusha is as strong as they come. Even without the years of Black Angel training, she's been kicking my ass during every workout. I've lost so much muscle mass since Colombia, I have yet to take her down. Break free of her grasp, yes, but slam her 165-pound body to the mat? No.

Anusha and I join the semicircle of a dozen Black Angels around the mat and let another group take their turn in the middle. Weak and thin and unfocused, I've found myself flat on my back at least a dozen times this week. When our turn is over, I can't help but hang my head, slink back to the circle, avoiding the agents' stares. I know what they're thinking. *This is Reagan Hillis? What a disaster.* Today I make the mistake of looking up. Each face reads the same. Grossly unimpressed.

My eyes find the floor once again and stare into the cracking blue plastic. I follow the spidery veins up and down the mat's weathered seams until I feel a warm hand on my shoulder.

"Don't worry," Cam says quietly next to me. "You're getting better."

"You're kidding, right?" I answer with a snort. "I look like shit. I'm performing like shit."

"No," he says, giving my shoulder a squeeze. "Your technique is there. Your muscle memory is there. You just need to build up your strength."

"I'm worse off than I thought," I reply, my voice hovering near annoyance, as I turn away from the two men practicing choke holds at the center of the mat. I walk toward the free weights, out of the operatives' earshot, Cam and Anusha following a step behind me.

"You're getting stronger," Anusha says as I reach for two twenty-pound dumbbells to begin my circuit training. "You really are. I see a difference already. You just need more training. We'll help you."

"Yeah, we'll train extra with you," Cam agrees. "Really. We could use the extra workouts. We want to make the academy as much as you do."

Doubtful. If these two don't make the academy, they'll both be placed somewhere in the military or CIA or FBI. Their lives will go on. This is my one shot. My only way. If I miss my chance and Torres lives, I sometimes wonder how I still can.

I watch myself in the floor-to-ceiling mirror as my biceps crunch the heavy weights toward my chest. My skin is definitely less gray, my cheeks are a little bit fuller (thanks to CORE's chefs' high-calorie, high-carb diet), and my body is beginning to regain a little of its shape following my unintended Despair Diet. But if I don't get stronger soon, I'm screwed.

"Thanks for the encouragement, you guys," I say. "I'm just pissed that I let myself get like this."

"Tragedy will do that to you," Anusha replies softly before quickly sucking her full lips in between her teeth. My eyes dart toward her face in the enormous mirror behind me as her brown eyes expand. They know.

"Who told you?" I ask, forcing my voice to be as causal as possible despite the initial urge to be knife-sharp.

Cam and Anusha share a look. After a few seconds, Cam finally answers. "We've heard bits and pieces around the compound."

"Which bits and pieces exactly?" I ask, dropping the weights on the floor. Despite the protective mat, they land with a crash that makes Anusha's shoulders flinch.

"Just that . . . that . . ." Anusha stutters before taking a breath and trying again. "That your mom died during a rescue mission in Colombia. One that you were on. That your automatic bid into the academy got revoked. And you had to face the Tribunal for some of your actions on the mission."

"You know, for being a bunch of top secret spies, the Black

Angels sure do like to gossip," I reply and reach for a thirty-pound dumbbell that I lower with both hands behind my head, my muscles straining and screaming under the weight of my triceps curl.

"I'm really sorry about your mom," Cam says, picking up weights of his own. I feel the nerve endings in my muscles clutch at the pity in his voice but push through the urge to full-out flinch. I never know quite what to say.

"I'm so sorry too," Anusha says, still standing behind me, watching as sweat begins to collect at my dark hairline. "I've heard from everyone she was great. Not just a great operative. But a great person."

"She was the best," I answer flatly and desperately search for a way to change the subject. "So what's your deal, Cam? You haven't told me why you didn't go back home after your Tribunal investigation?"

"I don't really have a home right now. My parents' cover was about to be blown," Cam answers, his words strained as he lifts the heavy weights over his head. "They had just been in the Middle East gathering intel from some of their sources. CORE was afraid we were being watched. I got woken up in the middle of the night, grabbed my go-bag, and we left."

"Been there more times than I can count," I reply and put my weights back in their stand.

"Yeah, me too," Cam says as he gently brings the weights down to the floor. He stands back up, puts his hands on his hips, his chest rising with steady breaths. "Always hard to watch your life get smaller and smaller in the rearview mirror. I really liked our last stop."

"Where was that?" Anusha asks.

"Stowe, Vermont," Cam replies, his eyes tinting with melancholy as he remembers his picturesque—albeit fake—life. "I loved it. There nearly three years. Almost all of high school. I was on the football team. Had friends. A life. After we had to leave, I told my parents I didn't want to start over again. I mean, high school's nearly over. And since I was planning on attending the Qualifiers in June, I asked if we could stay here in DC. Let me finish high school online. Couldn't stomach the thought of . . ."

"Pretending." I finish his thought as he trails off.

Cam nods. "Where were you?"

"I was in a suburb of Columbus, Ohio. Same thing. Real friends. Real life."

Gone now, my mind whispers.

"You guys just always leave in the middle of the night?" Anusha asks, lowering her body onto the floor behind us, pulling it into a stretch. "No warning or anything?"

"Yup. If you want this life, get used to it," I answer, my voice harsher than I meant it to be.

"Do you ever get a chance to say good-bye?" Anusha questions.

"Normally, no. We never get to say good-bye. We just disappear," I answer and take a seat next to her on the mat. "But I begged them to let me send an email to my best friend in Ohio. I didn't make a ton of friends at our other stops. But I just couldn't bear the thought of her wondering what happened to me the rest of her life. After everything that happened, I think they felt sorry for me and bent the rules."

When we reached DC, the Black Angels had allowed me to send one final email to Harper. One stating that my mother had been killed in a car accident overseas on assignment and my dad was injured as well. That he was to be transferred to a different city as soon as he recovered. I wrote that I was sorry that there was no time to say good-bye, but that I would think of her and love her always. The agents stood over my shoulder as I typed out the detailed lies, the achingly personal truths. The minute I hit send, they deleted all of my Reagan MacMillan accounts and made me turn over my cell phone. I never got to see her response. Any trace of the girl I was in Ohio has vanished. Another splintered shadow. Another ghost. I wonder if anyone even notices I'm gone.

"You guys miss the people you left behind?" Anusha says, reaching for her toes.

"All the time," Cam answers for us both.

I nod slowly, my chest throbbing with homesickness. I miss Luke, but he's so tied to the twists and turns of my tragedy that sometimes it's hard to think of him, to wish for his presence in my life. He was there when it happened. He watched her die in my arms. And as much as I care about him, I'm sometimes afraid if I hear his voice, see his face, I'll only remember her last moments in Torres's basement.

Harper is an escape. Thinking of her makes my head fuzzy with conflicting emotions, happiness and heartache tangled together. I miss dancing with her in the car and the sound of her singing voice, sweet and high and always in tune. I miss her wild hair and her sugar-and-lemon perfume and the way her arm felt when it hooked through mine.

"I miss everything about them," I reply and lie down on the mat, pulling my right leg toward my chest and stretching my throbbing hamstring. Cam and Anusha both look over at me, a shared sadness looming behind their half smiles. It's the first real thing I've said to either one of them. They've gotten one-word answers and half-truths. The pretender mask still firmly in place. Taking it off is terrifying. Even with my parents, when I should have been myself, I wasn't. I spent years pretending to be someone else. And with Mom gone, I'm still not sure who is under there. Or if I'll even like what's hiding beneath.

EIGHT

"COME ON, REAGAN," CAM'S VOICE YELLS FROM across the mat as I screw up a take-down for the third time in a row. "If you were on a real mission, you'd be dead right now."

I wipe my forehead with the back of my hand, my chest rebelling against new breaths, my muscles slack and weary. We've been training for hours and the exhaustion has more than settled in.

"I know. I'm sorry. This is freaking hard, man," I say, my normally steady voice edging toward exasperation. "I'm just tired."

"No one gives a shit if you're tired on a mission," Cam barks, playing bad cop trainer, as we train alone in a smaller martial arts studio, away from the prying eyes of the other Black Angels.

"Come on. Let's try it again," good cop Anusha says gently before putting me in a headlock. Air pushes from my body and I catch a glimpse of my brown eyes in the mirror, flashing with irritation—with myself and with Anusha for not letting me at least catch my breath. Finally, I peel her tight fingertips from my screaming flesh, lower my center of gravity, and flip Anusha onto her back.

"Yes, Reagan!" Cam springs up on his toes, giving me a slow and steady clap. "That's my girl." My lips can't help but spread into a small, thankful smile.

"Finally," I reply, my hand reaching down for Anusha's. "Let's end on a high note."

Anusha stands up and pats me on the back before walking across the studio to grab us both bottled water.

"I still don't know if they'll think I'm strong enough to be out in the field," I say, my hands settling on my narrow hips. I look up at myself in the mirror. I'm still too thin, but after a few weeks of hard training with Cam and Anusha, I'm starting to see the outline of the girl I used to be.

"You will be," Anusha declares, handing me a cold bottled water, which I open and greedily chug. "You're getting better every single day."

"Thanks to you guys," I say, wiping away the excess water that's dribbled down my chin. "Seriously. Thank you for training with me."

"Of course," Cam says, putting an arm around my shoulder and giving me a tight squeeze.

I look up into his kind eyes and wonder why. Why they're putting in all these extra hours with me. They don't have to. They could be resting or concentrating on their own weaknesses. But instead, they're spending their time trying to better mine. After the year I've had, it's hard to believe in kindness. It's hard to believe in good. Even when it's pure and real and holding out its hand, right in front of you. Torres made me like this. He made me search for the cruelty in others. And for that, I'll never forgive him.

"All right, I'm exhausted," Cam says, glancing at the digital clock that hangs over the floor-to-ceiling mirror. I follow his eyes. It's nearly midnight. "Showers?"

"In a few," I say and settle back down on the mat, my muscles seizing and in need of a stretch. "I've got to work out some of these cramps or I'll be up all night with charley horses."

"The worst," Anusha replies and takes a seat on the mat next to me. "I could use a stretch myself."

"Well, I'm beat," Cam says and walks toward the door. "Charley horses be damned. Catch you two at breakfast."

"Good night," Anusha calls after him, pulling her torso over her legs and reaching out for her toes. The door clanks behind him and Anusha turns back toward me, a smile inching up her face. "Do you think Cam has a crush on you?"

"What?" I ask, my voice rising. "No way. He's just a friendly guy."

"He always finds a way to touch you though," she says, her eyebrows arching. "He doesn't really do that with me."

"I'm not giving off more-than-friendship vibes, am I?" I ask, pulling my elbow behind my back. "Because he's great and all but I don't really have the headspace for anything more than that."

"Yeah, me neither," Anusha replies softly, her smile suddenly falling. She digs her teeth into her bottom lip and turns away from me. But I catch her face before it leaves mine. I know that look. I know that sorrow behind her eyes.

"You had to leave somebody," I say, the words slowly escaping my lips. "Didn't you?"

Anusha's light brown eyes glisten; flecks of gold and green inflame like fading fireworks. "Yeah," she finally says, her voice breaking slightly in her throat. "My boyfriend back at the Air Force Academy. I had to break up with him to come here. They made me cut off all ties with him to accept this position, but I wasn't allowed to tell him why. They told me I couldn't keep in touch with him so . . . I had to really hurt him. I broke the guy's heart."

Pain etches deeper around Anusha's eyes as she pulls her knees to her chest, and I'm back in that New Albany living room, letting the Australian soccer player kiss me in front of Luke while I swallow the scream in my throat.

Silence encircles us, the ghosts of our twin betrayals playing back like a bad movie in our minds. I wait for Anusha to expand. She's been the talker, I've been the listener. But her mouth stays pressed together in a thin line.

"I know it's hard to believe people when they say they know how you feel," I reply, pressing the backs of my feet together into a stretch. "But I do. I know what it's like to destroy someone while your heart just . . . cries out for them."

I'll never get over the broken look on Luke's face. The way his pale blue eyes turned glassy before his gaze left mine. The throbbing of every cell within me to explain.

"Did you leave someone behind too?" Anusha asks.

"I guess you could say that," I reply, my voice catching in my throat. Sometimes, I wish it was just my betrayal that made my heart constrict at the thought of Luke. If I had simply disappeared from New Albany at least I'd know where he was. I could lie awake at night and imagine him on our couch in the bonus room, running along our path early in the morning, dissecting something that makes Harper squirm in AP biology lab. At least I'd know he was safe. It's the not knowing, not being able to imagine pieces of his life, that causes my throat to itch with worry.

"Comes with the territory, I guess," Anusha replies with a sigh, her chin resting on her kneecaps.

"Yes, it does," I say. "This life isn't for everyone. It's freaking hard. Hurting people you love is only the beginning."

"It's a lot to get used to," Anusha says, her voice thin, like it's coming from somewhere else. This whole time, I've been so focused on my own struggles, I didn't even notice that the people who were trying to help me were struggling as well.

"You don't have to do this, you know," I reply quietly, reaching out to touch her arm. My fingertips rest against her dewy skin and I realize it's the first time I've reached out to touch anyone in months. "There are a lot of pros to being here. Take down the bad. Rescue the good. But when you're a Black Angel, your life belongs to the agency. Believe me, I've lived it. You could still go to the air force. Make a difference in the world. But your life will belong to you."

Anusha stares into the mirror across from us, carefully considering my words. She turns her face toward mine, resting her cheek against her knees.

"Why are you doing this? I mean, after everything you've been through, everything you've seen. Why are you still here?"

I stare down at the fading blue mat and the ember in my stomach flares. His face comes back to me; dark, penetrating eyes, salt-and-pepper goatee. I daydream about Torres every few hours, his mouth bloodied, his limbs tied in metal chains. I think about where I'll put each bullet. I muse on the color of his blood. I like to imagine it's brighter than the rest of ours. That God color-coded

Torres's wickedness so he could spot that blazing red color after the light faded from his eyes and know exactly where Santino Torres belongs.

But I can't say any of this to Anusha. I can't say it to anyone.

"You know I struggled last year with my decision to come here," I reply, my words measured. "Before my mom died. Before everything in Colombia. I wanted to be normal. I almost chose college over the academy. My parents had been saying for years that I was not normal and I guess . . . I finally believe them."

The words I'm saying are true. They're not all lies. Not a part of my Torres vengeance plan. My parents were right all along. I'll never be normal. Even if this never happened. Even if Mom was still alive and I had gone to college, something would have pulled me back. Mom worried I couldn't hear the calling, but I did. I always heard it, but I ignored it, afraid of what would happen if I actually answered. Now the very worst has happened. And I hear it louder than ever.

"I asked my mom once why she did this," I continue. "Why she risked her life for total strangers. She told me the people she saved, they were someone's daughter or mother or son. They meant something to someone. Now I know how all those people would have felt if my mom wasn't there to save them. And I don't want anyone else to feel like I feel right now. Not if I can help it."

A melancholy smile twitches on Anusha's face. Her bright eyes turn foggy as she opens her mouth to speak, closes it, then tries again. "I'm really sorry, Reagan," she says, her voice fragile and soft.

That hollow space inside of me shrieks, angry and unforgivingly cruel. Sometimes, my love for my mother betrays me. It makes me think I'm stronger than I am. But then that agony returns, punishing me for my foolish hope.

Hope. People have been saying that word to me a lot since Mom died. That I need to hold on to it. Let it drag me out of bed to face another day. But to me, hope is evil. Far crueler than fear or anger or hate. At least those emotions are honest. Not hope. It wraps us in the warmth of false promises until it's stripped and ripped and cut away, leaving mocking scars on our skin.

A jagged rock of grief, permanently lodged behind my sternum, breaks free, and tears scrape at my throat.

Don't cry. Don't cry. Don't cry.

I don't want to show weakness. Not here. Not even to Anusha. I try to get up before Anusha sees them, but her face changes, falls.

"Reagan," she says gently as I make my way toward the door. But I don't turn around. I open the door and throw myself into the dark hallway. My legs hurry down the North Hall, picking up speed with every step until I'm running. I hear the echo of Anusha stirring, getting ready to come after me. I slip into another dark studio and silently shut the door. My body pushes against the wall, sinking inch by inch until I'm on the ground. And only once I feel the cold concrete beneath my hands do I let the tears, the loss, fall all around me.

"I miss you," I whisper into the darkness. "I just miss you."

NINE

"THIS MUST BE WHAT THE FIRST DAY OF COLLEGE feels like," I say quietly in Anusha's ear as we sit on my bed and watch Black Angel trainee after Black Angel trainee drag her two CORE-approved duffels into our once-empty dorm room. We knew this day was coming. When the other ten legacies would join our quiet space. I feel like after months on my own, I just got used to having Anusha around 24/7. Adding ten more girls to the mix is going to be interesting.

Each girl is exactly what you'd expect a Black Angel child to be: strong, confident, and guarded. They've been pleasant enough, each greeting us with a tentative handshake and their Black Angel stats: name, legacy status, specialty, last "hometown." We're tied together by the double lives we've led and countless lies we've weaved, but even with that silent bond, we refuse to drop our pretender masks. We force our best smiles and feign genuine interest in one another's stories. But I know what we're all doing: mentally filing away our silent judgments. But instead of categorizing one another as "sorority girl," "pothead," or "study nerd" like we would if we were in a college dorm, we're labeling our competition, deciding who we're better than and who we could lose out to.

"Do you know whose stuff this is?" a girl asks, pointing to Anusha's already claimed bottom bunk. Tall and thin, dressed in an ivory lace jumpsuit, black booties, and a black leather jacket, she looks more like a high-fashion model than a highly trained child spy.

"Yeah, it's mine," Anusha replies and holds out her hand. "Hi, I'm Anusha. You're welcome to grab the top bunk. It hasn't been taken yet."

"Lex Morgan. How do you feel about switching?" she quickly replies, placing a hand on her slender hip and casting a glance down at Anusha's now awkward greeting. "I really, really hate the top bunk and all the bottoms are already taken."

"Well, I'm ... I'm pretty comfortable on the bottom bunk," Anusha answers, slowly withdrawing her hand and tucking it into her sweatshirt sleeve, embarrassed and confused by this girl's dismissal. "I kind of claimed it over a month ago. Sorry about that."

"How have you already been here a month?" Lex asks, narrowing her deep-set eyes, an almost too-bright-to-be-real shade of green. "This is the first day legacies were allowed to arrive."

"I'm not a legacy," Anusha answers, clearing her throat, growing increasingly uncomfortable with Lex's presence. "I finished my freshman year at the Air Force Academy and was invited to come here early."

"So you're just an EOP?" Lex scoffs, tossing her blond ponytail over her shoulder. "I don't mean to be rude, but I think legacies

70

should have seniority when it comes to bunks. I mean, I'm a fourth generation Black Angel. So how about you move your stuff?"

"You've got to be shitting me, right?" I say, unable to contain my smart mouth any longer. "Lovely first impression you leave."

"Well, how should I be acting?" she asks, shrugging her shoulders. "What do you want me to do, offer to bake cookies while we braid each other's hair? This is Qualifiers. I didn't come here to make friends. I came here to compete."

"That doesn't mean we can't be kind to each other during the process," I say.

"Are you going to be one of those people who is nice to everyone on the outside but is planning on how to stab us all in the backs on the inside? Or did you learn all this 'Kumbaya' crap in the air force too?"

"I didn't attend the air force," I reply. "I'm a legacy. But only a second generation. I bet that's probably not good enough for you either, is it?"

"You're a legacy?" Lex asks, her bee-stung lips forming a curious pout. "I thought I knew all the legacies coming to Qualifiers. What's your name?"

"Reagan," I reply, suddenly not wanting to say my last name out loud.

"Reagan what?"

"Hillis."

"*You're* Reagan Hillis? Are you serious?" she says with a laugh, her aristocratic face registering both shock and delight. "What the hell are you doing here? You were one of the elites. You had an automatic bid into the academy. What'd you do to screw that up? Kill someone?"

My lower spine throbs, each vertebra seizing, one by one, until the agony rattles my neck. Anusha's hand reaches out and touches the icy exposed skin on my wrist, immediately protective. Or maybe worried I'll get kicked out of Qualifiers before they start for punching this girl in the face.

One Mississippi. Two Mississippi. Three Mississippi.

I count my breaths, trying to stop the storm that is raging inside my tightening chest, and attempt to formulate a coherent thought.

"I broke a rule," I finally answer, my lips slowly and deliberately wrapping around each word, as Lex's mouth curls into a smirk. "Now I'm here. So go ahead and add me to your list of competition."

"From the looks of you, you won't be much," Lex replies with a snort, throwing her duffel bags back on her shoulders. "I've been hearing about you from my parents and the trainers for years. I guess it's like meeting a celebrity you really love. They never quite live up to the hype."

Lex looks my still-too-thin body up and down one more time before sauntering over to the other side of the room, where I'm sure she'll bully her way into one of the lower bunks.

"Is this chick for real?" Anusha asks, her face tight and mouth angry. "I mean, I've seen *Mean Girls.* I just didn't know I'd meet Regina George in the flesh one day."

I take in a breath, wishing for the days of New Albany High School and Madison Scarborough, where I could easily combat her bullying ways by hacking into social media accounts or the school's

72

mainframe to change grades. But here, everyone knows my tricks. My techniques won't work on a girl like Lex.

"Forget about her," I reply, waving my hand through the air and trying to take my own advice. "Typical Black Angel move. She's just trying to get inside our minds. Her parents must have hammered her with psychology but skipped the whole part about acting like something that resembles a human being."

Every person in this room is a product of their training, of their parents. My parents trained me to be confident and defiant and strong in the face of adversity. To think of others, the targets that need saving, before thinking about myself. Clearly, Lex Morgan's parents taught her to be ruthless. That winning was the most important thing. That her life and successes mattered most of all.

"She strikes me as someone who is proud to tell you about how her family came over on the *Mayflower* or something," Anusha says, still glaring at Lex. "She clearly comes from a long line of people who just take whatever the hell they want."

"Don't worry," I reply. "Girls like her get theirs in the end."

"You sure about that?" Anusha asks as we watch one of the other trainees remove her stuff from the bottom bunk so Lex can slide hers in. Lex looks over her shoulder at us, smiling triumphantly, as she claims her place in the Qualifiers hierarchy.

Head bitch. Let the games begin.

I hear him before I see him.

The rest of the girls have gone to lunch, but I opted for a big breakfast and the chance for one more training session before

Qualifiers orientation this afternoon. Behind the closed door of our dorm room, I hear the clunk of boots, the scrape of heels in the hallway. I'm tying my shoes when I hear his long, confident stride. When you're a Black Angel, you memorize weird things about people. Anyone can memorize a voice. But I know all the little pieces that make him whole. The way he bites his cheek when he's pensive. The way his voice rises an octave when he thinks I'm full of crap. And I know his walk. I'd listen for it as I sat in class. I'd smile when I'd hear it down the hall, knowing I'd see his face in a matter of seconds. But the sound of his distinctive cadence in the hollows of CORE stop me cold.

It can't be. It really can't be.

My neck slowly swivels toward the door, my lungs burning under the weight of anticipation as the footsteps get closer and closer then stop in front of the door.

Knock, knock, knock.

"Come in," I say, the words barely escaping my swelling throat. After a second, the door opens and there he is, a smile parting his full lips and crinkling his dimples, and I can't remember seeing a lovelier sight.

"Luke?!" I whisper, my lips trembling, tears burning my eyes. I blink hard, certain that when I open my lids the sight of him will be a cruel mirage. But when I open my eyes, he's still there, standing in my doorway. Before he can speak, my feet take off running. I jump into his arms, my limbs flailing and hair flying, getting caught between our lips as he laughs and I begin to cry into the curve of his shoulder.

"Hi, Reagan," Luke says, softly stroking my hair as I wipe my tears away.

"Am I hallucinating?" I ask, pulling myself away from his strong body so I can look at his face. I hold his warm cheeks in my cold hands. "Are you real?"

"I'm real," he whispers back.

"I'm so confused," I reply, taking a step back, both hands rising to my forehead. "What are you doing here? Where have you been? Is your family okay? Are you okay? Is everyone safe?"

"One question at a time," Luke answers with a smile, pulling me in for another hug. I breathe him in. Cinnamon gum and body wash and something new, something I don't recognize. I wrap my arms around his waist and let him hold me. I take in all the things I've been missing. The weight of his arms and curve of his defined chest. His sweet breath against my neck. The beat of his heart in my ear. I close my eyes, thinking back to all the nights at the safe house I prayed to a God I'm not even sure I believe in to let me see him one more time. To hear his voice just once. Even if it was a phone call telling me he was okay. And now here he is, his warm body enveloping mine, filling a small part of the aching emptiness that has hollowed me out. I squeeze him again and silently say thank you to whoever answered my selfish prayer.

"Okay, what is going on?" I ask, pulling out of our embrace, too ravenous with curiosity to hug him for a second longer. "I didn't know if I'd ever see you again. I've been so, so worried. Where have you been? Why are you here?"

"Let's just start at the beginning," Luke says, taking my hand and leading me over to one of the empty bunk beds.

Luke tells me that the Black Angels feared for both of our lives after Colombia. *We* were the faces captured by security cameras. We were the ones who killed Torres's brother. We were that monster's best targets for revenge. And that wasn't just speculation. CORE intercepted messages about a plan to find and kill us in the States. So when Luke was escorted off the plane in Virginia, he had a choice to make: be reunited with his parents and sister and immediately force his entire family into hiding, or spare them the danger, go into hiding by himself, and join the Qualifiers in June.

"I didn't want my family to face that kind of threat," Luke continues, his forearms leaning over his knees, his face tilted toward the floor and eyes shielded from me. But I can still see the pangs of distress, the torture of his choice on his face. "I didn't want my little sister to have to live in fear. It didn't seem fair. So I chose to go live in a safe house in New Hampshire. Had round-the-clock security. Finished high school online. And now I have the chance to join the Black Angels through the EOP. They said they normally only hold spots like that open for cadets who have finished their freshman year but since I had already proved myself on the mission, they wanted to give me an early shot."

"Luke, I'm so sorry you had to make that choice," I reply, putting my hands on top of his, a guilty knot twisting in my stomach at the thought of Luke alone in New Hampshire, torn away from his family and his friends and the life we both loved. He wasn't born into this darkness. He had a chance at a different life.

"It is what it is," Luke replies with a shrug, still avoiding my eyes.

"This is my fault," I say, my voice ragged and thin.

"No, it's not," Luke says, shaking his head. "I followed you to Colombia. I followed you into that house. You tried to keep me away, keep me safe. It was my choice to go. And my choice to be here now. And you know what . . . I'd do it all over again."

He slips his hand through mine and squeezes it three times. I squeeze back and try to smile, try to be happy that he's here. Because I am. But I can't shake the guilt that's pulsing through my veins, metallic and cutting. The lives I've altered and futures I destroyed that night in Colombia. Luke had a plan. He was supposed to be a West Point cadet. Serve his country. Follow in his father's military-boot-sized footsteps. Luke was not supposed to live a life of isolation. He was not meant to trade in his pins and accolades for a career in the shadows. His dreams are gone. The life he wanted stripped away. By Torres. By me. And how do you even start to say you're sorry for that?

TEN

"I THINK WE'RE SUPPOSED TO BE IN HERE," ANUSHA says, gently pulling at my arm and guiding me from the East Hall into one of the secure conference rooms. A few trainees are already inside sitting in high-back leather chairs that line a long, dark, wood conference table. They look up when we walk in and almost immediately return to staring at their hands, their laps, the shiny tabletop veneer in silence.

"Friendly," she whispers and I stifle a giggle.

We grab a pair of chairs at the far side of the room, waiting for our first official meeting as trainees to begin.

"Are you nervous?" Anusha leans over and whispers.

"A little bit," I answer quietly back, but in reality, my stomach is filled with a thousand lead-winged butterflies. "Are you?"

"I might throw up or shit my pants. Or both," Anusha whispers and I bite down on my lower lip to stop my laughter from shattering the silence.

"Have you given any thought to which team you want to be placed on?" I ask her quietly.

"You mean if I even make it past Qualifiers?" Anusha asks as she shifts awkwardly in her seat, her eyes lacking their usual confidence.

"I've seen you," I answer back. "You'll make it."

Anusha is everything the training academy would want. Strong, smart, and flush with raw talent, the trainers can mold her into the exact type of agent they need. But more than that, she has a military pedigree. She'll actually obey the Black Angels' every order while I'm still given the side-eye everywhere I go. *Insubordinate. Combative. Reckless.* The adjectives used to describe me may not be said out loud, but they're written on every face. Legacy status or not, I've got a long way to go in proving I belong here.

"One of the trainers told me with my military background I may be good at Forward Logistics," Anusha answers, tightening the band around her ponytail. "Do all the advance scouting and intel. Establish operations ahead of missions, bank accounts, housing, all that stuff. But it kind of sounds like bitch work to me. I think I'd rather be doing Counter Intelligence or Rescue/Take-down, but we'll see how much I suck."

"You won't suck," I reply. "You were chosen for a very good reason."

"Well, I'm no Reagan Hillis," she whispers, arching her perfectly sculpted dark eyebrows over her light brown eyes. "I guess I didn't realize how legendary you were before I went to lunch earlier today."

"Oh, lovely," I reply and roll my eyes.

After years of secret identities, this was one of the first times I could actually introduce myself as Reagan Hillis. But with each hand I shook, an unconscious tug at my tongue stopped me from saying my full name. Until Lex pressed me, I didn't say my last name out loud to even one trainee.

Anusha touches me on the arm and whispers, "What?"

"Nothing, it's just..." I begin but my voice trails off.

"What? Were you hoping you'd be anonymous here?"

"I don't know," I say and cross my arms over my chest, anxiety coiling around my already heavy stomach. "I mean, why does everyone know who I am and I don't know any of them?"

"That's what happens when you're the best," Anusha whispers, tapping playfully at my wrist with her fingertips. "They've all been measured up to you their whole lives."

"By who?"

"Trainers, their parents, people at CORE."

"Great, no wonder no one wanted to talk to me after lunch. They've probably all hated the sound of my name since they were eleven years old."

"Well, I wouldn't have," Anusha says, putting her hand to her chest, shaking her head, almost offended. "I would have just let it motivate me. But be careful. I know there's more than a few who will be gunning for you."

"Perfect," I say and play with the knotted-up cord of my sweatshirt. Just what I need: the leaders at CORE, my father, and now 80 percent of the trainees all against me.

When I was thirteen and having a particularly tough time at whatever new school, new life I'd been thrown into, I'd lie in bed every night, stare at my dark ceiling, and dream about going to the academy. I envisioned doing everything with my Black Angel friends that I never got to do with kids on the outside. *They will understand me*, I used to tell myself. *I can be Reagan Hillis with them. I'll never have to lie.* Never once in my daydreams did I imagine sitting among people who not only knew, but actually shared my deepest secrets, and still feel so alone.

"Reagan . . . they wanted to know why you're even in Qualifiers," Anusha whispers as more and more trainees file into the room. "Lex was peppering me with questions. Said the two of us looked close and I had to know the truth."

"And did you tell them?" I ask, worry altering my voice.

"Of course not," Anusha answers quietly, her sincere eyes meeting mine. "I would never."

My lungs pull in a deep breath, but it doesn't calm me down. My chest collapses with an even deeper sigh. "I guess it doesn't matter. They'll find out about Colombia and Torres and Mom soon enough. But thanks for buying me a little time."

"Don't worry," Anusha whispers, bumping her elbow into mine. "I've got your back, Reagan. Whether you want me to or not."

The muscles in my mouth twitch, forcing a small smile. I look up at the door as Luke walks into the room. He spots me, waves, and makes his way in our direction. Introductions are made, hands shaken. Luke grabs the seat next to me and automatically rolls it closer, the wheels scratching along the stained concrete.

"How are the guys in your dorm?" I ask softly. People are finally beginning to talk but I don't feel like broadcasting our conversation.

"I haven't met them all yet but they seem cool," he answers and nods his head. "How are the girls?"

"Uhhh . . . too early to tell," I reply with a shrug. "But apparently they were all talking about me at lunch. Trying to figure out why I'm here instead of at the academy."

"Don't worry about them." Luke shrugs, unconcerned. "It's just first-day jitters. You'll be fine."

Three loud claps interrupt the low hum of chitchat as Blue Scarf enters the room.

"Good afternoon, everyone." Her voice booms, attempting to quiet remaining whispers. I study her as she stands at attention, staring at us until she has absolute, complete silence. She's in black pants, black heels, a thin black sweater, and a sky-blue scarf. This lady really likes her blue scarves. I kind of want to break into her room and ransack her closet to find out just how many she has.

Blue Scarf takes three large steps to her left and stands directly in front of two guys who are still whispering to each other, burning holes into the sides of their heads until they shut up. Blue Scarf looks down at her watch. She shakes her head, disapprovingly, and launches into a lecture.

"Not good at all. It took a full seventeen seconds for this room to quiet down not only after I walked in, but after I commanded your attention. That is the type of behavior I expect out of kindergartners. Not Black Angel trainees. This is not high school. This is not college. This is a tryout for the most elite and powerful spy agency in the world. Lesson number one: when a senior leader of CORE, or anyone with rank over you for that matter, walks into the room, you shut the hell up. You stop whatever conversation you're having and you give us your attention immediately. If that's too hard for you to do, then there's the door and good luck to you." Blue Scarf waves her hand in front of the open doorway, her eyes searching the room, daring someone to get up. No one moves. No one breathes.

"My name is Victoria Browning," she says and the formal name fits her stiff, elegant, slightly bitchy face. "But you will address me as Director Browning. I am one of the senior leaders at CORE and will be helping to oversee all of your training and your development. Basically, I will be a crucial person to impress because I decide your fate."

Browning's eyes find mine and the muscles in my back wince, forcing my spine into a perfectly straight line. *Fantastic.*

"First things first. Qualifiers is a year-long tryout," Blue Scarf... I mean, Director Browning, continues. "Your first few months will be spent here at CORE where we will assess you on everything from your physical strength, your weaponry skills, and your martial arts training, to your strategic thinking and intelligence. If you don't meet our standards, you will be cut after the first round. Those who remain will rotate through all four of the primary leadership teams: Forward Logistics, Counter Intelligence, Intel Technology, and Rescue/Takedown. After your year at Qualifiers, we will decide who will receive an invitation to the prestigious training academy. Make it through the academy and *we* will place you on the team you best fit. You do not get to choose. From this day forward, your life belongs to the Black Angels. Do you understand?"

We nod our heads in fierce unison as Browning goes over the list of strict rules: No leaving the compound without permission. No drinking. No smoking. No drugs. Ten p.m. curfew. Lights-out at midnight. No phone calls except to our parents (and only once a week). No speaking out of turn in front of trainers or operatives. And absolutely no dating.

"We know what happens when twenty-four young, athletic teenagers come together. But this rule is firm. We do not want you distracted during your time at Qualifiers," Browning adds, placing her fingertips on the polished wood table. "Training should be your first and only priority. Clearly we encourage dating after Qualifiers, otherwise many of you legacies wouldn't be sitting here. But while you're a trainee, we better not catch you doing anything you wouldn't want to do in front of your parents. Do we understand one another?"

I nod, perhaps with a little too much enthusiasm, my lungs swelling with relief. Whatever is happening between Luke and me, it doesn't need to be defined because it's forbidden. At least for the next twelve months. My head can barely compute that he's actually here, let alone how I feel about him after all these months apart. A big, fat question mark is just fine by me. I try to catch Luke's reaction in my periphery. He doesn't look nearly as pleased.

"Your first physical assessment begins tomorrow morning at six a.m. Be late and you'll have points deducted from your overall score. Not to mention, you'll have to do extra chores around CORE. I hope all of you enjoy scrubbing toilets."

A few boys in the corner groan but stop as soon as Browning's eyes dart across the room.

"If you thought training with your parents was intense, you haven't seen anything yet," Director Browning says, clasping her hands together, a rigid smile cutting across her severe face. "Take a look around the room."

The trainees look to their left and right, eyeing one another, some with fear, some with arrogance, a few with both.

"There are twenty-four of you sitting in this room," Director Browning continues, pointing to the table.

"In three months, at least a quarter of you will be gone. And even if you make it through to the next round, we reserve only three spots on each of the four teams in the training academy. Now, you all have genius-level IQs and know how to multiply. So yes, your math is right. Only half of you will make it onto an elite squad. The other half will either be cut or be assigned a desk job at CORE or one of our other compounds. So unless you want to be downloading satellite photos or doing research in this dungeon for the rest of your life, I suggest you do your very best, every single day. Even when you think no one is watching, we are. Everything counts here. Am I clear?"

Everyone in the room nods in silence, terror etched on every trainee's face. Most of us have been training to be Black Angels since we were kids. We've given up sports and ballet and dances and sleepovers, spent every waking hour learning languages and martial arts and mastering knife skills and weaponry. All of us want a spot.

"Your entire life has been building up to this moment," Browning says, reading our minds. "Qualifiers: where you think you're just a year away from joining the training academy. Twelve months away from being sent off on missions around the world. Well, guess what? Your parents may have told you that you were special. But I'm here to tell you you're not. Prove to me you deserve to be here. Until then, you're nothing."

With that, she turns and exits the room, the sharp tap of her high heels echoing in the silence, reality plunging deeper and deeper into our brains with each rapid beat. I look around the room. Eyes are wide and mouths are open or twisted beneath wringing, nervous hands.

The room is silent until Anusha leans over and whispers in my ear, "Let the bloodbath begin."

ELEVEN

MY SCORCHING BODY SPREADS LIKE A STICKY STARFISH on the cool, blue mat. My sweaty pores are like a million suction cups, clinging to the plastic as I stare up at the two-story ceiling and wonder about the feat of engineering that went into building this place. Cam's upside-down face appears in my line of sight, leaning over my body, his mouth spreading into an upside-down grin.

"Did you know one of your nostrils is bigger than the other," he greets me, his head now tilting to one side, examining me at this very odd angle.

"Nice to see you too, asshole," I answer with a smile so he knows I'm kidding. I raise my eyebrows up at him. (Or would it be down? This upside-down face thing is confusing.) "All I know is that both of my nostrils are ginormous."

"Hey, that's a good thing," Cam says, still looking down at me. "You get double the oxygen to your heart than most people with those two caves."

"I guess I have my Sicilian grandmother to thank for that."

"Gotta love those Mediterranean noses."

"Let's just hope I don't inherit the matching Mediterranean mustache in about twenty years," I say and push my reluctant body back up. I reach my hands out for Cam to help lift me to my feet.

"I'll buy you an electrolysis gift certificate for Christmas," Cam answers and pulls me into a standing position. "Ya know, just in case the lip fuzz makes an early debut."

"I kind of hate you," I reply, the giggle in my throat muffled by the sting searing up my sore legs. After our Qualifiers meeting, I thought I should get in an extra run and practice some sprints before tomorrow's first assessment. I think I may have overdone it.

"You lie. You know you love me, Reagan," Cam says, throwing his arm around my neck and pulling me into his body.

"Stop, I'm all sweaty," I reply and playfully push him away but he only pulls at me tighter, which makes me laugh.

The hairs stand up on the back of my neck, an invisible pull, tethered to someone else's eyes in the room. I always know when I'm being watched. My smile falls. My eyes flick up. Luke is standing in the doorway of the training center. His sweet face from earlier has been replaced by a vacant stare that burns through me despite the ice in his glare. His pale blue eyes catch mine and even though I have nothing to feel guilty about, my skin pricks with a million fire-blazed pins.

"Luke," I call out, instinctively pulling away from Cam. "Come here. I want you to meet someone."

Luke stares at me for a second longer, the straight line of his lips deepening into a slim frown. He shoves his hands in the pockets of his maroon New Albany soccer sweatshirt and walks slowly toward us, his eyes fixed on the concrete floor.

What is he doing?

Once he finally makes his way across the gym, I start my overly enthusiastic introduction.

"Luke, this is Cam. He is a fellow displaced trainee like me, so we've been training together at CORE for the last six weeks. Cam, this is Luke. You've heard me talk about him before. He was my neighbor back in Ohio and ended up on the mission with me in Colombia."

"Oh, hey, man," Cam booms, his voice rising with surprise. He sticks out his hand to warmly greet Luke. "It's so nice to actually get to meet you. Heard a lot about you. I had no idea you'd be at Qualifiers."

"She didn't either," Luke answers coolly, shaking Cam's hand and nodding toward me. "Long story. Maybe I can tell you over a game of pool or something later tonight."

"Sounds great," Cam replies, glancing at the digital clock over the row of weight machines. "Hey, I'm gonna hit the showers before my meeting with my adviser. Great to meet you, Luke. I'll catch you later tonight?"

"You're on," Luke replies, bobbing his head and puffing out his chest. Like a total bro. A side to him I've never, ever seen. Even around his jock high school friends, he was consistent in his anti-bro-ness.

"I'll see you later, Reagan," Cam says, placing a warm hand on my shoulder before jogging out of the training facility.

Luke's eyes narrow, following Cam as he walks out the door.

89

When he's gone, Luke turns back toward me, his eyes still creased, waiting for an explanation. I stare at him for several beats, not sure what to say. Not sure if he even deserves an explanation.

I roll my eyes, annoyed by our silent game of chicken. "What?" I finally blurt out.

"Is he your boyfriend?" Luke asks, tilting his head back toward the door.

"What? No!" I reply, my voice a little louder than I meant it to be. "He's just a friend. What is with you?"

"He didn't look like just a friend to me," Luke says, his tone sharp and cutting as the words leave his mouth.

"Why are you acting like this?" I ask.

"Is that how you always refer to me?" Luke asks, bulldozing past my question. "Is that how you think of me? As your neighbor?"

"Of course not," I reply, running my fingers along my tight jawline, already exhausted by this conversation. "But what do you want me to do? Share my screwed-up sob story with every single person here? I mean, how do you refer to me?"

Luke casts his eyes to his feet and kicks the corner of the blue mat. "I guess I don't know now," he answers without looking back up at me.

"I really don't know what you want from me," I say, shaking my head and beginning to walk away. "I've got to shower."

I push past Luke and head for the door, the heat of his sudden, surprising jealousy evaporating any happiness I may have felt earlier today.

"Did you even think about me?" Luke calls after me, forcing me to turn around. "When we were apart? I know you said you worried about me, but you're a Black Angel. You know how to tell people what they want to hear."

"Are you serious?" I ask, my hands rising to the center of my stinging chest as I move back toward him. "How can you think something like that, let alone say it out loud?"

"So did you?" Luke asks.

"Luke, I thought about you all the time. I worried about you constantly. I used to put out an extra coffee cup on the counter and pretend you were in the other room so I wouldn't feel so alone. But when you got off that plane in Virginia, I didn't think I'd ever see you again. Thinking about you physically hurt. So excuse me if I had to pull myself together and try to get over you so I could make it through the day."

Luke's eyes shift from anger to a silent, private ache. He bites down on his lower lip, his chest rising as he gathers his words.

"Reagan, don't you know I'd do anything for you?" Luke finally asks, his voice quiet. "One of the reasons I chose to go into hiding and be away from my family was because it was the only way I'd ever get to see you again."

A tattered breath catches in my chest, oxygen molecules disguised as razor blades. *Does he even want this? Did he choose all this just for me?* The guilty knot in the center of my gut tugs and tugs and tugs until it's so tight I can barely move.

"I ran after you and into that house in Colombia," Luke says, his voice barely audible. "And I'll never stop running after you, Reagan. I guess I just wonder sometimes if you'd do the same for me."

It's like he ripped the words right out of my brain. Luke made the biggest decision of his life based on me. But I've never considered giving up my shot at the Black Angels for him. Not once. The guilt spreads, sharp and searing, through my veins. But even now, with him standing right in front of me, I'd make the same choice. I would never say it and hate to even think it. But as much as I care about him, Torres is my sole priority. There's no room in my heart for love. Only revenge.

"Look," I finally say, my brain struggling to string together the right words. "There's no denying how much I've missed you. How much you mean to me. But I've lost everything. I've lost my mother. I've lost my home. I've lost my friends. I've lost my father. I mean, he's so destroyed he can barely stand to be around me. And I thought I lost you forever. My world has been ripped into a million pieces. So becoming a Black Angel, focusing on making it through Qualifiers, has consumed me. It seemed like the only way to get over losing my life. I'm sorry if you think that I haven't thought about you. I have, but . . ."

"No, stop," Luke replies and closes his eyes. He shakes his head and runs his fingers through his hair before returning his eyes to me. "Don't apologize. There's nothing for you to apologize about. I'm sorry. I'm being a selfish jerk."

"No, you're not," I answer and reach out to touch him behind his elbow. "You lost a lot that night too."

And he has. I see it in the paleness in his skin. The way his eyes have lost their shine. Even the way he carries himself. He's different. Damaged somehow. And it was my choices that snuffed out the light that used to follow him wherever he went.

My lungs pull in a breath as I let my fingertips linger on his warm skin. "It's hard for me to see past one hour at a time," I say, moving closer to him.

"I understand," he replies as we walk together toward the door, his hand settling onto the small of my back. "I'll still be here."

And he would be, even if I told him to run away.

Back in Ohio, I was ready to open my heart to him. I nearly handed him a map of my deepest, most joyous and painful parts. And as he runs his fingertips along my spine, I know how desperately he still wants that map. But I can't give it to him. I can't give it to anyone.

TWELVE

"LADIES, LET'S MOVE IT." OUR TRAINER MICHAEL'S voice booms over the sound of two dozen pounding feet. "I'm not impressed. You're supposed to be Black Angel trainees. Right now you look like a bad high school track team."

I glance over at Michael, standing at the curve of the indoor track as we round the corner, a stopwatch in his hand, a frown deepening on his face. Part of today's assessment is timed intervals, and in true Black Angel form, we only get thirty seconds of rest in between each one. We've already completed a 400 then an 800 then a 200 followed by another 400. Despite my grueling training schedule with Cam and Anusha, my strength and endurance is still not where it was before Colombia. I've finished somewhere in the middle during every single race (and have received side-eyes galore from my fellow trainees every time I cross the finish line, *Really?* written in between their raised eyebrows). I have to finish near the top during this 800 or I'm going to dig an even deeper hole for myself at Qualifiers. But as our feet thunder toward the curve for our last lap, I'm boxed in between a group of girls in the inner lane. I try to find a way out but I'm completely trapped. As we get to the straightaway with another three hundred meters to go, I see a small gap between the two girls in front of me, large enough that I could sprint through and get to the front.

Go, go, go, my mind screams as I push my legs to move faster, dig harder. But as I move closer to the opening, a sharp jab to my right ribs knocks out the strained breath I have in my screaming lungs. I glance to my right. Of course. Lex. She sees the opening too and with one more wind-sucking stab of her elbow, she rushes past me, pushing her way through the opening and into the front of the group.

Fall on your face, fall on your face, my mind commands, my eyes narrowing and throwing invisible switchblades into Lex's back, as if my brain has the bewitching power to make it so.

As we round the last two hundred meters, I grit my teeth so hard, I fear they might crumble in my mouth. My muscles feel like they're pulling apart, tendon by tendon, as my feet pound harder against the rubber track. Blood swishes through my ears, urging me to fight my way to the front. But that last knock to my ribs has made it impossible for good air to find its way back into my lungs (even with my carnival-show-sized nostrils). And despite my speedy pace, I remain confined to the middle of the pack. I can't push my way through without pulling a Lex and sabotaging everyone else's time. And I refuse to play dirty.

"Almost there, kick your way through the finish," Michael calls out, jogging over to the finish line as the rest of us sprint through the last fifty meters. Lex crosses the finish line first and triumphantly pumps both fists in the air like she just won the freaking Olympics (way to be humble, Lex). I cross the finish line somewhere in the middle again. Not the worst. But so clearly not the best.

"All right, passable job, you guys," Michael says, looking down at his stopwatch. He's about forty with the unicorn combination of dark hair and piercing blue eyes. But what's even more striking about him are his dark eyelashes; they're so long and thick, he almost looks like he's wearing mascara. "It wasn't total shit, but I was expecting a lot more out of some of you."

His eyes scan the crowd of female trainees, clutching our stomachs and trying to hide the impulse to pass out. His gaze doesn't stop on anyone in particular, but the muscles in my neck seize anyway as I wonder if he's talking about me.

"Go ahead and take a short break while I time the guys in some of their runs," Michael continues, looking over his shoulder as the male trainees file through the doorway after their strength assessment. "Get hydrated. Stretch. Your run isn't over yet. Regroup and I better see some major improvement out of some of you."

Michael's eyes find mine in the crowd and hold them for a beat before he runs to the other side of the track, where the male trainees are waiting for their next test.

Shit. Shit. Shit.

I turn on my heel, hanging my head as I jog over to the long bench along the far wall where my enormous water bottle is waiting. I grab it and take several greedy gulps, wishing the water was ten degrees cooler, right on the edge of frozen.

"He was totally talking to you, ya know," a voice says from behind me. I don't have to turn around to know that raspy, irritating voice is Lex's. Water droplets roll down my lips and chin, splattering on the polished concrete floor. I wipe away the excess liquid and turn around to face her.

Lex's blond high ponytail swings from side to side as she shakes out her legs, her hands resting in her favorite position on her hips. Only she could make a state of rest look so aggressive. While I'm a sweaty mess in a pilling T-shirt and running shorts, Lex looks like a trophy-wife-in-training in her aqua Lululemon tank and tight yoga pants. I try to keep my expression as blank as possible, but clearly she sees agitation in my eyes because her lips part into a satisfied smile.

"I think we're all a little surprised and frankly disappointed," she presses as her eyes scan my body.

"And why is that?" I ask, trying to keep my voice calm and even.

"Well, you've been built up to be some type of god," Lex answers, her voice haughty. She bends her waist from side to side, her tank top riding up to show off her sharply defined stomach (I'm sure this little maneuver is all by design). "My parents were on the Rescue/Take-down team with your parents for years, so all I'd ever hear is 'Reagan Hillis got asked to train in Israel with Krav Maga specialists' and 'Reagan Hillis got asked to go to a weaponry camp in Russia this summer' and 'Why can't you be advancing like Reagan Hillis?' Frankly, it got a little old. So to see you in Qualifiers and sucking? Kind of makes me wonder why the hell everyone's been so impressed and why you were ever singled out as an elite."

"I probably could have run a faster time if someone didn't knock the wind out of me on the final lap," I answer, my voice feigning disinterest. I take another swig from my water bottle and pretend like her words don't bother me even though my blood runs hotter by the second.

"Yeah, right," Lex answers with a laugh. "I've been watching you. You're a middle-of-the-pack kind of girl. Which is fine with me. I want a spot on the RT squad so when I saw you were at Qualifiers, I'm not going to lie. Got a little worried. But looks like I won't have much competition after all."

"Why do you think you can talk to people the way you do?" Anusha says, appearing at my side from behind me. I hadn't even realized she was there.

"Listen, EOP," Lex answers, rolling her eyes. "I can talk to people however the hell I want. You are nothing. My family literally built the very floor you're standing on. What was your family doing four generations ago?"

"My great-grandfather was a doctor in Mumbai," Anusha answers, her arms crossing in front of her chest. "My great-grandmother raised seven children and ran a school for girls. But even if they were selling chicken curry out of carts in the street, I'd still be proud of where I came from."

"Talk to me when your family helped to change the world," Lex throws over her shoulder and saunters toward the other side of the room where a tiny clique of followers is watching and waiting for her.

"I don't understand," Anusha says, turning toward me and pointing over her shoulder with a hitchhiker thumb. "Changed the world? Built the floor we're standing on? Do you know what the hell she's talking about?"

"Holy crap," I answer with a nod, remembering my Black Angel history lessons, pieces of the puzzle that is Lex Morgan's self-important attitude snapping into place. "I didn't realize who she was. No wonder she's so smug. Her family practically invented this agency."

As Anusha and I stretch in the corner, I regurgitate the history that was hammered into my head over the years.

"America had always had spies, but they were disorganized, especially the elite spy sector," I explain as I reach for my toes. "When President Eisenhower commissioned the building of the CIA headquarters, inside that budget were hidden funds to build a proper underground facility for America's most secretive spy network. And to run this agency, Eisenhower chose an army lieutenant who was his special advisor during World War II. He helped him with everything. D-Day. Battle strategies. That man's name was Lieutenant James Morgan."

"Oh shit," Anusha says under her breath.

"Lieutenant Morgan brought in his son to be one of the agency's first directors and then that son brought in his son. And now, there is the latest Morgan descendant," I answer and tilt my chin up at Lex across the track. "She's not just a legacy. She's *the* legacy."

"I'm sorry. Does being *the* legacy just give you a free pass to be a total bitch?" Anusha asks, unimpressed by Lex's family history.

"Absolutely not," I answer and shake my head. "But it explains a lot. I mean, her family created strategies and ran missions that helped to end the Cold War. They've stopped a number of attacks that would have had devastating effects on the United States. I hate her. But Lex's family members have been vital to the success of this agency and the safety of this country."

"But that doesn't mean a girl like Lex will get a top spot in the Black Angels over someone who is truly deserving like you," Anusha says.

"It might," I answer, looking down at my outstretched, aching legs. "It just might."

How could the Black Angels not give an RT spot to Lex Morgan? Her family members have walked these halls for decades. They've sacrificed normal lives to save millions more. Even with her horrible attitude and complete disregard for human decency, she'll get in. She has to. And that means there's one less spot, one less chance for me. Even if they took away Lex's family advantage, that girl is highly talented and annoyingly strong. I'm nowhere near her level right now. And as I watch her perfect Black Angel body curve into a stretch, I can feel my one shot to kill Torres fading, and fast.

The ember blazes in my stomach, its vengeful smoke polluting my lungs. My heart suddenly races and my chest seizes, and I feel like I'm a few breaths away from a panic attack.

I need to get out of here.

Despite the dizzy fog encircling my skull, I push myself off the ground and walk away from Anusha, Torres's heartbeat gaining strength in my ear. It beats and beats and beats against my brain, like a ticking time bomb. Without me, the Black Angels may catch him. Bring him to the US to stand trial. Lock him away for life. But that's not enough. Almost nothing will be enough. And my chance to see Torres's cold, dead eyes diminishes with every mediocre race, every middle-of-the-pack test. I must get stronger, better, faster. Because average, even among the very best, might as well be dead last.

THIRTEEN

"NO, LUKE. TURN LEFT," I SAY AND MOTION TOWARD the next fake stoplight on the closed CIA course in the mountains of Virginia. "Let the team behind us pick the target up. We've been behind him too long. He'll get suspicious if we follow him for much longer."

"You're the boss," Luke answers, pulling down on the turn signal as we approach the next light.

"Team two," I say into my earpiece. "We are making a left on Elm Street. Subject is still in a blue Honda Civic in the far right lane. We need you to pick him up."

"Picking up," I hear Anusha answer from three cars behind us.

"On it," Cam echoes. He's driving while Anusha plays strategic navigator, her eyes never leaving the target.

Our first week of assessment was all physical: timed runs, endurance tests, obstacle courses, lifting measurements, martial arts maneuvers. Sixteen hours a day of this stuff. My strength is back to only 75 percent after Colombia, and holy crap—every muscle, every tendon, even my skin is rebelling with exhaustion. Thank God this week has let up a bit; still grueling training and tests but only half the time. The other half, we're being tested on our strategy and intellect, and I'm finally hitting my stride (much to the dissatisfaction of Lex).

Luke makes a far too cautious left onto Elm Street, his eyes still on our target.

"Luke, you can't do that," I try to say as gently as I can, but my voice is tight with insistence. "Turning too slow makes you stick out. We need to remain hidden or the target is totally going to call us out and we'll fail the test. You've got to swing the car like you normally would. You can't do anything that draws attention to us."

"You're right, you're right," he says, nodding his head with frustration. I've had countless hours of training on surveillance from my parents and summer camps. But for Luke, this is all very new. "I'm sorry. This is just really bizarre. I feel like we're shooting a movie or something."

The CIA built a small town in the middle of nowhere, Virginia, for secure training just like this. There are several different avenues and streets, but the buildings are hollow or even completely flat. It's like maneuvering through the backlot of a Hollywood studio or Disney World or something. Still, CIA operatives and Black Angels have filled the streets with other cars and even fake pedestrians to make it feel as real as possible.

"I thought we were supposed to do this test in Georgetown," Luke says, glancing over at me.

"I know. Me too," I answer. "I guess they like to keep us on our toes. Okay, turn right onto Main Street up here so we can run parallel with them," I instruct, pointing Luke toward the right-hand lane. I look in the side mirror, knowing there are Black Angel trainers tailing us, watching our every maneuver. I touch the talk button in my earpiece and say, "Team two, we are taking a right on Main Street and will pick you up after two blocks, copy?"

"Copy," Anusha answers. "But be advised, target is now making a right-hand turn onto Shirley Street. Repeat, Shirley Street. You'll need to pick us up earlier."

"Copy that," I say back into the earpiece, silently motioning to Luke to turn right on Main Street, but he can hear Anusha in his earpiece too and is already making his way toward the right-turn lane. I switch off the microphone on my earpiece so I can speak privately with Luke. "Crap, maybe I shouldn't have had you turn earlier if he was going to turn so fast."

"No, that was the right move," he reassures me, nodding his head. "We were getting too close to him. He would have flagged us soon and then we would have failed."

"Team one," Cam says into my ear. "Be advised, target is parking on Shirley Street next to a park. This could be the drop. Request pickup."

"We're on him," I say as we turn onto Shirley Street. "Team two, check your mirrors. Can you see if he's getting out of the car?"

"Affirmative," Anusha answers. "He is getting out of the car and approaching a small playground. He's in a gray T-shirt and jeans. Black baseball cap. Sunglasses. Shaggy brown hair."

"Shit," I whisper to Luke. "Okay, you've got to let me out as close to the park as you can, but without drawing attention to us. I just don't want to lose him and miss the drop."

"Here, I'll pull down the alley up here," Luke says as he floors it down Shirley Street. I can see the park on the right-hand side and a man with his hands shoved in his pockets approaching the swing sets.

"Stop, stop, stop. You're going way too fast," I reply and touch his arm, his tense hands gripping the steering wheel at 9 and 3, just like they taught us in driver's ed. Luke releases his foot from the gas and we ease our way toward the alley, a block away from the park. I spot the target's gray T-shirt and shaggy hair as Luke pulls up to the curb. Without saying a word, I jump out of the car as soon as it's stopped.

Once I shut my car door and start casually walking after the target, Luke says in my ear, "Reagan, I'm going to circle the block and keep an eye on the target."

"Okay, but only circle once," I say back and push a dark pair of sunglasses up the bridge of my nose. "Pretend you're looking for parking, but when you find a spot after the first circle, park."

"Copy," Luke answers and I can hear his car engine fading as he pulls farther down the block.

"Team, be advised I'm now crossing the street and going to walk along the south end of the park but I won't enter it yet," I say into my earpiece as I casually stroll across the street without taking my eyes off the target. Black Angel trainers and agents are playing the role of pedestrians on the sidewalk and I do my best to blend in with them.

"Reagan, we are parking now one block over," Cam says into my ear. "We will be there soon with backup."

"No, no, hang back, you guys," I answer and shake my head. "I think the less people physically out here, the better. I've got this."

"Copy that," Anusha says in my ear as I watch the target remove an envelope from the pocket of his jeans. He turns around, looking over his shoulder, scanning the pedestrians in the park and on the sidewalk. I immediately turn away. When I look back, he has turned around and is walking toward a large slide at an empty area of the playground. I press my talk button. "Target has removed an envelope and is now approaching a metal slide at my three o'clock. There are no other citizens in that section of the park. Looks like this is a lone drop."

"Copy," Anusha and Luke both say at the same time in my ear.

I circle around the opposite end of the park and head toward a fence where several young "couples" are paired up, peering into the park. I pick a spot and rest my elbows up on top of the chain-link fence. My head is pointed toward the swing set, but my eyes are staring straight at the target, hidden behind my dark sunglasses.

The target stands next to the slide, his elbow resting on the hot aluminum. He looks over his shoulder once more then seamlessly tucks the envelope underneath before shoving his hands in his pockets, backing up and walking away.

"Got him," I say into my earpiece, still watching his large frame from behind my dark lenses.

"Awesome. Don't move in too fast, Reagan," Anusha replies into my earpiece.

"I know," I answer and watch as the target walks out of the playground and toward his car.

"Target is approaching his car," I hear Luke say in my ear, parked somewhere nearby. My eyes follow his body as he approaches his blue car, climbs in, and pulls out of his spot.

"Am I clear?" I ask my team.

"No. Hold on," Luke says, clearly watching the target closely. "Okay, go, Reagan. You're clear."

My eyes scan the park one more time, making sure there is no one else ready to intercept the envelope. The trainers didn't say anything about being on the lookout for a second target, but this is the Black Angels. You'd be stupid to not expect the unexpected.

"Making my approach," I say into my earpiece as I push away from the fence and walk toward the slide where the target stuck his envelope. "Thirty feet away. Twenty feet away. Ten feet away." I update them on my progress. I reach the slide, feel for the spot with the envelope, and pull it away. "Got it."

"Excellent job, team," I hear Jack, our surveillance and tactical trainer, say in my ear. "You are the only team to complete the surveillance test on the first try so far."

"Awesome work, guys!" Luke says in my earpiece and I can hear Anusha and Cam celebrating on the other end too.

"Yeah!" I exclaim and throw my hands up in the air as I walk toward Luke's car, now parked where the target's used to be.

"Reagan, fantastic leadership," Jack says in my ear. "You really helped to steer the team in the right direction and keep everyone hidden."

"Thanks so much, sir," I reply, breathing a sigh of relief. After my horrible performance last week, I'm elated to finally be excelling at something. "I really appreciate that. Everyone did amazing."

"Agreed," Jack answers. "You were the last group. So you four can drive the practice cars back to base. Grab something to eat. You need to refuel before our last test tonight."

"Perfect," I say and open the car door. Luke beams proudly at me as I climb into the passenger seat.

"Freaking awesome, Reagan," he says, opening his hand to me, inviting a high five. I hit my hand into his palm and hold it there for a second too long. My skin ignites, tingling like tiny champagne bubbles, as my fingers drag against his skin and pull away.

There it is, my mind whispers. That unquestionable heat. I wasn't sure if it'd ever return.

When I've touched him over the last week, I've felt warmth. I felt care. But let's be honest. I have so many emotions stacked on top of one another that it's hard to breathe. Hate on top of hurt on top of sorrow on top of fury. So, love? I wasn't sure if it was still in this car, still in me. It's hard to find the good when you're emotionally suffocating from all the bad. But as my eyes linger on his strong hands, I realize just how badly I want his fingers laced through mine. How much I need to feel that touch, that burn again.

"I need food so badly," Luke says, breaking my trance as he pulls out of the parking spot.

"Uhh . . . yeah . . . yeah . . . same," I stutter and shake my head to clear it. "And an ice cream sundae. Will you make one for me?"

I like the way Luke makes my sundaes. Always have. When we lived in New Albany, he'd come up with the best creations. It was a little game we'd play trying to outdo his last wildly creative concoction.

"Of course I will," Luke says, pulling down Shirley Street, the Black Angel watchers directly behind us.

"Do we get radio in these cars?" I ask and Luke flips on the radio to a classic seventies rock station. Boston's "More Than a Feeling" comes blasting through our speakers.

"Yesssssss," I say and Luke's full lips separate into a wide smile, his dimples creased so deeply, they could hold pocket change. We both love all kinds of music but have a special place in our hearts for the rock bands of the seventies.

"More than a feeling," I jump in on the chorus.

"Till I see Marianne walk away," Luke sings.

"I see my Marianne walkin' away." I belt out the last line of the chorus and then bend my fingers into a fierce air guitar, shredding my imaginary solo, my head banging and hair flying.

Luke laughs and for a second, I forget where we are, what we're doing, and the life that lies ahead of us. For the three-minute car ride back to base, it's just us.

FOURTEEN

"READY. AIM. FIRE!"

CORE's firing range explodes with the rapid blasts of bullets. Twelve of us are lined up in the shooting range, two Glock 22 pistols in our hands, firing at a difficult target several hundred feet away.

The explosions end. I count while I fire, so I know my clips are empty, but I can hear a few other trainees still pulling on the trigger, the click of an empty chamber giving them away.

"All right, bring them forward," Jules Puleri, our shooting instructor, shouts and the machines bring our paper targets forward for her to inspect. A former military sniper shooter, Jules was awarded several presidential medals before being recruited to join the Black Angels a decade ago. I've heard people say she's the best shooter in the entire country.

We put our weapons down and stand next to our dummies, bracing for Jules's comments. I spy a look down the line. Several dummies are sprayed with bullets. Mine has two giant holes. One to the head, one to the heart.

"Nice work, Mr. Conley," Jules says as she inspects his target before moving on. "Mr. Weixel, getting better, happy to see that. Miss Venkataraman, you're still all over the place. An extra hour of shooting tonight, please."

Anusha nods her head and examines her dummy. Some of her bullets didn't even hit the target.

"Lex Morgan," Jules says as she comes closer to my end of the shooting range. Lex's green eyes widen as Jules gets closer, an expectant smile tickling the corners of her mouth, causing her lips to twitch under her restraint.

"Yes, Agent Puleri?" Lex responds, her put-on voice slick with saccharine. I have to resist the constant urge to roll my eyes whenever Lex is around.

Jules stands in front of Lex's target, examining it from top to bottom before shaking her head. Lex's face falls before the words reach her.

"This is a joke, right?" Jules's gravelly voice is wrapped in serrated blades, cutting through Lex's overly confident demeanor. Which is fine by me; Lex has only grown more insufferable as the weeks of testing and training have gone on. "This is atrocious. You've seriously been shooting since you were seven?"

"Yes, ma'am. I can shoot any type of weapon you throw at me," Lex answers, her voice with an edge that borders on defensive. *Uh-oh.* Jules's neck begins to change colors.

"Well, I just gave you one of the easiest weapons in the world to shoot and you can't shoot for shit, so let's bring that confidence down a notch or two. Or twenty," Jules declares, stabbing her finger through several bullet holes that didn't come close to hitting the outlined target. "Three hours of extra shooting practice tonight."

"But, Agent Puleri," Lex says, looking across the shooting range at the clock on the far wall. "It's already ten p.m."

"Are you questioning me, Miss Morgan?" Jules's voice swells.

"No, ma'am," Lex answers and shakes her head, her long, blond ponytail swaying back and forth.

"Sure sounds like it," Jules huffs. "You've been in Qualifiers for over a month. You should know by now when a trainer says something to you, the only response we want to hear is yes. There are no excuses at CORE. I don't give a shit if you're tired. I don't give a shit if you're hungry. No one put a gun to your head and forced you to be here, so if you want out, there's the door."

Jules's strong arm stretches out and points toward the door that leads to the North Hall and the rest of the training rooms.

"Yes, ma'am," Lex responds and puts her arms behind her back. She bows her head and her ivory cheeks streak crimson. But I've been around Lex long enough to know that flush isn't from embarrassment, but anger.

"Next. Reagan Hillis." Jules makes her way toward me and my dummy. She looks it over, her hands penetrating the gaping wound at the target's chest. "As close to perfect as you can get. Anybody who needs extra help, talk to this one."

Jules pats me on the shoulder and I wince under the weight of her compliment. I started out more than mediocre when it came to my strength and endurance but my shooting skills have always been at the top of the group. Just another reason for some of these people to dislike me. Especially Lex.

"All right, that's enough for today," Jules announces, looking down at the watch on her wrist. "One last thing: I know tomorrow is your one free day and some of you have requested to go into DC for the day but Director Browning wanted me to pass along that all of those requests have been denied and we need you to stay put."

"Why?" one of the male trainees asks.

"I don't need to give you a reason why," Jules answers curtly and turns back to the rest of the group. "If any of you need to refuel before bed, kitchen is open for another hour, so make your way there. Otherwise, hit the showers. Lights-out at midnight. Except for you, Lex. I better not see you leave the range until one a.m."

"Yes, ma'am," Lex mutters.

Jules claps her hands two times, signaling the end of training, and walks toward the exit. I want to follow her out, grab some food, and hide. But before I can make my way toward the door, my friends are gathering around my target.

"Holy crap," Anusha says, sticking her fist through the hole in the chest. "You really tore the hell out of this guy."

"Way to go, Hillis," Cam says and gives me a high five.

"Yeah, you're showing us how it's done," Luke adds, wrapping his arm around my shoulder and squeezing me closer to him.

"And she's so humble about it too," Lex says under her breath, but loud enough for us all to hear her.

"What did you just say?" Anusha asks, whipping around to face Lex.

"Nothing," Lex responds, her so-sweet-I-might-puke smile

crawling up her face. "Congrats, Reagan. You make the rest of us look like total amateurs."

"That's your problem, Lex," Anusha snaps, always quick to defend me. "It's called work harder and get better. This is a competition, you know."

"Oh wow! I didn't realize that," Lex says, bringing both hands to her cheeks. "Thanks so much for letting me know how the Black Angels work, Anusha. Especially since you've been here a whole five minutes and all. Enjoy it. You'll be cut and back flying your little planes in no time."

With that, Lex heads toward the weapons room to grab more ammunition.

"What is wrong with that girl?" Anusha says, spinning back around to us, her thumb pointing over her shoulder at Lex. "Why does she think it's okay to talk like that to people in a room full of guns? I seriously just want to—"

"Screw her, Anusha," Luke says, gently grabbing on to Anusha's wrist to stop her from running after Lex. "She's not worth it. Come on, let's go get something to eat."

Cam takes over from Luke, pulling at Anusha's arm to quell the brewing confrontation. Anusha, like Lex, likes to have the last word. Luke and I follow a few steps behind them, our pace set at "Luke and Reagan" speed so we can have a few minutes to ourselves.

After a few silent steps, I say what I've been thinking all week. "Everybody hates me."

"Everybody does not hate you," Luke replies quickly, his fingertips gently wrapping around my forearm. My skin pulses and he pulls away. "People are in awe of you. You're finally getting back your strength and catching up and everyone is starting to see what you can really do."

"I'm not even close to where I should be," I answer firmly. "We did intervals the other day. I'm still middle of the pack. Granted, I'm at the front of the middle now, but still the middle. I just don't know if the trainers will think I'm field material after seeing my performance. Definitely not Rescue/Take-down material, that's for sure. You've got to actually . . . you know . . . run and stuff. Kick in doors. Lift heavy objects."

"You'll get there."

"It took me years of training to get there," I answer and shake my head, disappointment continuing to bankrupt my meager stash of hope and faith. "It's hard to get that back after just a couple months."

"But you're doing awesome at shooting," Luke counters. "And all the strategy tests, you're killing it. You've come in first in all of them."

"I guess," I answer and shrug my shoulders. "It's good I'm doing well in those tests to make up for my poor standings in strength and endurance testing but kind of bad news as well."

"Why?" Luke says as we walk slowly around the intel center and make our way down the West Hall toward the cafeteria.

"Because it just gives Lex more of a reason to hate me. Admit it. Lex and her little friends would rip my throat out while I was sleeping if they thought it would help them get ahead. Hell, they'd probably do it just for shits and giggles if they thought they could remove my body without getting caught."

"Don't let her get under your skin," Luke says, shaking his head.

"That's all she's trying to do. She's trying to get in your head so you'll screw up."

"I know it," I answer. "Only three spots on the RT squad. You know I want one of them. But she's a shoo-in between her skills and the Morgan family legacy."

"You've got just as good a chance as she does. Just watch your back. She strikes me as someone who plays dirty," Luke says, placing his hand between my shoulder blades, the warmth of his hand seeping into my cool, exposed skin. I adjust the strap of my tank top, forcing his hand to slide down my spine and return to his side.

"I will," I say and look up into Luke's kind eyes. My body leans into his, inviting him to put his arm back around my shoulder. He smiles at me, slips his hand along my skin, and tightens me in his grip. "But even when I can't, you've got my six, right?"

"I like it when you talk military to me." Luke's dimples crease deeper as I use the military term for *back*. He squeezes my shoulder and says, "I've got your six. Always."

And I know he does.

FIFTEEN

MY HAIR SMELLS DIFFERENT. I STARE AT MYSELF IN THE tiny, cheap mirror over one of the sinks in the girls' dorm bathroom. I pull my wet locks to my nose and sniff. Yup, fruity notes of apple that remind me of fall. My shampoo is cleaner with a hint of lavender. I shrug my shoulders at my reflection and pull my robe tighter around my waist as I towel off my dripping dark tresses. I'm so exhausted right now I must have grabbed someone else's shower stuff by mistake.

"Reagan," I hear a familiar voice say from behind me.

My body turns around slowly, half convinced I imagined it. I haven't even heard from her since the Tribunal over three months ago. But there she is, dressed in black leggings and a gray zip-up, her blond hair in a messy bun on top of her head. I study Sam's face. She's pale with graying circles cradling her blue eyes. She must have just gotten off a plane.

"Hi, stranger," I say, my voice softer than I thought it'd be. The mournful knot lodged beneath my sternum flares as our eyes lock.

My pseudo-aunt. My mother's best friend. I wonder if she feels the twin ache in her chest when she sees me, a reminder of what we've lost.

Mom's disappeared a little bit at a time. It's like she's made of sand, and every day I watch as pieces of her get picked up and swept away, stolen by the wind. I used to call her cell to hear her voice, but the Black Angels disconnected her number in December. When I'd hear a creak in the safe house, I stopped mistaking it for her around Valentine's Day. The worst was when her clothes lost her scent, a mixture of Olay face cream and the perfume Dad bought her every Christmas. Once a week, I'd rifle through her go-bag and greedily smell her favorite sweater. Each time, it grew fainter and fainter and fainter until one March day, it was gone. *She* is all but gone, a face in a photograph, a series of tattered memories. No grave site to visit or ashes to hold on to. All that remains are the people who loved her. And that will never, ever be enough to fill the gaping wound that has wrecked us all.

"What are you doing here?" I ask, re-cinching my robe around my waist. "I haven't heard from you in ages. I thought you were deep in the trenches or something."

"I was," she answers and walks into the empty dorm bathroom, the door squeaking shut behind her. "Sorry I haven't been allowed to reach out. I've missed you."

"It's okay," I answer. I've grown accustomed to her going radio silent on me when she's on intense missions. Dad, too. "I know how it is. So how long are you back for?"

"I'm . . . I'm not sure yet," Sam answers, her tired eyes shifting anxiously around the bathroom, avoiding mine. The hairs on the

117

back of my neck stand up. Despite her decades of training, I know Sam too well. We read each other like few can.

"Sam, what's going on?" I ask, reaching out for her arm. I know this look. She's trying to hide it, but I've seen this restrained terror before. I saw it on my parents' faces, heard it in their words, after the mission that killed Torres's son. Something is wrong. "Did something happen on your mission?"

"No, no. I'm fine. I'm just exhausted," she answers quickly, rubbing her face into clusters of stress lines and wrinkles. She glances down at her watch. "I've been up for like thirty-eight hours straight. I just wanted to see you before I crashed. How is it going here?"

"Okay, I guess," I respond, pushing my lips into a pensive pout, my mind filtering through the last two months of Qualifiers. "My strength is still not where it was before. So I'm definitely not blowing anyone away with the endurance testing. But I'm getting better every day. Doing really well on the strategy, operations, and intel side. So I think that's promising."

"So I've heard," Sam says softly. Her eyes finally lock back up with mine, tinted a shade darker. She bites down on her lip, but brick by brick her walls begin to fall.

"Sam, what is it?" I ask gently, reaching out for her again. Before I can touch her, she pulls away, her face cast down. She steadies herself, both hands drawn to her hips, and takes in a weighty breath.

"You don't have to do this, you know," Sam finally utters, her voice quiet, her eyes fixed on the chipping floor tile and flaking beige grout.

My body bends backward, thrown off by Sam's sudden declaration.

"What are you talking about?" I ask, my voice uncharacteristically wispy.

"You can still have a normal life. Isn't that what you've always wanted? Weren't you ready to choose that before Colombia?"

"I don't understand why you're saying this," I reply, shaking my head. "After what, like five solid years of pushing me to go to the academy, now you don't want me here? You don't think I'm good enough to be a Black Angel?"

"No. That's not it at all," Sam answers, looking back up at me and furiously shaking her head. "Things are just...Look, I know your strength and your mind and your talent and what you could do for this agency. The Black Angel in me wants you here. But the part of me that loves you like a daughter is absolutely terrified right now."

Right now. Right now. Those two words echo inside me, like they were screamed into a canyon, and the knot of fear pulsing in my stomach pulls more taut.

Sam takes a step closer to me and grabs my hand, threading her fingers through mine.

"Your mother was my...my..." Sam's eyes gleam as she sniffs back unexplained tears, threatening to fall. "I promised her I'd always protect you. So the thought of you doing this job and something happening to you too...I hate to say it, but I just want you to be normal now."

"But why now, Sam?" I press her again, narrowing my eyes and squeezing her hand. "Something must have happened. Why are you saying all of this now and not months ago?"

"It's something I've been thinking about for a while..." Sam's voice trails off; she stares at the wall behind me, a memory or scene or moment playing out against the white cinder block. She shakes her head, erasing its projection. "But just . . . an alarm has been ringing in me for days saying run, run, run."

Torres. It has to be Torres.

I let go of Sam's hand and grab her by the shoulders. Her eyes turn back to me, wild with worry. "What aren't you telling me?" I say, my voice tight. "I know you. I know something is wrong."

Sam's shoulders lift with another heavy sigh and she slowly shakes her head. "Nothing is wrong—"

"You're lying." I cut her off and squeeze her shoulders tighter. "I know when you're hiding something from me. Tell me. Is it Torres? Have they found him?"

Sam's face stays stoic, but I can feel her shoulders flinch in my palms at the sound of his name. She pulls away from my strong grasp. "No, it's not Torres. I told you, I'm exhausted and I've just been worrying about you is all. The things you see in the field . . ." Sam looks through me, her mind still replaying a movie she doesn't want to see. She closes her eyes for a moment, then opens them again. "It changes you. And I guess sometimes I just want a different life for you."

"Don't you think with all I've already seen, if I didn't want to be here, I'd have left by now?" I reply. Before I can stop it, I hear the weighty clank of rusted chains. The dark blood on her clothes. The smell of gunfire. And my body goes numb.

Sam nods slowly, unconvincingly, her hands smoothing out the bumps and stray hairs along the crown of her head. "Just . . .

promise me you'll be careful, Reagan. Follow the trainers' every instruction. You're still a ... wanted woman."

The muscles in my back constrict. That pause. The way her mouth almost formed another word, then stopped before it could escape her throat. She wasn't going to say wanted. She was going to say hunted. I'm a still a hunted woman.

"I know," I answer, shaking off the panic I can feel thickening my throat, restricting my breath. I stick out my chin and give her my most confident nod. "I'll be okay, Sam. Promise."

Sam holds my gaze and thinks, a sad smile tickling the corners of her lips. "Okay," she finally utters. "Please. Stay safe, Reagan."

With that, Sam turns and walks out of the dorm bathroom in search of a free single bedroom to rest her weary body. As the heavy door whines closed, a chill races through me, like a thousand tiny spiders under my skin. And that black cloud of dread camouflages itself as air, a Trojan horse ushered back inside with my next breath. It tightens my lungs, releases its poison.

Something is wrong. Something is very wrong.

SIXTEEN

DESPITE SEVERAL MINUTES OF TRYING TO DEEP
breathe my way out of a panic attack behind a closed bathroom stall
door, I still can't pull in a full breath. My lungs sag, like a half-filled
balloon, the dark cloud refusing to let go. And if not being able to
properly breathe wasn't bad enough, the muscles in my back rebuff
every effort to untangle them. Carrying my empty tray down the
breakfast line takes a considerable amount of effort.

"Rough training week?" Simon, CORE's head chef, asks me as
he loads my plate with the soft and creamy scrambled eggs he knows
I like.

"Oh . . . yeah," I lie, rolling my shoulders and stretching my back,
trying in vain to find relief that just won't come.

"Take a hot shower," Simon answers. "And pop ibuprofen like
Skittles. You'll be all right."

"Thanks, Simon," I respond with a strained smile as he hands
me my plate of eggs, bacon, and toast. "I'll give that a try."

I grab a couple packets of jam from the breadbasket at the end of the line and snake my way through the cafeteria toward our table in the far right corner where Cam and Anusha are already eating. It's not just us who have a self-assigned seat. Everyone does. CORE senior leaders always eat at tables toward the front, operatives in the middle, Black Angel trainers in the left-hand corner in the back, and trainees to their right. It's almost like we know our positions, our rank in the powerful chain of command. And we are the lowest of the low. That's why we sit by the trash cans.

When I reach our table, Anusha's and Cam's shoulders are angled sharply toward each other; their tones are hushed.

"Where's Luke?" I ask, nodding toward his empty seat.

"Already ate," Anusha answers. "Had an early meeting with his adviser."

"Maybe Reagan knows why," Cam says softly as I take my seat.

"Maybe I know why what?" I reply and open my packet of jelly.

"They canceled our training exercise in Georgetown today *again*," Anusha answers, her large eyes narrowing. "Don't you think that's weird? That's like the third or fourth time they've done that in the last few weeks. And I got special permission to meet my parents in DC tomorrow night, but this morning Browning told me the request has been denied even though it was approved two weeks ago."

The pain in my shoulder deepens and I have to force my body to stay upright.

"Something is going on," I reply, my voice dropping along with my stomach.

"How do you know?" Cam asks, his face tightening with shared worry.

"Sam's back."

"Your pseudo-aunt slash watcher lady?" Anusha asks. They've heard me talk about her ad nauseam but have yet to meet her face-to-face.

"Yes," I confirm. "She's back and she's acting super weird and emotional and just . . . something is wrong. I know it. I have this feeling it has something to do with Torres. And that we're in danger. All of us."

"Why? Did she say something?" Cam probes.

"No, but . . . I just know," I reply, my body leaning in closer to them. "I can't explain it. When I brought up his name, she said no, but I could feel it. Cam, you've been around Black Angels long enough to know when something is wrong, am I right?"

"Yeah," he says quietly with a soft nod.

"And you feel it too, don't you?"

"I do," he whispers, his eyes holding mine, a silent understanding passing between us.

When you're a Black Angel trainee, every sense is heightened. It's what you're practically programmed to do. To not only be aware of your surroundings through what you see and hear, but what you feel. Our parents have been on enough missions that we know immediately when things go well and when things go terribly wrong. It's not just by tight smiles or how they hug us hello, but by their energy. A bad mission changes the molecules that surround their bodies. The tension expands the gases in the room, diluting the oxygen, until it's hard to breathe, hard to feel anything but their fear. They try to hide it, but we know. Most of the time, I'd let it go. I wouldn't push for details. I'd simply give Dad an extra kiss or

124

hold Mom's hand at the kitchen counter for a few beats longer than normal. It's like we've signed a silent policy where we don't ask and they don't tell. But we always know. We were designed to know.

"What do we do?" Anusha asks, tapping her fingers nervously on the table. "How can we find out if that's true?"

"I'll hack into the files," Cam answers, his eyes still on me.

"Are you sure about that?" I ask, reaching out for the top of Cam's wrist. "What about the Tribunal? You almost lost your spot once. I don't want you to risk losing it again."

"This time I won't get caught," he replies.

"You think you can even get in?" Anusha asks.

"I don't know," Cam says with a sigh. "But I want to at least try."

———

"Let's just grab it and go down to one of the secure conference rooms," I say quietly to Cam as he pulls his Black Angel–sanctioned laptop from underneath his bunk bed. He opens his nightstand drawer, digs around, and pulls out a tiny envelope. He examines it for a moment then shoves it into the pocket of his sweatshirt.

"What's that?" Anusha asks, eyeing the envelope's exposed white corner.

"You'll see," Cam answers, pushing the envelope deeper into his pocket, hiding it completely out of view.

"What are you guys doing?" a voice says from behind us. Anusha and Cam turn around, their faces streaked with alarm. I swivel my head slowly, knowing his voice. Luke.

"Just come with us," Cam answers, tucking the laptop under his arm and walking briskly toward the door. The three of us follow

Cam's quick pace down the hallway, trying to look as inconspicuous as possible. I look down at Mom's watch on my wrist. We still have about twenty minutes before our morning training begins.

Once we reach a small, soundproofed conference room, Cam ushers us in and we quickly close the door behind us.

"We don't have a ton of time to do this," I say as Cam takes a seat at the conference table, the metal frame whining at the changing weight.

"Do what?" Luke asks, his eyes searching each face for some type of answer. We all stare at one another, not sure what to say or who should explain.

"I think Torres has resurfaced and . . . I don't know what, but something is happening with the Black Angels," I answer, walking closer to Luke. "They keep canceling all training sessions outside of CORE. Plus, Sam is back and seems really upset and weirdly protective and worried and I just . . . I just know something is going on and we want to find out what it is. So Cam is hacking into the secure files."

"That's a terrible idea," Luke replies curtly, shaking his head at me. He steps around me to get a better look at Cam, who is already typing away at his computer. "Weren't you almost kicked out of the Black Angels for hacking?"

"Slap on the wrist," Cam answers without tearing his eyes away from the computer, seemingly unmoved.

"Well, don't you think we should wait until the trainers tell us what's going on?" Luke presses, turning back toward me.

"Yeah, right," I snort, my face contorting with the impossibility of trainees being looped in on something so highly confidential.

126

"They're not going to tell us anything. Especially if it has something to do with Torres. And if it does, I think we, of all people, should know."

"Why?" Luke asks, crossing his arms over his chest. "Reagan, don't you think there are protocols in place for a reason?"

"Look, if you want to be all military and follow the rules, then you don't have to be here," I answer, the words sounding much harsher out loud than in my head. But I don't really have time for this. "Cam and I have people we love on the front lines in the Black Angels. We deserve to know what's going on. We're doing this."

Luke's full lips disappear as he squeezes them in a thin line between his teeth. "Fine. Do what you want, Reagan. I'm just trying to protect you," he answers quietly, taking a seat on the other side of the table while I rush back to Cam's side.

"Okay," I say, standing behind him and peering at his screen. "What do we do?"

Cam walks us through the hacks. He has already bypassed a restrictive security program put into place for all trainees. Now the computer is free to be accessed by any Black Angel operative. Next security protocol to bypass: biomechanical. Facial recognition is hard to fake. Thank goodness Cam's laptop only has a tiny clear rectangle on the right. It wants a fingerprint. But not Cam's fingerprint. A higher ranking Black Angel fingerprint. Someone who can actually get into the CORE database.

"How the hell are we going to get a senior leader's fingerprint?" Anusha asks, rolling her seat closer to Cam. He smiles at her mischievously and pulls out the envelope tucked in his pocket. He holds it up and waves it in the air with about the same enthusiasm he would if it contained the secrets of the universe.

"Director Browning should be more careful where she places her hands," Cam answers and unseals the envelope, pulling out a tiny piece of pink latex. My jaw becomes unhinged.

"You've got to be shitting me," I reply with equal parts astonishment and respect. The lengths Cam had to go to in order to get that print defies all rational human behavior. He probably had to lift her prints from multiple surfaces (without getting caught once, mind you), take a high-resolution photo of a perfect fingerprint, secretly access CORE's computer labs to print its inverted form on a transparent sheet with a thick toner setting, then sneak latex out of one of the engineering labs. Jesus. I know the basics of how to do it, but lack the balls. That kid is brave.

"I knew it'd come in handy one of these days," Cam states, carefully pulling Browning's latex fingerprint closer to his face, moistening it with his breath. "Here goes nothing."

Cam places the fingerprint to the screen and my heart pounds anxiously against my chest as the security scan begins. *One Mississippi. Two Mississippi. Three Mississippi.* The laptop screen flashes two words: *Access Granted.*

"Yes," Cam whispers and kisses that little latex print.

"You're an evil little genius," Anusha says, patting him on the back.

Cam pulls out a slip of paper tucked inside the envelope. I stare down at a series of numbers, words, and letters. Browning's passwords.

"How the hell did you get those?" I ask, grabbing him from behind by both shoulders.

"Easy. I was in her office a few weeks ago for a status meeting and she left for a minute to grab some reports, so I installed a keylogger that recorded her keystrokes," Cam answers. "She never suspected a thing. After a week of recording, I analyzed it and narrowed down her list of passwords."

"You're kind of insane, you know that, right?" Anusha says, a small smile creeping up her face. "Like the good kind of insane but still . . . Jesus."

"Okay, now what?" Cam says, more to himself than to us. My eyes scan the laptop screen, landing on a red circle with a pair of angel wings in the right corner.

"There," I answer and Cam clicks on the symbol. A screen pops up, requesting his password. "How do you know which one?"

"I don't," Cam replies, his chest rising with a nervous breath. "I should get a couple tries though."

"What happens if you type in one too many wrong passwords?" Luke asks, his hands steadily climbing up his face with each stressful minute. When he sat down they were at his chin, then his cheeks, now they're hovering around his eyebrows.

"Then we get locked out," Cam replies, staring down at the list of passwords. "Oh, and bonus . . . CORE will be alerted of suspected theft of information."

"Perfect," Luke answers, his hands now sliding up to his temples.

"It's cool," Cam utters with a confident nod but a cracking voice. "I've got this."

Cam types in the password, marked with a star, on his tiny sheet of paper. He double-checks every letter and number, then hits enter. My chest tightens and I hear Anusha suck in an anxious breath as we wait for the CORE mainframe to let us in.

One Mississippi. Two Mississippi. Three Mississippi.

The screen suddenly fills with activity.

"We're in," Cam says, his hand pounding triumphantly against the table. Satellite photos come in live in the left corner of the screen while white lines crescendo and fall on the right. Cam clicks on the box and we hear a man's voice speaking in Russian. A phone call interception. A spinning, blue globe in the center has icons that pinpoint where the call is coming from, where the satellite photos are being taken. It's like having an inside view of CORE's secure intel center that I've never been allowed to see. Down at the bottom, tiny blue folders are marked with mission code names. I scan the list. Sniper Five. Operation Big Ben. Driftwood Rebellion. Metal Spear. Huxby Light. Traitor Terror.

"Traitor Terror," I say and point to the bottom of the screen. "Think about it. Former Black Angel turned traitor. That's got to be it."

Cam clicks on the blue folder and a screen pops up, requesting a password.

"Which password is it?" Anusha asks, peering down at the list in Cam's hand.

"I don't know," Cam answers and shakes his head. "I knew that first one would be her log-in because she uses it all the time. I don't know which password is for the Torres folder. Or if that password is even on this list."

"Shit," I say under my breath.

Luke stands up from his seat across from us and silently walks to where we're huddled on the other side of the table. We all stare at the list, narrowing down the possibilities.

"Well, it could be two options," Luke says, pointing at the paper. "Diablo919. *Diablo* is the Spanish word for *devil*. I feel like that's fitting for someone like Torres. Or, maybe it's Wings160. You know, in reference to the Black Angels since he was a former agent?"

"Good thinking, Luke," I say, relieved to have him with us and not against us. Not that I gave him much choice in the matter. "Let's try those."

Cam types Wings160 into a tiny password bar, triple-checks it, and hits enter. The screen immediately blackens, the laptop's speakers blaring with three warning beeps. *Access Denied* pops up on the screen in thick, red type.

"Crap," I say, mentally crossing that password off the list. "Try the diablo one. Luke may be right. That one might be it."

Cam slowly and purposefully types in the last password, his fingers shaking slightly with every keystroke. The four of us check and check and check again.

We don't have to do this. We don't have to do this, my mind whispers. I shake my head, drowning out the doubtful noise trying to stop me. We need to know where Torres is. What he's up to. If he's coming after us.

"Okay," I say softly and touch Cam on the shoulder. "It's right."

The room is silent as we collectively hold our breaths. Cam hits the enter key. I close my eyes as pinpricks race across my spine, my stomach heaving as each second passes.

One Mississippi. Two Mississippi. Three Mississippi.

I open my eyes. The screen lights up. *Access Granted.* We're in.

"Oh, thank God," I boom, my hands grabbing at my throbbing stomach and massaging the knot coiled around my intestines. A steady stream of air escapes through my gaping mouth and an un-expected laugh bubbles up my throat.

"I seriously almost blacked out," Anusha interjects, shaking out her hands.

There are dozens of files in here. We scan their names: Recorded Phone Calls, Banking Reports, Digital Tracking, Surveillance Videos, Known Associates, and Satellite Photos. Cam's cursor hovers over the Satellite Photos file and clicks in. The first satellite photo that comes up is Torres's ranch in Tumaco. I remember the layout from our mission. The satellite photos are dated three days ago. There are no lights. No guards. No activity. He's not there.

My eyes settle on a file labeled Attacks. "Wait, what's that?" I answer and point toward the file. "Attacks. What does that mean?"

"Click on it," Luke says, leaning in closer to the computer. Cam clicks on the folder and a Black Angel report pops up. It's marked with yesterday's date. The words *Highly Classified* are written in red block letters across the top. My eyes scan the report.

Black Angel operative shot and killed.

Assailant fled.

Surviving operative: Samantha Levick.

Surveillance photos retrieved.

Assailant identified. Torres White Angel.

Second attack on Black Angels.

Torres at large.

Extreme threat.

Reagan Hillis. Luke Weixel. Highest targets.

Trainees locked down.

All Black Angels on high alert.

No. Oh lord, please no.

My head begins to shake back and forth in furious bursts, like that could erase the words on the screen. But when I look again, they're still there.

Bile rises up my throat as the fragments of what I just read paint a terrifyingly clear picture. Torres is targeting and killing Black Angels. Because of me.

The room spins, my stomach throbs with the twist of a thousand knives. Bile rises farther and farther up my throat until I cannot contain it. I sprint across the room toward a metal trash can and throw up for the first time in years. The acid burns my throat and the biting, sour smell makes my eyes sting with tears. I heave once more, throwing up what little breakfast I was able to force down, and then there's a hand on my back, rubbing my clammy skin.

"It's okay, Reagan," Luke's voice says gently from behind me. "It's okay."

"No, it's not okay," I cry out, my voice echoing against the hollowed metal. I stay bent at my waist for a second more, making sure I'm not going to throw up again, before standing up and wiping my rancid lips with the back of my hand. "People are *dying* because of what I did. He's coming after Black Angels for no other reason than what happened in Colombia."

"What are you talking about?" Luke says softly, turning me

around. "He came after you and your family two years ago. He came after you again in the fall. He's always been targeting Black Angels."

"Yeah, but I started this attack," I reply, pointing toward Cam's computer, hot tears still burning my eyes. "I killed his brother. He wants us both dead and if he can't kill us, he's going to kill somebody else. And that's not fair. It's not fair that other Black Angels are in danger because of me. I wish he'd just killed me in Colombia. Ended this whole mess."

"Listen to me, Reagan," Luke says, clutching both of my shoulders. "Santino Torres is an evil man. He'd come after the Black Angels even if we both died in that storage room. This is what he wants. He wants us to be scared. And he won't stop until the Black Angels find him."

"Well, what the hell is taking so long?" I answer and throw my hands up in the air. "How is Torres completely off the grid and yet he's able to track *us* down? That doesn't make any sense. This is supposed to be the best spy agency in the world. How is he beating us at our own game?"

"Pain can make you superhuman," Cam replies, his voice monotone, his eyes unfocused, caught in a stare he can't break. "He's lost his son, his brother, his freedom. And he wants us to pay for that."

"I hate to even say this, but training starts in five minutes," Anusha says, glancing up at the clock over the soundproofed door. "How are we supposed to get through the day knowing all this is happening?"

"We just have to," I say, clearing the lingering emotion in my throat and forcing the fear and sorrow and panic back into their little box. "We can't breathe a word of this to anyone. You guys understand? No one can know."

The three of them stare back at me, nodding their heads, silently accepting that this is our dangerous secret to keep. And right now, there's nothing we can do but watch and wait. That fire, that anger that consumed me for months has grown inexplicably cold. I feel paralyzed, helpless. The only cure for this sickness is action. But I have no idea what to do or where to begin.

SEVENTEEN

THEIR BREATHING HAS BECOME MY NIGHTLY SOUND-
track. I lie awake and stare into the black while their breaths wrap
around one another, like a symphony, each with their role to play.
Lex's is unmistakable. Erratic, she alternates between low and
quiet, then deep and noisy. She's the percussion. Anusha sleeps one
bunk over. She broke her nose playing lacrosse two years ago and
suffered a deviated septum. When it's quiet, I can hear the slightest
whistle. She's the wind instruments. Hannah, the girl who sleeps
on the bunk above me, has steady, dependable breaths. Quiet and
calm, almost sweet. She's the strings.

It's after two o'clock in the morning and I have yet to fall
asleep. My brain refuses to turn off for the fourth night in a row.
Ever since we found out about Torres, what he's doing to Black
Angels, I can't sleep. I long for Sam's sleeping pills, for the imaginary
hand that pushes me deeper into the heavy fog of drug-induced
slumber.

It's no use. I push my body quietly out of its nest of blankets, pull on my robe, and find my slippers at the end of the bed. I tiptoe across the room, careful not to disturb anyone, and slip out the door.

The lights are switched off throughout most of the compound. Only every other overhead light lining the residential hallway is switched on, their relentless fluorescent hum reduced to a level that's only semi-annoying. Late night wandering has its perks.

My legs carry me down the dimly lit hallway and past the closed doors of the boys-only dorm, the tiny single bedrooms of high-ranking CORE officers, and bathrooms. I loop around the intel center, I'm sure still buzzing with Black Angel operatives despite the late hour. As I turn down the West Hall, a streak of manufactured light and muffled conversation spill out of the rec room. I hope someone left the TV on. I don't feel like chatting. As I get closer, an upbeat melody of wind instruments echoes into the hall, a cheerful theme song I recognize but cannot place. I creep along the hallway's edge, thankful for my silent slippers. I poke half of my face around the door's concrete casing and see Luke, dressed in his ragged New Albany soccer hoodie, staring intently up at a couple proudly showing off a painting. I immediately cringe. A clown with a painted white face, disturbing eyes, and red, malicious grin.

"What are you watching?" I ask, my shoulder leaning against the doorway.

Luke turns around and smiles when he sees me, revealing a pair of dimples I'd like to carry around in my pockets and take out anytime I feel sad.

"*Antiques Roadshow* on PBS," he responds.

"You a big fan?" I reply and flop down on the cocoa-brown leather couch next to him.

"Becoming one," he says and nods toward the TV. "These people don't even know what they have. This stupid clown painting has been in their basement forever. Piled with junk. This art dealer guy just told them it was worth one hundred and fifty thousand dollars. Can you believe that?"

"Not really."

"I'm terrified by that clown's face . . . yet I cannot look away."

My lips separate and I feel a smile spread across my face for the first time in days. My fingers reach up and touch my raised cheek. I pinch at the fleshy apple, just to make sure it's real.

"Can't sleep?" Luke asks, still not taking his eyes off the clown who looks like he cuts people's throats for fun.

"No. Way too much stuff in here," I answer, pointing to my skull. "I just needed something to numb my brain."

"Well, you've come to the right place." Luke grabs the controller and begins flipping through. He flips past CNN, ESPN, and HGTV. He stops on Bravo, where they're playing a repeat of one of *The Real Housewives of Wherever.* "Bravo? They're the masters of cotton-candy-for-your-brain TV."

"Mmmm, nah," I reply and shake my head. "I hate to admit that I like a good martini-and-champagne-fueled cat fight as much as the next person. But not in the mood for their petty crap tonight."

That's the thing I'm discovering about pain. You scoff at other people's problems. Who *cares* if someone said you were a bitch behind your back. Who *cares* if somebody didn't come to your stupid party. The last few days, I've found myself wondering how the people around me are still walking fast. Talking loud. After my mother died, it felt like the world deafened and spun at an agonizing speed. Carrying this dangerous secret about Torres has brought on the same excruciating sensation. Especially down here. Without the sun or moon to help keep time, hours tick by at half speed. Like one long, sleepless night.

Luke flips past a channel playing a horror movie, an old episode of *Cheers*, and QVC.

"Stop," I reply and touch his arm, my fingertips immediately pulsing when I feel his warm skin. I quickly pull away. "Go back to QVC."

He flips back one and the late-night QVC crew tells me all the reasons I cannot live without an aqua-blue skillet. They speak in eager tones as they slide a perfect pair of sunny-side up eggs onto a waiting plate and wipe away the nonexistent mess with a paper towel. On air, these people live in a constant state of total amazement.

"I love QVC," I reply and hold my arms across my chest, wishing my robe was a little bit thicker. "Even though I don't own a house or know how to cook or whatever, I'll flip it on and find myself saying, 'You know what, I really do need a knife that can cut through a sponge *and* a tin can.'"

"They are marketing geniuses," Luke replies, putting down the controller. "And I don't usually throw that word around. But anyone who can speak about a cake pan or a blender with unflinching enthusiasm for fifteen straight minutes is a special kind of human."

"Agreed. They should become politicians after they're done at QVC. Like, if that guy from *In the Kitchen with David* ran for president..."

"You mean... David?"

"Yes, David. I bet he'd find a way to win. He'd talk about foreign policy with the same gusto he talks about cookies and stockpots and we'd all be hypnotized. Like, 'Yes, yes, you're so right, *In-the-Kitchen-with-David* guy. That *is* a great idea to bring Palestinians and Jews together in Israel.' He'd win by a landslide."

A laugh bubbles up Luke's throat as he stacks his hands on the top of his head, and for a minute, the leather couch beneath us feels exactly like the one in the Weixels' bonus room where we've shared a million and one stupid conversations. And though it's just for a second, I'm happy to forget where I am.

"Do you miss home?" I ask, picturing the Weixels' brick Georgian house, Luke's empty bedroom, the record player that's been silent since we left for Colombia.

"New Albany isn't home anymore," Luke answers, the surprising statement punctuated by a deep sigh.

"What are you talking about?" I ask, turning toward him.

"CORE moved my parents to North Carolina a month ago," Luke says, his eyes still on the television.

"What?" I ask, my voice breathy. "Why? Because of Torres?"

"Yeah," Luke says, chewing at the inside of his cheek. His subconscious, nervous tic. "They had a watcher on them in New Albany but decided to take them to a more secure location on a military base. Dad's the only one who knows the reason. Claire and Mom just think Dad took a new military job there."

"Why didn't you tell me?" I say, grabbing at his wrist.

Luke finally tears his eyes away from the blond host with too much blush and looks in my direction. "I didn't want to upset you. Give you a reason to worry."

"Have there been threats made against them? Is that why they got moved?"

Luke stares at me, pressing his lips together. Not wanting to answer.

"Tell me," I push.

After a few seconds, he reluctantly nods his head.

God damn it. Not them too.

The panic returns to my body quickly, too quickly. It doesn't trickle in, it floods. Like I'm drowning, sparking a sense memory I've long forgotten.

I'm five years old, in a crowded pool and walking too far from the shallow end. Suddenly, the water is too high. My feet have lifted up. I can't find the floor. I'm splashing and swallowing water. My mind is screaming but I can't breathe. I can't cry out for help. I try to find something to hang on to. But there is nothing. Suddenly, there's an arm around my stomach, pulling me back, telling me I'm going to be okay. It was my mom.

I try to breathe next to Luke, but the air gets caught in my throat. And I realize this time, there's no one here to save me. No one to pull me from the flood.

"I'm sorry," Luke says, reading the change in my face. He slides his hand on top of mine. "I shouldn't have said anything. You came here to escape."

"You should have told me when it happened," I reply and close my eyes for a moment, trying to release the noose wrapped around my rib cage. "God, I'm so sorry. This is my fault."

"You need to stop saying that," Luke replies gently, his thumb and forefinger stroking the top of my hand. "You are not responsible for any of this. You're not responsible for my parents having to move. You're not responsible for your mother's death. And you're certainly not responsible for the fact Torres is coming after Black Angels. *He* is the monster. Not you."

"I get that," I say and stare past Luke, that dark field coming back to me. I can almost smell the sea, feel the firm ground beneath my feet as I run toward the house. "I just can't help but go back and wonder what I could have done differently. My mother dying is one thing. The fact that he's threatening your family. That he's tracking down and just, like . . . picking off Black Angel agents . . . it just makes me think, my God, what have I started? How much worse can this get?"

Tears burn at the corner of my eyes, the panic and sadness clash to form a suffocating balloon in my throat. Luke slides from his side of the couch and pulls me into his arms. I've done my best to swallow my tears in front of him since our days in the safe house. But as he holds me, cradling the back of my head with his hand, my face contorts, my lower lip trembles, and a few tears escape.

"Reagan, would you really not make the same choices?" Luke says quietly into my ear. "If you had to do it all over again, would you not still sneak down to Colombia? Still leap out of that van when everyone else was ready to abandon the mission? Not run after your mother and try to save her?"

"I don't know," my voice squeaks out. As I open my mouth, tears slide in, filling my tongue with salt.

"Well, I know you," Luke replies, pulling a wet strand of hair away from my face and tucking it behind my ear. "And I know if given the chance to redo everything, you could never just sit and do nothing. You are a fighter. You fought to save your family. You fought your way in here. And you'll fight to see Torres brought to justice. There is not a doubt in my mind that you will help bring an end to all this."

I don't know how he does it. After days of feeling powerless and incapacitated, that ember at my core suddenly flickers, pulsing from dark to light. Luke is right. I can't sit in this black and hopeless hole. I didn't fight my way here to be paralyzed by Torres. My mission has been singular since the moment he pulled that trigger.

Sam has tried to warn me about revenge. She told me that its flame doesn't just destroy your target. It blisters you from the inside, then trickles out, and before you know it, everything you touch is damaged. All that is good burns and blackens. I pretended to agree. But the intense heat cradles me, soothes me somehow. I know it could destroy me in the end. But if it means ending this terror, if it means protecting the Black Angels, then I'll gladly wake up blackened and broken. I long for the taste of ash in my mouth.

EIGHTEEN

"THANK YOU FOR RESCUING ME TODAY," LUKE SAYS, pulling his elbow behind his head to stretch his sore muscles. "I had no idea what I was doing on that simulated mission."

"You're learning fast," I answer, pulling my feet together on the ground, my long limbs creating a butterfly. "I've been doing this forever. You've only been here a few months. Don't beat yourself up."

"I know, I guess I just get nervous about being behind everyone else," Luke replies, his right knee bent in front of him, his left leg stretching behind. "Especially with Qualifier cuts this week and everything."

I glance at the clock over the double doors. It's eleven p.m. Lights-out in an hour. The training center is empty. The rest of the trainees have already hit the showers and are getting ready for the next day. But Luke and I still need work.

"You'll make it. You have so much raw talent," I say to ease his mind. But in reality, I have no idea who the senior leaders will choose to let go. I'm not even sure if I'll make it. But I do worry about Luke. I've been training every day since I was five—but for someone like Luke who has just baseline military training, it's tough. While I'm slowly improving, the cracks in Luke's training are beginning to show. I see the frustration etched around his mouth and burning in his eyes. He gave up so much to be here: West Point, a military career, a normal life. I refuse to let him fail or see him stuck at a desk at CORE for the rest of his life when he could have been a colonel like his dad. So every night this week, when the rest of the team heads out, I stay with Luke. I teach him new skills, help him refine old ones. And it's my job to cement his place here.

"How are you feeling about things?" Luke asks, taking a seat next to me to stretch his hamstrings.

"With the training?" I ask and give a quick shrug of my shoulders. "Okay, I think."

"No, you're doing great," he says, his fingertips pulling at his toes. "You're getting so much stronger. Anyone can see that. I mean the stuff we can't see. You seem ... I don't know ... different. Like your body is here but you aren't."

"I do?" My eyes widen with surprise although they shouldn't. This is Luke I'm talking to.

"Yeah," he answers with a nod; his eyes look past me. "Ever since our late night in the rec room last week you've just seemed sort of ... robotic. Everything you do is precise and perfect. But even outside of training, it's like you're acting out a role. Playing the Reagan everyone wants you to be or something."

Ever since that ember reignited, I've forced my body back into old, mechanical Reagan. While part of me is suffocated by the

145

robotic rigidity of who I used to be, the other half is comforted by the numbness. Like slipping back into an old, worn sweatshirt. I know just where the pulls are, the pills in the fabric. I'm mindful of the exposed threads, one pull away from unraveling. The numbness anchors every part of me. But it's a trade I have to make.

"I guess I am," I reply and run my hands along my defined quad muscles. "I need to be perfect. I need to make this next round. You're the one who said it. That I could help stop Torres. I don't want to miss that chance because of lost points during the assessment phase. I have to be like this or I'm afraid I'll get cut."

"I know. But you don't have to be like this around your friends. Around me."

He's right. My personality has shifted. Even when we're alone. I smile less. I stand up straighter. Weigh my words. Cut them into precise syllables when I finally do speak. But I just don't know how to jump between the two.

"It's hard, Luke," I finally answer and point toward my head. "I've got two versions of myself in there. I can't just switch them on and off. When I commit to one, I'm all in. So if I want to make it, Zombie Reagan is who I have to be."

What I really want to do is hack back into those files. Find out where Torres might be. Load up my weapons, hop a flight to South America, and stick my Glock down his throat. But I can't do that. Not yet. My mind is playing constant defense on the real me. She's just too dangerous for this place.

Just thinking about Torres causes that flame at my core to pulse. The heat rises, licking my organs, blistering my skin from the inside out. I see her face. Hear her scream. Gunpowder fills my nose, then iron-rich blood, like clumps of wet pennies.

Stop. Stop. Stop, my mind pleads. My eyes snap shut, snuffing out the threatening anger. My body presses into a deep stretch, my muscles aching. I take in a breath and slip back into the cold.

"I get it," Luke replies after several moments of silence. When I look back at him, he's retying his shoe, creating perfect bunny ears. "You do what you need to do. There's no one who wants to see you succeed more than me."

"Same," I answer and try to swallow, but my throat is dry and scratchy.

"I need to get better with my ground defense if I'm going to make it all the way to the academy," Luke says, shaking his head. "With military training, you don't really practice a lot of those moves. I totally embarrassed myself yesterday."

"You did great for your first time," I answer and grab the bottle of water next to me. I take a long swig before standing up. "Come on. Let's practice. That's the only way you'll get better."

I hold out my hands for Luke to take. I pull him up and as we make our way to the center training mat, his fingers glide down my hand and lace with mine. The hollows of our palms kiss, just for a moment, and my heart pounds in my ears. He squeezes my hand once, then pulls away, knowing we can't. The creases in my fingers throb without his pressed against mine, but I shake my wrist, force the buzzing to fade, and grab one of the fake knives from the side of the mat.

"Okay, I'm going to show you how to do this first," I say,

handing the plastic blade to Luke and laying my body down on the ground. "Then it's your turn."

"Got it," Luke says, straddling my torso and holding the knife at his side.

"Okay, come at me," I say, motioning with my hands.

Luke hesitates for a moment and then plunges the plastic blade toward me. I instinctively push one hand up to his eyes, careful not to actually poke him, and with my other hand, I brace for his arm before he can make impact. I jam my hand up his chin, snapping his neck back and rolling him on his side. Once he's on his back, I push his knife-wielding hand down and fake punch him in the face until his legs release their grip on my body and I can get away. Three seconds and I'm out.

"Damn, you make that look so easy," Luke replies and rolls onto his knees, his hands resting on his thick, muscular thighs. "You're almost graceful when you're kicking someone's ass."

My hands grasp at my hips and I smile, thinking about Mom. That's how she was too. There was an Audrey Hepburn quality to her. Long neck, fluid limbs, perfect form. She made martial arts almost look like a ballet. The memory of her burns my throat. I cough and force her face away.

"Okay, your turn," I answer and point Luke to the floor. He lies on his back and waits for me to assume my place above him. "Ready and go."

I plunge the knife toward him and he fumbles, reaching for my face with one hand but forgetting to block me with the other. I touch the plastic blade to the side of his neck and make an obnoxious noise, like a game show buzzer.

"You're dead," I say, tapping the knife to his flesh, and he shakes his head. "Concentrate. You've got this, Luke. You've memorized the moves. I know you have. Stop overthinking. Just let your mind go. Your body knows what to do."

Luke nods and we try again and again and again until he nails it.

"Amazing," I say and high-five him. Luke smiles and grabs at his knees, slightly out of breath from my heavy body forcing him down over and over.

"Thank you for teaching me." Luke straightens back up. "I couldn't do this without you."

"That's why I've got to be all numb and stuff," I say with a smile. "I've got to be good so I can stay here with you. Now, let me show you how to get off the ground a little sooner after you flip the assailant over."

I hand the knife back to Luke and lie down on the ground. Luke hovers over me in the attack position. I nod to signal that I'm ready and he plunges the plastic blade toward me. I start off doing everything right. I push his face away with one hand and brace for his attack hand with the other. But after I flip him over and try to get up quickly, I stumble and fall on top of him.

"Sorry," I say with a giggle. Luke is laughing, his stomach heaving against mine. He throws his knife to the side and once our laughter begins to slow, his eyes lock with mine.

Get up. Get up. Get up, my mind pleads. But it's too late. Luke holds me with his eyes, our breaths settling into parallel gasps, his sweet and warm on my aching lips. My body melts into his, even as my brain continues its plea. But I don't want to move.

His fingertips slowly find the back of my neck and as he touches me, every nerve ignites, the universe unravels in a matter of seconds. My lips tremble as I say, "Thank goodness the trainers weren't here to see that."

"Yeah, thank goodness," Luke replies, his voice soft and jagged. His fingers dance across my shoulder blades and find the exposed skin of my arm. And there it is. Stronger than ever. An unmitigated heat that instantly liquefies every organ. I thought maybe it was a fluke back in the car during training. A reaction to the stress of Qualifiers. But it wasn't in my head. It's here. And as much as I don't want it to be, it's very, very real.

I want to get up, walk away. But Luke's touch has hypnotized me into a state of paralysis, and the memory of our kiss at Templeton floods my body. My mouth throbs. My tongue tastes of cinnamon. Every inch of me vibrates, like my skin is made up of a thousand little heartbeats.

Pulse. Pulse. Pulse.

"I know we can't," Luke finally says, his fingertips brushing against a spot above my elbow that weakens my limbs. "But tell me one thing. Can you feel this?"

Yes. A million times, yes, my mind whispers, the words caught somewhere between my heart and tongue.

The heat from his hand singes my flesh. Our breathing stops almost in unison until all I can hear is the buzz of the overhead lights. Luke's head lifts off the mat and like a magnet, my face is pulled closer and closer to his. My stomach burns with a different kind of heat, a swirling, aching blaze. A feverish tornado. My nose grazes his and the air between us smells like it did before, like milk and honey. His bottom lip brushes against mine and . . .

Boom.

Down the hallway, a door slams, the crack rattling against my chest and sending my body flying straight into the air at record speed. I look down at Luke, his eyes still on me, waiting for me to return or at the very least, answer his question.

"I think that's enough for tonight," I say quietly, even though every part of me wants to touch him. Kiss him. But it's far too risky. On so many levels.

I turn my back on Luke and walk toward the open door that leads to the North Hall. My body tingles, my limbs weak and fighting against me with every step. I settle my hand on my still-burning stomach as I try to suck in new air. I can feel Luke watching me, but I don't look back. I can't. I reach the door, turn into the dark hallway, and free-fall into the night.

NINETEEN

"I FEEL LIKE I'M LEGIT GOING TO THROW UP," ANUSHA says as we take our seats in the conference room where we had our first meeting at the start of Qualifiers. "How many people are they cutting today?"

"I don't know," I answer and shake my head as I settle into the high-back leather chair next to her. "I think at least six."

"Any idea who it's gonna be?" Cam asks, taking a seat next to me.

"I have no freaking idea," I reply. *Maybe me.* The heavy knot in my stomach tightens at the thought of not hearing my name called for the next round. I haven't been what the Black Angels expected. I know I haven't lived up to the legend, the myth that seemed to doom me before I even set foot inside CORE. The only thing worse than high expectations is falling so fantastically short.

"You look pretty nervous over there, Hillis," Lex says from across the table, her pink lips curled into an insufferable smirk. "But then again, I'd be nervous if I were you too."

"Lex, why don't you shut the fuck up," Anusha quickly snaps.

"Why must you be so vulgar all the time, EOP?" Lex answers, lifting her long fingers to her lips and feigning disgust. "Do they teach you to talk like that in the slop halls in the air force?"

"Do they teach to act like a total bitch at prep school?" Anusha counters just as Director Browning walks through the doorway.

Browning claps her hands three times in the air, the open pockets of her palms creating a thunderous strike, startling everyone who hadn't noticed her presence. She narrows her gray eyes and glares back and forth between Anusha and Lex. "That's enough out of the two of you," she declares, her angry eyes now focused on Lex.

"I'm sorry, I don't know what you're talking about," Lex answers sweetly, her hand at the center of her chest. "I was just wishing Anusha and Reagan well today."

"Yeah, right," Anusha says under her breath but loud enough for Director Browning to hear.

"I said that's enough, Miss Venkataraman," Browning replies, shooting her a silencing glare. "This is a serious agency that conducts very serious work. This is not a place for high school bullshit, so if you'd like to go play mean girl somewhere, perhaps you still have time to send in your application to college and join a sorority. Do I make myself clear?"

No one speaks. Anusha gives Browning a tiny nod of her head while Lex glares across the table at me, as if to say *See what you made me do?*

"All right. Now, for what we really came here to discuss," Browning says, pulling at her black blazer and taking her place at the head of the conference table. "Thank you very much, trainees, for your hard work during the last several months. We know Qualifiers can be rigorous. We are pleased with the improvements we've seen in many of you, but for some, you've fallen short. And I'm sorry, but this is the end of the road. Any questions before I call out who will be moving on to the next round?"

Lex's hand shoots up. Browning nods, adjusting the dark blue printed scarf around her neck. I haven't seen her wear it before. Must be new.

"Will we be finding out our ranking among the other trainees today?" Lex asks, her hand still raised in the air, even after she's been called on and her question phrased. Overeager much?

"No, Miss Morgan," Browning answers, shaking her head. "Your status could very well change during the next round, so there's no point in celebrating or feeling defeated just yet. We won't just be looking at your raw talent and skill level during this next phase of Qualifiers. We'll be assessing your communication, your leadership, your ability to follow orders, and your teamwork. All very crucial elements to being a Black Angel. Even more important than your skill level. Some of you may even be sent out on real missions with Black Angel operatives. This is our chance to test you and see if you're truly equipped to handle stressful moments in the field."

"Very well," Lex says, her voice obnoxiously proper in front of officers and trainers. She places her hand delicately in her lap and shoots me a look. Her eyebrows rise above her giant, upturned eyes and I know what she's thinking. *Gotcha now, Hillis.* Everyone knows what happened in Colombia. How I was called combative. Reckless. A rule breaker. With Lex of course leading the gossipy

154

pack. The extra glint in her eyes tells me she's counting on me screwing up this round. If I even make it, that is. I dig my fingers into my hip bones and turn back toward Director Browning, refusing to alter my blank stare, give Lex any kind of reaction—good or bad—to cling to.

"All right, if I call your name, you will be moving on to the next round of Qualifiers," Browning states, balancing a pair of reading glasses on the bridge of her nose as she unfolds a sheet of paper from her blazer pocket. "Hannah Adams, Luke Weixel, Cameron Conley, Anusha Venkataraman, Matthew DeVillers, Alexis Morgan..."

Lex's eyes light up at the sound of her name and the lack of hearing my own. I can feel her intrusive glare from across the table but refuse to give in to her. As Browning rattles off name after name, I pinch my fingers against my thumb, counting the number of trainees that have been called, mentally computing just how many spots are left.

"Elisabeth Kelley."

Four.

"Anay Patel."

Three.

"Jackson Yuzwa."

Two.

"Luca Angellini."

Oh my God. One. Please say me. Please say me. Please say me.

My entire face goes numb, my tongue swells inexplicably in my mouth as I realize this could be it. My end. No more training. No justice for my mother. Torres will end up free or in a prison cell, which is grossly more than he deserves. The acid in my stomach solders my organs together. This can't be it. This can't be the way it ends for me.

Anusha reaches out, touching me gingerly on my wrist as if to say, *It's okay. It's okay.* But it won't be. Not if I don't hear my name. Her fingers encircle my bone, and my skin wilts with clammy dew beneath her touch.

"And the last remaining spot goes to," Browning begins, pausing theatrically as if she's the host of an old-school game show. I can nearly hear the dramatic rattle of a drumroll only to realize it's just my heart pounding in my ears.

Please God. Please God. Please.

"Reagan Hillis," she finally announces. Browning's eyes catch mine as her lips flinch into an almost indistinguishable smile that I'm not quite sure how to take.

Anusha's fingers slide up my wrist, squeezing my hand, and I finally remember to take in a breath. I'm in. I somehow squeaked through.

"To the trainees who didn't hear their names, I'm sorry but that means you have been cut," Browning reports flatly, removing her glasses and tucking them into the pocket of her black blazer. "Please return immediately to the dorms and pack up your things. Flights have already been arranged for your transport back home. We wish you well."

Browning folds her list in half, turns on her heel, and walks briskly out of the room. Three male trainees whose names were not called quickly stand up and, with their heads lowered, slip out of the room behind her. Olivia and Kathryn, two of the female trainees who didn't make it, stand up almost in unison, hugging their arms to their chests, and hurry into the hallway. But Savannah, one of Lex's little followers and closest friends, sits frozen across the table from us. She stares blankly past me, her mouth pressed into a thin line, her dark, stunned eyes glazing with tears. She hasn't been particularly kind to me. She's been quiet and distant, her head halfway up Lex's ass. Giggling after every dig or rude comment thrown our way. But still, I feel sorry for her. She's a third generation Black Angel. Trained her entire life to be here. She gave up everything to follow in her parents' footsteps. Now she has to return home and tell them she's not wanted here. Explain why she failed. And as the news begins to sink in, shame reddens her cheeks and forces those tears to fall.

Lex pulls her body into a hug, hiding Savannah's face from our view.

"It's okay," Lex says quietly in her ear. "It's okay, love. You'll be all right."

I never imagined seeing Lex as anything but ruthless, but as she lightly strokes Savannah's dark hair, I realize that maybe there is a heart somewhere in there.

"You don't deserve to be here, Reagan," Lex snaps, her emerald eyes now fixed on me.

Okay. Perhaps scratch that.

"I'm very sorry you feel that way," I reply gently, not wanting to get into an argument with Lex in front of a girl who in one hour will be on a plane back home. I stand up with Anusha and we begin to make our way with the rest of the trainees toward the conference room door. Luke and Cam lean against the cinder block walls near the doorway, waiting for us.

"They kick agents out of here for what you did," Lex calls after me but I keep walking. "You manipulated and bullied your way onto a mission. You disobeyed orders. You spit in the face of all the Black Angels that came before you. Your own mother died because of what you did."

Her final words stop me in my tracks. Trainees who aren't yet out the door slow their pace or turn around. Every nerve in my body sparks. I'm surprised I cannot see glowing, incandescent particles leap off my skin. I try to move but can't. I try to breathe, but no air comes. Luke is now at my side with a hand on my back, trying to guide me out of the room, but my feet are sinking, like quicksand, into the acid-stained cement floor.

"No one else will say it to you, but I will," Lex calls over her shoulder. "Savannah deserves that spot. Not someone like you. Not someone who is so combative people actually die."

My lungs inflame and I feel like my body is on fire.

"Let's just go, Reagan," Luke says quietly into my ear, pulling me by the arm, but my feet still won't move.

"No," I respond, yanking out of his grip. I slowly turn and look at Lex. "Santino Torres put a gun to my mother's head and pulled the trigger. Not me. I didn't kidnap my parents. I didn't take them on a plane down to Colombia. I didn't tie my mother up in a basement and beat her. Santino Torres did."

"But don't you think things would have turned out differently if you'd actually followed the rules?" Lex replies, letting go of Savannah and turning her chair around to face me. "Don't you replay your mistakes in your head?"

That hollow spot inside me shrieks as that night comes back to me in fragments. Dad's bruised face. The sound of gunfire with the guards. The feel of death, pressing against my neck. Mom's desperate face. Torres's loaded gun.

"Every day, Lex," I finally whisper as a searing pain balloons against my chest. "Every single day."

"See, you don't think you deserve to be here either," she replies, her eyes narrowed into almost indistinguishable slits. "So why the hell are you?"

"To make your life as miserable as humanly possible when she gets a Rescue/Take-down spot over you," Anusha says, pushing me forcefully toward the doorway and into the hallway, Lex's question still echoing in my brain.

We walk in silence for a few seconds before Luke grabs me by the elbow and says, "Don't listen to her. We all know you deserve to be here."

I nod, keeping my eyes on the floor and watching my feet as I force them to step one in front of the other. I don't want them to see my doubt, my panic.

Do I deserve to be here? Am I only here for revenge? Is killing Torres a good enough reason to take a spot from a Black Angel child who truly wants this? Who has trained so hard and dreamed of nothing else?

Selfish girl. The words most frequently used to describe me whisper in my ear and slip in between the gray looping coils of my brain. Perhaps I am selfish. Perhaps Savannah could do more good in the world by being a Black Angel than I could.

Maybe Lex is right. Maybe I am unworthy of this spot, this chance. Maybe she's the only one who sees me for what I really am: A rule breaker. A manipulator. A killer.

TWENTY

"WHAT FLOOR DO YOU THINK THE OFFICE IS ON?" Luke asks quietly next to me as I mentally scan the floor plan that was shoved in our faces for only sixty seconds before our test. Thanks, Mom, for the photographic memory.

We're standing on the ground floor of a busy bank. Well, at least it looks like a busy bank. It has a few tellers, men and women scribbling their names on the backs of checks, and bankers dressed in suits and ties. It's just another Qualifier test at one of the CIA's many training facilities, one hour outside of Langley.

I love these exercises. It's the only time we get to see the sun or breathe in air that's made by trees and not machines. That underground bunker is starting to shrink with each passing week, and I'm actually starting to long for my days cooped up at the safe house. At least there I had the luxury of a window to the outside world.

"They really go all out for these tests, man," Cam says next to me, pretending to look down at his cell phone but eyeing the two dozen low-level CIA operatives posing as actors for this assessment. "It's hard to tell who is who in here."

"That's the whole point of the exercise," I respond, still mentally scanning each floor on the blueprint, trying to figure out our next move. "You think when we're in the field people are going to have *terrorist* or *target* sewn onto their collars?"

"Point made," Cam responds, looking back down at his phone, trying to blend in with the other "civilians" in the crowd.

Our mission today: download the contents of an executive's laptop to find a dirty money trail. My eyes quickly look over the roaming agents, wondering who could be our targets: bank insiders looking to catch us before we reach the crucial data. Dressed in an array of suits and jeans and hoodies, I have no clue who has their eyes on us. What I'm looking for is body language, shifting eyes, nervous hands.

Focus, Reagan. Focus. The office.

My mind mentally crosses off locations inside the building. According to the blueprint, the basement holds the vault and safety deposit boxes. An executive's office wouldn't be down there. And it wouldn't be up on the main floor either. Way too much traffic. Far too easy for someone to steal information. The second and third floor house all the banking offices. And the better the view, the higher the salary.

"Third floor," I answer confidently. "The only thing we were told is that the target has a VP level title at this bank. Seems only right he'd have a nice office on a high floor."

"Corner office," Luke surmises and nods his head.

"Not necessarily, but maybe," I reply and look down at Mom's watch ticking away on my wrist. We've been standing here for far too long. "We need to get going. We can't all use the same staircase or that's going to look super suspicious. Cam, you take the south stairs. Luke, let's take the north stairs and all meet up at the top of the third floor. Everyone have their earpieces in?"

"Got it," Cam answers, shoving the almost invisible sphere deeper into his ear canal.

"Don't talk to anyone if you don't have to. Act like you belong here," I instruct and eye Luke's hands in his pockets. "Take your hands out of your pockets. That makes you look like you have something to hide. The targets will spot that in two seconds."

Luke removes his hands from his pockets, hanging them awkwardly at his sides, and gives me a sheepish nod.

"Okay, let's go," I reply and turn on my heel to head toward the north stairs. Dressed in black pants, a blue button-down, and a light black jacket, I blend in among the bank employees much better than Luke, who is dressed in jeans and a long-sleeve T-shirt. I tried to convince him to wear something different this morning but he dismissed me. "Listen to me. If we pass someone on the stairs, do not make eye contact. Just talk to me about something that's not very memorable."

"Like what?" Luke asks, beginning to shove his hands into his pockets again until I give him a look.

"Something age appropriate," I reply as we slip out of the lobby of the bank and reach a heavy steel door that leads to an internal stairwell. "A party we're going to this weekend. We need to look like we're meeting one of our parents for lunch or something. Got it?"

"Got it," Luke answers.

"Good, now let's go," I reply and open the stairwell door. The door closes behind us with a weighty clank and I hear the sound of high heels on the concrete steps. I hold up my hand and listen to the *clack, clack, clack* to determine if the footsteps are going up or down.

Clack, clack, clack, they echo at a faster tempo. Crap. They're going down. We'll have to pass her.

"I know, right?" I say to Luke as if we're already in the middle of a conversation. If we're in the middle of speaking, we have a strong chance she won't stop us. It's Black Angel psychology. Even in the most dangerous circumstances, people don't like to appear rude. "Do you think Levi is going to make it to the party?"

"He texted me and said he was coming," Luke answers, playing along as we climb the first flight of stairs. "He asked if he could bring his new girlfriend. I haven't met her yet, have you?"

"Yeah, I met her last week," I answer and the clacking-heeled actor/operative comes into view. My eyes immediately tear away from her and stay stuck on Luke. "She's super sweet. I think you'll like her. I'm so glad Levi finally picked a good one. The last few girls he's dated have totally sucked."

As we reach the second-floor landing, I can feel the woman's eyes on us. I look at Luke, waiting for him to pick up the next part of the conversation, but he just stares at me, his mouth hanging open, like a fish about to swallow bait and get wheeled into a boat. My eyes widen and I want to slap him. He's giving her an in. *Say something. Say something!*

"Can I help you two?" the woman asks as we reach the stairs to the third floor.

I turn toward her and smile politely. "We're good. Just meeting my dad for lunch," I answer quickly and turn back toward Luke, hoping she'll think twice before rudely interrupting our conversation. "I hated the last girl he dated. She was so demanding and rude. I seriously threw a small party when they broke up. Remember, over a Christmas present?"

Clack, clack, clack. The woman is continuing her journey downstairs. Thank God.

"Well, I mean, who can really blame her," Luke responds as we reach the final steps. *Almost there. Almost there.* "He gave her one of those Open Heart necklaces from Kay Jewelers."

"True," I say with a genuine laugh. "I think I'd break up with someone if they gave me one of those necklaces too."

Clack, clack, clack. She's reached the first-floor lobby. I hear the door downstairs swing open and then slam shut behind her just as we reach the third floor. I swing open the door, ushering Luke through with dramatic, annoyed flair.

"Jesus Christ, Luke," I hiss, finding it impossible to hide my irritation. "Our cover may be blown now. You have to keep talking, you know?"

"I know, I know," he answers, his eyes frustrated. "I'm sorry, I just froze."

"Well, you cannot stare at me with your mouth hanging open," I reply quietly. "That was the worst moment you could freeze up at."

"I'm aware, Reagan," Luke answers, his voice low and tight in his throat. "Come on, we don't have time to argue about what I did wrong."

"Yeah, especially not now," I respond as we spot Cam at the other end of the hallway walking toward us. "She may be a target and could be reporting us for all we know. Let's find the office and get out of here."

But which one? The long hallway is lined with open and closed doors. It's eerily quiet up here. Like they're waiting for something to happen. I feel for my fake gun beneath my light jacket. We're to simulate the violent moves we'd use to get out of a dangerous situation but not actually hurt any of the operatives. With my adrenaline pumping and muscles twitching, that might be a little tough. But I'll aim for no broken noses.

My eyes scan the walls of the hallway. Above a drinking fountain is an eight-by-ten poster of faces and titles, men and women dressed in black or gray suits, pearl earrings or colorful silk handkerchiefs completing the banker look. I walk quickly toward the sheet of paper, careful to keep my footsteps light and not draw attention to us, and pull it off the wall. Each face has a name and a title. Cam and Luke look over my shoulder as I scan each title.

Associate Director of Operations

Director of Communications

Executive Director of Commercial Loans

Vice President of Internal Affairs

"That guy," Luke says and points toward the VP of Internal Affairs photo. "He could be our guy. He's a VP."

"Not so fast," I answer and hold up my hand. "He's a VP but he's not the right type of VP. He just deals with internal bank stuff. He won't have access to dirty money trails on his computer."

My eyes keep scanning.

Executive Director of Mortgage Loans

Managing Director of Client Services

Vice President of Investments and Client Acquisitions

"Him," I say and point toward his name. James Lacaillade. "Vice President of Investments and Client Acquisitions. He has access to the actual investments. He transfers money in and out. He's our guy."

I fold the sheet of paper into squares and shove it into my pocket as we quietly walk down the hallway, my eyes scanning the names on the gold plates posted outside every door. We pass door after door after door. No James Lacaillade. My throat thickens, unnerved. Perhaps I had this all wrong? Maybe he's not even on this floor after all. We reach the very last office.

"Found it," Luke says, pointing toward James Lacaillade's plate. "See . . . corner office."

The office is empty, door open. I peer across the hall at the other open door. No one there either. We're clear. But for how long?

"Come on, let's get this done," I say, pushing Luke and Cam into the room and shutting the door. I close the blinds that look out into the empty hallway. Pins prick at the back of my spine. Something is not right. There is not a single person in the hallway. I look down at my watch: 12:22. It's lunchtime, so maybe in the real world everyone would be out. But as my stomach spirals, I can't help but feel like this is a trap.

"Cam, start doing your thing," I say and look down at the door handle. No lock. Shit. We need to stop someone from coming in here. At least give us a chance to download the file. I look around the room. The floor is carpeted so we could slide something heavy across it without sending off alarms (any other type of flooring, you might as well just scream out "Hey, we're stealing confidential files in here!"). I spot a short, gray file cabinet in the corner. Perfect. "Luke, help me with this."

"What are we doing with this thing?" he asks as I begin to pull it out of its spot in the corner.

"There's no lock on the door," I reply as we tug the heavy cabinet from its spot and slide it toward the door. It fits seamlessly beneath the long handle. "So God forbid someone comes up here, not only will the weight block them from pushing their way in, they won't even be able to move the handle."

I pull down on the piece of curved metal and it immediately strikes the cabinet. The lock won't even slip past the doorjamb.

"Brilliant," Cam says from his seat behind the laptop. "I want you permanently on my team."

Thanks, Mom, my brain whispers. She taught me how to use my surroundings to my advantage; how to look for clues or escape routes or tools that may seem completely ordinary, but could save my life. She knew it all. Even more than Dad. She saw what others could not.

"How are you doing on the files, Cam?" I ask, making my way behind the desk so I can get a better view of the laptop screen.

"Good," Cam answers without looking up, his eye glued to the screen as his fingers frantically type. "I've gotten past all the initial security measures and I'm just hacking into some of these encrypted files right now. This is where the money trail has got to be."

Luke and I watch in amazement as Cam types out a series of numbers and letters and symbols, the blue screen filling with codes

I cannot understand. My hacking skills are basic. College level. Cam has the equivalent of several PhDs.

"Just give me a couple more seconds," Cam says, pounding at the keys, the screen giving way to more and more screens until boom. The words *Access Granted* flash in large, green letters. "Got it. Now I just need like ninety seconds to upload. Luke, give me the drive."

Luke fumbles in his pockets for the fake cell phone that holds the chip we need for the illegal download.

"Luke, you need to have that stuff ready," I scold, trying to hold back my frustration.

"I know, I know, I'm sorry," Luke answers, the lines around his eyes and mouth deepening, clearly rattled by his series of mistakes. I desperately fight the urge to sigh. Luke finally opens the secret compartment in the back of the cell phone, revealing a wire and tiny chip that we've been instructed to use to download the files. He hands it to Cam. I glance down at my watch.

"That just wasted thirty freaking seconds," I comment, biting down on the flesh inside my cheek in an attempt to keep my voice as calm and even as possible. "That's time we need."

"Reagan, I know," Luke answers curtly, shooting me a glance that says *Back the hell off.* And I do. The trainers are listening in on us. I shouldn't make him look bad. I don't mean to. I just want high marks on this mission. Since the first round of cuts last month, I've been doing everything in my power to prove that I belong. That I didn't get the last spot because I manipulated or bullied my way in here. I need to prove to Lex, to the other trainees, to the senior leaders, that I deserve to be here. Because before Qualifiers is over, six more trainees will be gone. And I didn't fight this hard and get this close to gaining access to Torres to be kicked out.

Cam plugs in the wire and chip into the computer and it immediately begins to download. A blue bar pops up on the screen, filling with the passing seconds.

10% complete. 15% complete. 20% complete. 25% complete.

I stare at the computer, my eyes burning from lack of blinking. Just as the bar reaches 40% complete, I hear footsteps in the hallway. I grab ahold of Luke's arm and we listen. The steps are the heavy clunk of polished dress shoes. A man.

45% complete. 50% complete.

They get closer and closer and closer.

55% complete. 60% complete.

"Someone's coming," I whisper, gripping down on Luke's flesh. I scan the room, immediately looking for an escape route. The window.

I pull up the blinds to reveal a tiny metal fire escape.

"Sixty-five percent complete," Cam reports quietly as the footsteps get louder and louder.

I unlock the window, pull it open, and lean my body outside. There's a rusty ladder that hangs off this sad excuse of a balcony. I stare down between the rudimentary fire escape bars. We're at least forty feet off the ground.

"Seventy-five percent complete," Luke whispers. The footsteps grow louder and louder until they are just feet from outside the door.

Shit.

The metal door handle jiggles, immediately slamming into the file cabinet. The three of us are silent, our lungs burning with held breaths.

"Hello," a deep voice says from the other side. Then there's a panicked knock followed by another jiggle of the handle. Again, it slams into the metal file cabinet, buying us time but its boom causing alarm. "Is someone in there?"

I look back at the computer screen. *80% complete. 85% complete.* Luke and Cam look at me and I immediately put my finger to my lips and point toward the narrow fire escape.

90% complete.

"Who is in there?" the voice roars. The panicked knocks turn into violent pounding as the man struggles to move the handle again. It bangs and bangs and bangs against the cabinet, the sharp sound scraping against my ear canals. "Whoever is in there, you have ten seconds to come out or I'm calling security. Ten . . . nine . . . eight . . ."

95%. 96%. 97%. 98%. 99%.

"Seven . . . six . . . five . . ."

The blue bar finally fills. *100% complete.* Cam grabs the wire and chip and shoves it into his pocket. He types in a few codes, completely erasing any evidence of his hack, and slams down the laptop screen.

"Four . . . three . . . two . . ."

"Let's go," Cam whispers and I begin to climb out onto the fire escape. Luke climbs out after me and the metal balcony sways under our collective weight.

"Come on, come on," I say and begin to climb down the ladder, my heart pumping so loudly in my ears, I can no longer hear the angry voice on the other side of the door. But as I reach the windows of the second floor, I hear gunshots and the sound of breaking glass. Security must be shooting out the internal hallway window (or at least fake shooting out the window).

Shit. Shit. Shit.

"Move!" I yell up at my guys as we climb down the ladder, careful not to slip off and die.

Twenty more feet. Fifteen more feet. Ten more feet.

A few more rungs and I reach the ground. I scan the street, looking for Anusha in our getaway vehicle, and spot the gray sedan parked fifty yards away.

Gunfire and voices can still be heard in the office above us. I turn around and watch as Luke jumps to the ground followed closely behind by Cam.

"Run!" I scream and start sprinting for the car.

The air is much colder than normal for late October in Virginia and I can actually see my breath heaving out of my lungs, its puffy clouds forming in front of my face. My high-heeled boots dig into the hard ground below me as Luke's and Cam's long legs nip at my heels.

Go, go, go, go, my mind screams at me. We are so close. My muscles tighten, moving faster and faster with each passing yard.

Twenty yards. Fifteen yards. Ten yards. Five yards.

Finally, I reach the passenger-side door and hop in. Luke and Cam open the back doors and slide into the backseat.

"Go, Anusha, go," Luke says, hitting the back of her seat before he even has his door fully closed. Anusha pulls out of her parking spot and races down the fake street. I turn around, watching the outside of the bank for security as Anusha reaches the first fake stop sign, takes a right, and we disappear from view.

"Fantastic job, team," RT trainer Michael says in our ears. "You are the first group to get out of the bank without getting caught and with all the information."

"Holy shit," I whisper, sinking into my seat and taking in a full breath for the first time in ten minutes. I smile and high-five Anusha as she pulls into the CIA's makeshift base in this little fake town.

"Reagan, I got to hand it to you," Michael says in my ear. "Some of those moves were genius. The file cabinet under the doorknob was a smart, tactical solution."

"Thank you, sir," I reply with a smile. "It was an Elizabeth Hillis move."

"Some girls get their looks from their mamas, you got your smarts," he replies with a sad little laugh. He knew my mother well. Worked with her on the RT squad for years. I see it in his eyes whenever he brings her up. He misses her immensely.

"Well, guess what?" Michael says in our ears. "Since you guys passed the test on your first try, you are done for the day. Actually, you're done for the rest of the week. Not sure if you guys have planes to catch for home or if you're coming back to CORE but, hey . . . enjoy your long weekend. It's one of the last breaks you'll have for a while."

"Thanks, Michael," I answer before taking the earpiece out of my ear and switching off my microphone.

"Oh my God," Cam says, grabbing me by the shoulder. "Freedom! I am so damn excited."

"Me too," Anusha says, putting the car into park and sinking back into her black leather seat. "No training, no meetings, no anything for three full days. I cannot wait."

"Me either," I say and clap my hands together. "What are we going to do, you guys?"

Anusha and Cam begin listing off all the ways we should relax and unwind with our few precious days off. Sauna, many sundaes, epic pool and Ping-Pong tournaments, a movie marathon.

I turn around to smile at Cam, and it's then I realize only three of us in this car are happy. Luke sits in the backseat, his dimples nowhere to be seen. His light blue eyes have darkened, his full lips sinking into a frown. He presses his head against the windowpane and silently stares out at the hollow buildings of our pretend town.

Tiny knots begin to loop in my stomach and I fear that scowl and vacant look has everything to do with me.

TWENTY-ONE

"IT'S CLOSE TO MIDNIGHT AND SOMETHING EVIL'S lurking in the dark," Anusha sings along to Michael Jackson's "Thriller" in our empty dorm room. She turns up the volume on her laptop and keeps singing.

"You try to scream," Cam and Luke sing in unison, their big feet landing with simultaneous thuds as they each spring through the open doorway, making me jump and laugh. "But terror takes the sound before you make it."

I spring from my bed, grabbing Cam dramatically by the shoulders and spinning him around as I finish the rest of the lyrics.

"'Cause this is thriller, thriller night," the four of us belt out the chorus, jumping around and walking like the undead while Anusha surprises us all, shaking her shoulders and legs from side to side. She looks like she should be standing right next to Michael Jackson in the music video.

"Anusha, you're officially the coolest girl I know," Cam says, grabbing her by the shoulder once she's finished her final, impressive spin move. She squeezes Cam around his waist before shimmying out of their embrace.

"How do you know the entire dance?" I ask, trying my best to copy her spin move but failing rather ungracefully.

"My friends and I may or may not have memorized the choreography a couple years ago," Anusha replies, dancing her way to the other side of the room. "I love Halloween. This is the first year I haven't dressed up. I want to go to a party so badly."

"I know. Me too," I say, flopping down on my bed next to Luke. "I'm sure our friends are having the time of their lives right now at some college Halloween party."

"Beer and girls dressed in lingerie and animal ears," Cam says, nodding his head, his eyes vacant, watching an imaginary scene in his head. "What's not to like?"

"Hey, I would not be slutting it up if I was at a college party right now," I insert, throwing my pillow at Cam's face.

"I would," Anusha announces, fixing her ponytail at the small mirror over our shared dresser. "Cat ears and the shortest black dress I could get my hands on."

"Meow," I say and claw at her as she passes me on the way back to her bed.

"Okay, guys, don't shoot this down right away," Anusha says. "But . . . what if we snuck out and went to some type of Halloween party tonight? Georgetown has got to be crawling with parties."

"Anusha . . ." I begin, sitting up straighter on the bed, but she holds up her hand, silencing me.

"No, wait. Think about it," she says and sits down next to Cam on the opposite lower bunk. "It's some of our only time off during training. All the other trainees flew back home for break. Director Browning and a ton of the senior leaders were called away on a mission. We're kind of here by ourselves."

"Us and like twenty other full-time CORE operatives," I reply.

"Yeah, but they're not paying attention to us," Cam says, waving off my concerns. And it's true. The operatives at CORE right now are so wrapped up in missions, they have no idea which trainees are here and which ones went back home for the short break.

"Come on, I'm so bored," Anusha whines, flopping dramatically onto her back. "We already watched movies and played pool and Ping-Pong all day yesterday. I'm running out of stuff to do in this underground prison. I need some time in the real world or I think I might lose it."

"What about the threat, you guys?" Luke states cautiously. He leans his body forward, resting his forearms on his strong thighs. "Torres is still out there, you know."

"Yeah, but something must have happened to make them all calm down," I argue. "They never would have let all the trainees go home and be out in public if there was still a serious threat. Plus, it's Halloween. We'll wear masks or something. No one will know who we are."

Luke turns his face toward me, his eyes narrowed, and quietly says, "I can't believe you're actually considering this."

"Cam, think you could hack into the security system and make it look like we never left?" Anusha asks, picking herself up off the bed and bouncing up and down on her knees, giddy with the idea of escaping.

"For sure," Cam answers.

"What about all the cameras?" Luke asks, pointing up at the ceiling. I follow his index finger. There aren't any cameras in the dorm rooms or bathrooms, but I've definitely noticed them throughout the compound.

"There aren't as many cameras in here as you'd think," Cam replies. "The Black Angels don't want their actions recorded. Plus, they're not really that concerned about what's going on inside here. Their focus is on the terrorists and kidnappings and murders on the outside. Not what the four of us are doing with our free time."

"What do you think, Reagan?" Anusha says, turning toward me, the corners of her mouth lifting into an apprehensive smile.

My lips pinch together and push to one side as I gather my thoughts. I don't want to get in trouble. But I'd kill to get out of this concrete bunker. Have a small taste of a normal life.

"You really think we can get out of here without getting caught?" I question Cam.

Cam nods his head. "Totally."

Anusha's and Cam's eager faces stare back at me, eyes wide, mouths primed with smiles. Finally, I return their grin. "Okay, let's do it."

Anusha jumps off the bed and tackles me with a hug. "Oh my God, I love you," she squeals and I squeeze her back, laughing into clumps of her dark curls.

"This is a really, really stupid idea," Luke says sharply, quickly getting up from the bed.

"Damn, way to kill the vibe," I answer, pulling out of Anusha's hug.

"Reagan, you of all people should know this is a terrible idea,"

Luke says, shaking his head disapprovingly, his hands on his hips, like a condemning father. "I'm telling you right now, do not go."

"Excuse me?" I answer, my voice harsh as I stand up from the bed. "Who are you to tell me what to do, Luke?"

"Are you kidding me?" Luke says, throwing his hands up in the air. He shakes his head again and turns around, walking toward the door, but not before throwing in a final dig. "All you do is tell people what to do."

"What is that supposed to mean?" I ask, my long legs chasing after him, my hand grabbing his forearm. He stops and turns around. "You've clearly got something to say. You've been acting totally weird the last couple days. So come on. I'm right here. Say it!"

"Okay, kids, that's enough. Mommy and Daddy haven't had their five o'clock cocktail yet," Anusha says in a high-pitched voice, trying to lighten the mood. But it doesn't work. Luke pulls out of my grip and walks out of the room.

"Luke," I yell and chase after him into the hallway. I follow him into the boys-only dorm next door that's completely empty. "Luke!"

He flips on the light, ignoring me, and walks toward his bunk. He calmly goes about his evening routine of putting away his freshly laundered training clothes, as if I'm not even in the room, which irritates me even more. I've never gotten into an argument with Luke, but I can tell that's where this is heading. That uneasy knot coils again around my stomach, but that doesn't stop me from blocking his path as he turns to walk toward his dresser, my acidic tongue demanding a confrontation. "What is your problem?"

He tries to walk around me, but I move to block him again.

Finally, he stares down at me, his jaw tight, eyes angry. An emotion I've never really seen in him before. Hurt, yes. Angry? Never.

"What's my problem?" Luke finally says, his voice low. "You should know. You only pointed out every damn problem I was having during our test the other day. And thanks so much for that. As if I wasn't already last on the list of the trainees. As if I wasn't struggling enough to stay here. With you, by the way. Do you know what it's like to constantly feel like you're one mistake away from being kicked out? And thanks to you and your bossy, big mouth, the trainers had to hear every single little thing I did wrong."

"I was only trying to help you," I answer, playing back the number of times I yelled at him on the mission.

"No you weren't," he replies quickly, finally stepping around me. He opens the drawer of his dresser, carefully placing his clothing inside before slamming it shut. "Your only concern was making sure we came out on top. You only gave a shit about whether we were number one, even if that meant I looked like a complete and total incompetent asshole."

"Well, excuse me if I want to make sure we make it into the training academy," I say and point at the center of my chest. "So sorry I cannot play the sweet midwestern girl that bats my eyelashes at you and pats you on the head and tells you you're perfect all the time and that your shit doesn't stink. Because sometimes, it freaking does."

"See, right there," Luke replies and points at me with both index fingers, his eyes lighting up, like he's caught me with my hand in the proverbial cookie jar. "That's another one of my problems with you. You've become cruel. And you were never cruel."

"Or maybe you didn't know me as well as you thought you did," I reply and cross my arms over my chest. "I was the girl everyone else wanted to be back in Ohio. I was sweet and funny and charming and whatever the hell I needed to be to get through the day. I was playing a role. I made you believe I was Reagan MacMillan. Well, I'm not that girl. I'm Reagan Hillis. And I guess I'm becoming the person I really am. And if that means I have to be bossy and bitchy and cruel to get the job done, then screw it. That is the person I'm going to be."

"But you're *not* this person," Luke says, his voice quiet, as he steps closer to me. "I've seen the real you. I saw her in New Albany. I saw her in Colombia. And I've seen glimpses of her here. I don't understand why you're doing this, what's made you like this."

As soon as the words leave his lips, his tight mouth drops back open and his face softens. I can see his eyes searching for the words hanging in the air, wishing he could pull them, one by one, back into his mouth.

"You of all people should know," my voice squeezes out as I slowly back away from Luke and toward the door. "I hope it never happens, but if your mother ever dies in your arms, maybe report back. Let me know how it changes you."

As I reach the door frame, my body begins to shake and my lungs feel like they might just pull apart. I turn and walk out of the room. Luke calls after me but my legs pick up speed until I'm running. I don't stop until I reach an empty, secure conference room. I slam the door, tear at clumps of my hair, then cover my scorching face in my even hotter hands. I miss my mother so badly sometimes I can barely stand it. I'm surprised some days that I can walk and form sentences, let alone think and run and train. I can feel my million shattered pieces clanging together somewhere inside me every time I move, cutting into my lungs every time I breathe. There's no going back. I'm way past repair. So why try to go back to the girl Luke fell in love with? Why even try to be good when all I feel is bad?

TWENTY-TWO

"IF YOU'RE GOING TO SIT HERE AND TRY TO TELL ME that KISS is the best rock band of all time, then I seriously don't think we can be friends anymore," Anusha argues loudly with Cam from the front seat of our "borrowed" Black Angel Jeep. Getting out of CORE was much easier than I thought. All Cam had to do was bypass a few codes, upgrade our security clearance, and we were out the door.

I had to get the hell out of there. The concrete walls felt like they were collapsing in on me. After our argument, Luke disappeared. He had initially called after me, but he didn't run after me. He didn't try to find me to apologize. So why should I even think about sticking around? Outside of the dungeon, I can finally suck in a full breath. But the oxygen is doing very little to stop the acidic bile that is eating away at my stomach lining. I feel sick about what he said. I feel even worse about what I said. Not just today, but on the mission. Some moments you can't undo.

"Well, who would you suggest should take the top spot?" Cam says.

"Ummmm, I don't know, like a hundred other bands," Anusha says, rolling her eyes, her mouth separating into a smile as she argues. "Led Zeppelin, AC/DC, Pink Floyd, Queen, Nirvana, the Who, the Doors, Black Sabbath, the Clash, Radiohead, the freaking Rolling Stones . . . need I keep going?"

"I get goose bumps every time I hear 'Rock and Roll All Nite,'" Cam replies. "Especially some of their live versions."

"Oh, Jesus," Anusha says, hanging her head in her hands. "You cannot compare 'Rock and Roll All Nite' to a masterpiece like the Stones' 'Gimme Shelter.' You just can't. When Merry Clayton hits that high note in the chorus, it makes me believe in God."

"Who's Merry Clayton?" Cam asks.

"And you say you know rock and roll better than me," Anusha says, knocking the back of Cam's headrest and laughing. "Don't even try, Cam!"

Somewhere between my argument with Luke and locking myself in one of the secure conference rooms, Cam hacked his way into a Georgetown club's computer system and scored us free VIP passes to watch one of Anusha's favorite bands from Chicago: Last Night in Sweden. I've never heard of them, but then again I never exactly had my finger on the pulse of the coolest bands. Without access to Harper every day, I'm even more out of the loop. That girl knew everything about the latest rising bands. She was always dragging me out to shows or to her room to listen to her latest find.

"So who does this band sound like?" I ask from the backseat.

The Jeep passes a streetlight and I can see Anusha's lips pushed into a pondering pucker as she goes through the catalogue of her favorite bands. "I'd say they're like if Walk the Moon and Twenty One Pilots had a baby," she finally answers.

"Oh, nice," I reply. "Two Ohio bands I like."

"Look at you hitting me with that musical knowledge," Anusha says, reaching into the backseat and pointing her finger at my forehead.

"I have my moments," I answer, my right shoulder rising into a sluggish shrug.

"I cannot wait to dance," Anusha replies, stomping her feet onto the carpeted floor of the front seat with anticipation. "You look like you could use a night out too."

"Yeah," I answer with a sigh. "I definitely could."

"Want to talk about it?" she asks quietly.

"No. Thanks though," I answer and stare down at the Catwoman mask cradled in my hands. I had absolutely nothing to wear besides training gear, so I dressed in head to toe black and somehow found this mask out of the very slim pickings at the Halloween Express on K Street. The Torres threat level has clearly dropped (otherwise, they'd never have let trainees out on break) but Luke is at least somewhat right. I should always try to hide my identity and protect myself.

My eyes turn to look out the window, scanning M Street. The sidewalks are packed with college students and young professionals. Women in tights, men in scarves, dressed up and ready to drink. No one is wearing a warm enough jacket. Men shove their hands in the pockets of their jeans, their bodies rigid, arms tight against their sides, doing their best to conserve heat. The girls travel in tiny packs, clinging to one another for warmth, or balance. Or both. The last of the autumn leaves cling to scattered parkway trees. These leaves are ugly, a disgusting shade of brown. The showstoppers have already fallen. Red, yellow, and orange leaves litter the sidewalk, trampled by boots, punctured by high heels. Autumn is all but over and soon the next desolate season will settle in. I roll down the window a few inches, the chill in the air striking my skin like a warning.

As Cam pulls up to a stoplight, a threesome of girls stumble out of an open club door, their arms linked together, an inebriated chain. I think of Harper and Malika, the pit of my stomach throbbing with homesickness.

I like to imagine what they're doing. I pretend sometimes that they write me emails about college. In my fantasy correspondences, Harper is obsessed with her film classes at NYU and is in love with all things New York. Malika is trying to pick a major but has her heart set on rushing a sorority at University of Georgia (something Harper teases her about mercilessly). I know it's kind of crazy. I know I can never reach out to them again, never know what's happening in their lives. And it makes my heart twinge with a potent mixture of resentment and sorrow.

Five minutes and twenty dollars for a parking spot later, we push our way inside the Loose Groupie with our VIP passes. Everyone is dressed in well-planned, elaborate Halloween costumes. Our costumes are slightly less impressive. A Venetian mask hides Anusha's face while a Teenage Mutant Ninja Turtle mask hides Cam's (a mask Cam seemed super pumped about). We look more like teenagers who have outgrown the acceptable age for trick-or-treating but still run around the neighborhood in search of free Reese's Peanut Butter Cups and Twix bars. But at least our identities are hidden.

An escort helps to clear the way for us and we get about two hundred dirty looks as we brush past the show-goers who have been standing around for hours, trying to grab the best spot in the small, packed club.

The Loose Groupie gives Columbus clubs a real run for their money. In Columbus, most clubs are just big black boxes with a bar in the corner. But the Loose Groupie's black brick walls are covered in white and silver graffiti (clearly a graffiti artist's work, but it's made to look like it was taken off the street), two neon bars anchor either side of the room, and giant album covers of every amazing rock band that's ever lived canvas the low ceiling. Anusha catches me looking up, follows my eyes, and then nudges Cam.

"Funny, I don't see KISS up there," she yells over the house music.

"I can take that VIP pass away from you, you know," Cam says, pointing at the pass dangling around Anusha's neck.

"You would never," she says with a smile, grasping the pass protectively between her hands.

"Our passes get us backstage for a meet and greet before show-time," Cam hollers over the loud bass. He looks down at his watch. "It's like ten minutes until they're supposed to go on. So want to give them a try?"

"Hell yes!" Anusha practically screams.

We snake our way through another small crowd of VIPs and make our way to the side entrance of the stage.

"Do we have time to run back and just say hi?" Anusha yells in the bouncer's ear, flashing her VIP badge.

"Yeah, quickly," he says, ushering us up the stairs and through a set of black curtains.

Backstage, there's a flurry of activity. Guys tuning guitars and checking lights. A few sit at soundboards, fiddling with levers and switches and knobs. The security guard leads the way, passing by roadies in dirty jeans and black T-shirts, their muscles tight against the fabric. We brush past a man and woman, both dressed in expensive tailored suits and nearly identical tortoiseshell glasses. They stand with their backs against the black curtains, trying to blend in but looking completely out of place.

"Record execs," Anusha says in my ear with disdain after we've passed them. "Only they would wear suits to a show."

We follow a line of white, glowing tape made to resemble arrows against a black painted floor to a back room where four guys and one girl are lounging on a pair of beat-up couches, smoking cigarettes and having a final drink before the show.

"Couple VIP meet and greeters," the security guard announces before disappearing out of the room.

"Hey, come on in." A man in his late twenties with shoulder-length dark hair waves us through the door and stands up from the scratched-to-hell chocolate-brown leather couch.

Anusha rushes through and holds out her hand, which he takes. "I'm so excited to meet you guys," she says, her voice an octave higher than normal. "I'm a huge fan. I used to come watch you guys when you played in clubs around Wicker Park."

"Awesome," he replies, slapping her on the back and turning to the rest of the band. "We've got an original fan right here, guys. Where you from in Chicago?"

"Bucktown," Anusha answers even though I know she lived in a west suburb called St. Charles. Trying to up her cool factor. And it works.

"Bucktown is where it's at," the girl in the corner answers and takes a swig of her beer, then holds her bottle in the air. "How rude of us. You guys want to have a preshow beer?"

"Absolutely," Anusha answers for us and they pass around bottles of a microbrew I've never heard of before. It tastes much more hoppy and bitter than the cheap Natty Light I occasionally sipped back in New Albany.

The band makes easy conversation with us about what we're doing in DC (we say college, of course), where we're all originally from (Ohio, Chicago, Vermont), and how we like living in the nation's capital (love it). We ask them about how long they've been together (five years), their influences (the Who, David Bowie, and Talking Heads) and where they're heading next on their tour (Richmond, Charlotte, and Charleston).

"Guys, it's time," a man says from the doorway. Forties with black-rimmed glasses and tired eyes, I have to assume he's their manager. The band stands up from their lounging positions, shaking out their arms and stretching their legs, like they're getting ready for a marathon. And I guess they are.

"Thanks for the beer, you guys," I say and set my half-empty beer down on the beat-up coffee table.

"Yeah, it was awesome to meet you," Cam answers, setting his beer down near mine.

"You guys can totally watch backstage for a couple songs if you'd like," the girl says, placing a pair of cat ears on her head and picking up a pair of drumsticks. A chick drummer. With a thick purple streak through her black hair and tiny star tattoos wrapped around her wrists. I kind of want to be her.

"Really?" Anusha says, her smile wide. "That'd be fantastic."

"Yeah, just follow us and hang out by the curtains," drummer chick answers, waving us through the door and into the darkness.

We follow the white, glowing tape that leads us back to the stage. The houselights have dimmed, the stage lights and music have been turned off, and the crowd breaks out into frantic cheers, eagerly awaiting the band.

"Stand right there," the girl shouts over the noise of the crowd, pointing with her drumsticks to a corner, covered by more black curtains, near the front of the stage. She smiles and disappears into the darkness with the rest of the band.

"Ladies and gentleman," a voice comes over the loudspeakers and the crowd cheers even louder. "Please welcome for the first time to Washington, DC . . . Last Night in Sweden."

Bright lights flood the stage and the band immediately launches into their first song. Anusha jumps up and down, pleased by their intro selection. The lead singer launches into the lyrics and I'm surprised by how crystal clear his voice is despite the fact he's jumping up and down on the stage, his exposed arms in his sleeveless shirt beginning to glisten with sweat.

A song later, I've finally let go. I've forgotten about Luke and our fight and the threat of Torres. I'm clutching Anusha and swaying my hips to the sound of the electric guitar. The crowd is cheering and screaming and so at first when I hear a louder scream, I think it's just someone who's really into the music. But then I hear it again and know that someone in the crowd is screaming out of fear or pain. Or both.

Anusha hears it too and pulls back the curtain. A fight has broken out at the front of the stage. Two men, one dressed as Batman and one as Superman (how's that for irony?) are punching each other while a girl dressed as Malibu Barbie tries to step in between them and break them up.

Oh no, no, no. Stop, girl. What are you doing?

The girl immediately gets thrown to the ground by the man dressed as Batman, and Anusha turns toward me, her eyes wide and eyebrows raised as if to say, *What should we do?* I shake my head at her, not wanting to get involved quite yet. After Superman lands a hard right jab to Batman's chin, the man dressed as Bruce Wayne's alter ego pulls out a knife.

Shit.

The band's song begins to slowly sputter into miscued drumbeats and guitar plucks as people turn their attention toward the violent fight in front of them. Batman brings his knife up, closer to his face, and as it shines against the stage lights, more people begin to panic and scream. But the crowd is so tightly packed in, there's nowhere to turn. Nowhere to run. The man lunges toward Superman with his knife. He plunges the knife toward his chest, but Superman dodges out of the way just in time, the knife slicing at his arm and drawing blood.

"We have to stop this," I say and move toward the edge of the stage. "Someone's going to get killed."

Batman lunges again with the knife, this time making contact with Superman's stomach, sending him stumbling backward. Batman pulls the bloody knife out of his flesh and steps forward, like he's ready to finish the job. I jump off the stage and between the two men as Superman falls to the floor.

"Put down the knife!" I scream over the scattered music, holding out my hand, trying to stop this lunatic from killing this guy.

"Fuck off," the drunk Batman screams at me, the knife dripping with fresh blood.

"Put down the god damned knife!" I scream again but he pulls his hands into an exaggerated shrug.

"Make me, little girl," he yells, the knife growing loose in his drunk hands. Too easy.

I kick him in the groin as I simultaneously hit his hand with the knife, sending it spinning across the stage. Then I grab him by the neck, pull him toward me, forcing his knees to give out, and slam his tall body to the ground.

"Holy shit!" someone in the crowd screams out.

I turn around. Superman is sprawled out on the ground, blood gushing from a gaping wound in his stomach.

"Somebody call 911," I call out and run to Superman's side. I pull his cape off from around his neck and try to press it into his wound to stop the bleeding.

"Reagan, we've got to get out of here," Cam yells, now off the stage and behind me, his voice shaking, and I know why. If the police come, we'll get questioned. They'll want to know who we are. How I knew how to disarm this asshole and knock him to the ground. Our cover could be blown. The Black Angels publicly outed. We might as well pack our bags. He's right. We have to leave.

"Somebody, help me," I cry out and a group of bouncers and concertgoers jump to help the bleeding man and hold down his assailant.

I look back at Anusha and Cam, their eyes so wide I can see the white around both of their irises. My muscles are tingling, nerves firing, fresh panic settling into my chest. I don't want to leave him. But we have no other choice.

With one nod from me, they slowly begin to walk back up the stage steps.

"Come on," I say, pulling at Anusha's wrist, my hands sticky with the stranger's blood. "Let's go."

We sprint into the darkness of the backstage, out the back door, and through the narrow alley. The cold fall air pierces my already heavy chest as my legs carry me down a crowded sidewalk. We hear sirens rushing down M Street but don't stop running until we reach our car, three blocks away.

TWENTY-THREE

THE THREE OF US WALK IN SILENCE THROUGH THE underground garage, down the secret elevator to the compound, and toward the dorms in the South Hall, our hands in our pockets, our teeth digging into our lips. We've ditched our masks at a gas station on our way back to CORE. I ran inside the bathroom, washing Superman's blood off of my hands while saying a silent prayer that he'd live. That he'd be okay.

Cam's hacks worked flawlessly, getting us through the gates and into the garage without anyone giving us a second glance.

"I'm gonna go wash my face," Anusha says quietly, bypassing our dorm room and walking toward the girls' bathroom. "Maybe take a shower. Clean some of this night off me."

"All right," I answer and grab her shoulder. "Are you okay?"

"I guess," she says and shrugs. "I've just never seen anyone hurt like that. They prep you for it in the air force and everything. It's just... it's different when it actually happens. You try to put up those barriers, but it breaks through and I can't help but feel scared for that guy. I can't stop seeing all that blood."

Her eyes look past me, vacant. I pull her body into my arms. I've seen far worse than Superman bleeding out on a club floor. But witnessing violence, facing death, it doesn't get easier. That's something I learned from my mother. You'll never truly become immune. As much as you try to hold missions away from you, as much as you try to turn your emotions off, they still seep into your skin, rattle you when you least expect it. No wonder she barely slept. I would hear her footsteps in the hallway. I'd fall back asleep to the sounds of her insomnia: a lamp switching on, the buzz of a TV, the clank of a coffee cup in the kitchen. The darkness she buried rose up in her dreams, jolting her awake at all hours of the night.

"Take a shower. Go watch some mindless TV," I advise, rubbing my hands up and down Anusha's arms. "That may help."

"Okay," she says quietly before disappearing into the bathroom.

When I open the room to the girls' dorm, Luke is dressed in pajamas and sitting on my bed. He stands up when I walk in.

"What are you doing in here?" I ask, my voice thin and tired. I don't have the energy to argue with him anymore.

"I was waiting for you," he answers, carefully sitting back down on the bed, unsure if he's a welcomed guest.

"Were you waiting in here so I could tell you that you were right?" I ask, tearing off my black jacket and flinging it on top of my dresser. "That we never should have gone. It's okay. You can say it. I know you're dying to say 'I told you so.'"

"No, I wasn't," Luke says, shaking his head, his eyes growing concerned. "I don't know what you're even talking about. What happened? Is everyone okay?"

"We're fine, I guess," I answer, zipping off the boots I borrowed from Anusha. I pull them off of my feet, each one landing with a thud on the concrete floor. "A fight broke out at the club we were at. First, it was just a fist fight. But then a guy pulled out a knife and stabbed the other guy and I had to jump in between them to stop them from killing each other."

"Jesus, are you okay?" Luke answers, his eyes following me as I walk around the room, grabbing a sweatshirt and socks.

"A little shaken up," I say and cross over to the small mirror above my dresser. I pull my makeup remover out of my tiny makeup bag. I dab the clear liquid on a cotton swab and rub it across my eyes, my mascara melting off in long, black streaks. "But I'm okay. I don't know about the guy that got stabbed. It was scary. That guy was going to kill him. You could just tell."

"You saved his life," Luke states quietly from my bed.

"I don't know," I answer with a sigh. "I should have jumped in sooner. We were all wearing masks, but still, I didn't want to risk blowing our cover, you know? I just hope he's okay."

The image of him lying in his Superman costume comes back to me. The pool of blood, growing with each heartbeat, at his side. People screaming. His chest heaving with desperate breaths.

"So what are you doing in here?" I ask again, looking back at Luke in my small mirror. He's still beautiful to look at, but I don't remember his skin looking quite this colorless back in New Albany. His pale blue eyes are dulled, and he looks like he's aged about ten years instead of one since our perfect kiss back at Templeton.

"I couldn't go to sleep without apologizing to you. I said some . . . some . . ." He stammers and looks down at his hands. "I'm so sorry for what I said to you. It wasn't fair. And it wasn't true."

"Maybe it was," I answer, wiping my face clean and walking across the room toward him. "Sometimes the truth comes out when we're backed into a corner and angry. So maybe that really is how you think of me. Cold and cruel."

"But you're not cold or cruel," Luke says, grabbing my hand. I let him pull me onto the bed next to him. "I don't know why I even said that."

"Because it's probably at least partially true," I reply, turning my face away from him, scared of what may be written in my eyes. "I know I've changed, Luke. I know I've hardened. But I don't know how else to be. I don't know how to go back. It's like the moment he killed her, he flipped some type of switch. And I'm left with all these broken pieces. An angry heart. And I'm sorry for that. I'm sorry I humiliated you during our test. I'm sorry I lash out at you. I'm sorry I'm not the girl you—"

"Reagan, it's okay." Luke interrupts my shaky voice, moving his body closer to me. His fingertips reach for my chin and only when he touches me do I realized it's trembling. He pulls at me gently, bringing my face toward his.

My eyes catch his and I can't help but want to cry and scream and kiss him all at once. He traces my jawline with his thumb and my body begins to tingle.

"You're still the girl I fell for," he whispers, his cool breath creating a tiny tornado on my inflamed lips. My face instinctively moves toward his, magnetic and familiar, and a flood of happiness and helplessness rushes through my body as my lips move closer and closer to his.

The door on the other side of the room swings open, hitting the cinder block walls with a bang, pulling Luke and me apart. Anusha crosses the room in her robe and grabs a second towel. She eyes us and it's clear she knows she interrupted something.

"Sorry," she says sheepishly and scurries back out of the room with her eyes focused on the floor. I move away from Luke, scolding myself for getting lost in the moment. We were lucky it was Anusha on the other side of the door and not a senior leader or trainer or a tattletale trainee.

"Reagan," Luke says lightly as I push myself off the bed and farther away from him. I turn around, wanting so badly to press my aching lips on his sweet mouth and let my world spin into darkness.

He looks up at me, his eyes pleading, his fingertips still lingering on my wrist, sending tiny bolts of electricity through my already buzzing body.

"We can't," I whisper and shake his touch, along with those tiny lightning bolts, away. But I immediately miss it the moment my fingertips slide past his.

Before he can say another word, I turn back around and walk out of the room. I can't bear to watch his face break. I can't bear to hear him say something sweet, something so "Luke."

I hurry down the hallway, away from the dorms, away from Luke, away from all the feelings in that room. The warmth I felt next to him begins to fade and as my blood returns to its chilly temperature, I wish for a different life. I run my fingers along the cinder block walls, wishing they were part of a college dorm. That my class schedule was Biology 101, Modern European History, and Advanced Play Writing instead of Surveillance Tactics, Advanced Hacking, and Threat Elimination. That Luke and I could actually be together. Or at least try.

I turn the corner and pass by the wall of fallen Black Angels. I usually walk by the wall quickly, never wanting to take in what those black stars really mean. But tonight, I slow down. I look. I let my hands run across the white marble, my fingers tracing the latest dark star as I wonder which one is for Mom. Each star is blank. No name or label to pay homage to those who died in the line of duty. Their heroism, secret and silent, even in death.

A tear breaks free and I push it aside before it has a chance to run down my cheek. The scar tissue around my heart flares, its stitches pull tighter. And I remember why I'm here. What Torres has done. And why Luke and I must stay apart.

TWENTY-FOUR

"SHIT, SHIT, SHIT, SHIT, YOU GUYS." A VOICE STIRS me from a sleep I swear I just fell into. The overhead lights flick on, pulling me out of my dreamless state.

"What?" I say, rubbing the remaining sleep out of my eyes as Cam and Luke take large, panicked steps across the empty dorm room toward our bunk. Cam is holding his laptop in one hand and grabbing at his hair with the other.

"What time is it?" Anusha asks weakly next to me, her bed-springs whining under her shifting weight. I glance at the clock on the nightstand but before I can report the fact that it's 5:32, Cam cuts me off.

"Screw the time," Cam says, his voice harsh and heavy, like he just ran down the hall. And from the look on his face, he probably did.

"Reagan, you're everywhere," Luke says and every muscle in my body locks up.

Luke and Cam sit on the edge of my bed, not caring that I'm still wrapped up in blankets.

"What do you mean she's everywhere?" Anusha replies, dragging her comforter with her and wrapping herself up like a burrito as she joins us on my bed.

"I mean there's videos of Reagan breaking up the fight from last night everywhere," Luke continues as Cam scans through website after website, each featuring grainy photos of me in my Catwoman mask knocking Batman to the ground.

"Oh shit," I say under my breath, my heart now pounding out anxious, rapid beats.

"A few people took cell phone videos of what happened last night," Cam explains. "Of the fight, of the guy pulling out the knife and stabbing the other guy. Of Reagan knocking the knife out of the guy's hand and slamming him to the ground. And the fact that you were dressed up as Catwoman and took down a guy dressed as Batman is just too ironic for this story not to get picked up around the world. The video is shaky and dark and since you have on a mask, you can't really tell it's you. But you can hear your voice."

"Here, just watch," Luke says, hitting the play button on CNN .com. The white button spins and then a pretty, blond anchor pops up on screen.

"The search is on this morning for a real-life superhero who was able to stop a violent, nearly deadly fight at a music venue in Washington, DC," she says into the camera before grainy video of the concert plays. "Over two hundred and fifty people packed into a Georgetown club to watch rock band Last Night in Sweden on

Halloween night when two men dressed as Batman and Superman got into a physical altercation. After the suspect dressed as Batman pulled out a knife and began stabbing the victim, a very brave woman dressed as—get this—Catwoman . . . leapt off the stage and was able to disarm the twenty-five-year-old suspect, stopping what police say could have been a homicide. Take a look."

The anchor stops talking and there I am, jumping off the stage, demanding he put down the knife, and then knocking it out of his hand and slamming his body to the ground. You can then hear me screaming for someone to call 911 from down on the ground next to Superman. It's shaky and grainy and dark, but it's me.

"Oh, holy Jesus," I mutter, my voice muffled by the hand over my mouth before the anchor continues.

"A member of the band, drummer Roxie Lennon, reported that the hero who jumped to Superman's rescue was an area college student she met before the show. The victim, twenty-six-year-old Rich Davidson, suffered stab wounds to his stomach but is listed in stable condition. The real mystery this morning . . . Who is Catwoman? Police report she took off before they arrived on the scene, which has the Internet buzzing. Perhaps Gotham isn't the only city with crime-fighting superheroes after all."

Cam clicks out of CNN and scrolls through dozens of news websites.

"Look at all these," he says, pointing at the screen. "CNN, Fox, NBC, ABC, CBS, Huffington Post, Reddit, the *New York Times*, *Daily Mail*. Check out these headlines: "Catwoman Takes Down Batman," "Catwoman Rushes to Superman's Aid," "Catwoman vs. Batman: The Real Superhero Story." You name it, you're on it, not to mention the fact that you're trending on Twitter with the hashtag #CatwomanHero. Everyone is trying to figure out who you are."

"I might be really screwed," I say, my hands cupping my shaking head. "Maybe we need to find someone. Tell them what happened before they—"

But before I can finish my sentence, a fist pounds at our door and it flies open. My father is standing in the doorway, dressed in a black sweater and jeans. His eyes are jagged slits and his cheeks are streaked scarlet.

"Dad," I say, my body knocked backward, shocked by his presence. "What are you doing here?"

"Just flew in," he answers, then points at me. "You and I need to talk. Tribunal chamber. Now."

With that, he turns on his heel, walking toward the East Hall, leaving the four of us in stunned silence, our lungs empty, our mouths open.

"Now!" I hear him yell from down the hallway, and whoever was sleeping in the private rooms is up now. I scramble off the bed, grabbing my sweatshirt and slippers.

"Do you think he knows?" Cam asks.

"Of course he knows, you idiot," Anusha answers for me, slapping Cam across the shoulder.

"We should come with you," Luke states, grabbing for my hand as I slip my arms through my sweatshirt.

"No," I say, shaking my head and pulling my long hair out of the neck of my sweatshirt. "There's no point. I'm the one on that video. There's no way I'm going to let you guys get in trouble. Especially you, Luke. You weren't even with us."

"I know," Luke answers with a small shrug. "I just don't want you to be alone."

"Cam and I should go with you," Anusha says and starts getting up off the bed. "We were there too. You shouldn't be the only one who gets in trouble. Let us help at least take some of the heat off you."

"Absolutely not," I say over my shoulder as I make my way toward the door. "I won't let you guys risk your spots here. Stay put. Please."

Before they can argue with me, I walk quickly down the hall, knowing my father will get only more annoyed with each passing minute he's left waiting for me. I wonder who else will be in the Tribunal chamber. If the entire senior leadership team knows what happened last night. If they'll all be sitting in various states of dress on their imposing throne, waiting to kick me out, my fate sealed by catchy headlines and shaky cell phone videos.

By the time I reach the closed, imposing steel doors, I'm out of breath, fear tightening its grip on my lungs, forcing me to swallow air in sporadic gasps.

I close my eyes for a moment, trying to calm myself down, but my hands are shaking as I pull down on the cold door handle. It swings open with a noisy creak. When I force my legs to move inside, my father is standing alone in the center of the room, his arms crossed, his mouth twisted into a livid scowl. I scan the imposing senior leadership seats for Director Browning or Stony Face, but they're not there. We're alone. And that might be even more frightening.

"Sit," my father barks, slapping the steel table where I sat during my trial. My little white, wooden seat is gone, so I make my way around the table and hoist my body up onto its sturdy surface. The chilly metal immediately soaks through my thin pajama pants, triggering a shiver I cannot suppress.

"Do you know why you're here?" my father asks, his fingers gripping at his wide, imposing hips as his body leans forward, like he's ready to pounce on me, rip me to shreds. I tell my tongue to speak, to string together a sentence or two. But it won't move. I stare at him, frozen, gripping the edge of the table. My silence only pisses him off more and he presses louder this time: "Well, do you?!"

"Yes. I think so," I answer quietly.

My father picks a Black Angel tablet off the table and flips it around so that the grainy photo of me knocking Batman to the ground is staring me right in the face. Above it, a headline reads: "The Search for a Real-Life Superhero."

"Do you have any idea what you've done?" my father says with a bitter-soaked tongue. "Do you have any idea how stupid it was for you to not only sneak out of CORE without permission, but then get involved in a public fight?"

"Yes," I answer, my voice weak. "But I couldn't just let him die. I had to help him. That's what you and Mom taught me. That's what you would have done."

My father's face suddenly softens. I study him as he looks me up and down. His chestnut hair has given way to hundreds of strands of gray in the last few months. The lines around his eyes and mouth have deepened, and he's lost weight since the last time I saw him. He puts the tablet down on the steel surface and pulls himself on the table next to me.

"What am I going to do with you, Reagan?" he says, shaking his head with both disapproval and confusion. His body is close enough for me to touch, but there's still a divide between us, an imaginary wall he's built up over the last year, brick by impassable brick. "Part of me is proud of you for saving this man. The other part of me wants to strangle you for being so irresponsible. You know you could have blown your own cover and more important, put the entire agency in jeopardy, right?"

"I know," I answer quietly.

"We are able to do these dangerous jobs because we are protected by secrecy," he says, his hands gripping the table, his eyes staring straight ahead. "You could have blown the cover off of an agency that has been performing undercover tasks for this government for decades. Do you understand the responsibility that comes with being a Black Angel? This is not a joke. We are not role-playing here. This is real life. Every day, we are risking our lives to keep this nation safe from terrorists and drug bosses and human traffickers and a very long list of criminals, and you could ruin all of that because you wanted to sneak out and see a god damned concert!"

My blood feels like lighter fluid racing through my veins. But it isn't anger that's causing the heat. It's shame. For breaking the rules. For ignoring my gut. For endangering the secrecy that surrounds the Black Angels.

"How did you even leave the building?" Dad continues, turning toward me. "Trainees need permission and passes."

"I figured out a way to sneak out," I finally say, not wanting to get Cam into trouble.

"Why did you do it?" my father asks, shaking his head. "Forget risking your place here and jeopardizing the agency. You know you have a price on your head. You know you're a target. I just don't understand why, after a year of us all trying to protect you, you'd risk your life by leaving the safety of CORE."

"I don't know," I answer and stare down at the dark, acid-stained concrete floors. "I guess I just needed a moment to breathe. It's so heavy down here. It's all so hard. I haven't felt even a trace of normalcy in over a year. I guess I wanted to be in the real world. Even if it was just for a couple of hours. Because at least then, I could breathe."

My father and I stare down at the ground in silence, our legs swinging almost in unison as we sit next to each other on the cold metal table.

"Who else knows?" I quietly ask.

"No one," my father answers with a sigh. "I got in around three in the morning. The video was sent to myself and a few senior leaders from a contact in the CIA asking if this could have been one of our people. I watched the tape, realized it was your voice, and then immediately went into our security system and erased everything."

"You covered for me?" I ask, my eyebrows rising with surprise. I thought my father wanted me out of the Black Angels. This was his chance to ban me from this life.

"Does that surprise you?" he asks.

"Yes," I answer and follow his eyes back down to the ground. "After everything that happened with your testimony in the Tribunal and our fight this spring, I . . . I guess I didn't expect it."

"You're my daughter," Dad answers, his voice surprisingly small. "It's my job to protect you. That's why I gave the testimony I did in the Tribunal in the first place. That's why I said you didn't belong here. I was trying to keep you safe. You're a smart girl. Couldn't you pick up on that?"

"No. I thought you were punishing me."

"Why would I punish you?"

"Because Mom is dead and I'm not," I answer, and the jagged rock of sorrow beneath my breastbone shifts and scratches at my flesh. "Because maybe in the deepest parts of your soul, you think it was my fault."

"I've never said that, Reagan," Dad answers defiantly, his fingers gripping the steel table even tighter.

"You've never had to," I say, rubbing the tops of my freezing thighs with my hands. "It's been over a year since she died, and do you know how many times you've hugged me?"

"I've been away."

"Even before that."

"I clearly don't keep track of hugs like you do."

"I've felt really alone, Dad." I say the words that have been sewn on my soul for months. They've been pulled at, fussed with, and torn apart so many times that the pain barely registers anymore. I swallow hard and take a breath. I need to get this all out. "I thought after the Tribunal, you just wished I'd disappear. You wished it'd been me who died instead of her."

There. I said it. As the words leave my body, my limbs begin to shake and my lungs feel like they might just pull apart. Whether he meant to or not, Dad has made me so much worse. This last year, maybe I could have gotten through it with him. Maybe I would have lost some of my anger, toward myself, toward Torres, if he'd just tried. Hugged me. Kissed my forehead. Told me it was going to be okay. He couldn't have fixed me, but just trying may have stopped me from wanting to fall apart.

When I look back up from my spot of nothing on the ground, Dad's smoothing something away from his face.

"I would never wish it was you who died instead of your mother, Reagan. Never," Dad answers, finally looking up, and now I know what he was pushing away. It was tears. His light brown eyes are glassy and when he blinks, a fresh tear falls down his face. "I have never wanted to punish you. I just couldn't bear to lose the last thing I love."

My body falls backward, my mouth gaping open. All this time I thought he was pushing me away because he was angry. Because I brought him pain.

"But, I don't understand," I say, my voice barely above a whisper. "I don't understand what happened in the Tribunal and then the way you acted toward me at the safe house. You haven't even checked on me during Qualifiers. Not once. I know you could. But you haven't. Not an email, not a message, nothing. You're not the father you've been the last seventeen years before any of this happened."

"I know," he answers, the tears coming faster now. And I realize it's only the second time in my life I've ever seen my father cry. "I don't know how I can ask you to forgive me, but I was only doing it to protect you, Reagan."

"Protect me from what?"

"From the Black Angels," Dad answers, sniffing and swatting at the tears that keep falling down his cheeks. "I don't want you to be

208

here. That's why I testified that you didn't belong. I was hoping the Tribunal would vote to kick you out so that you could just go to college. Get away from all of this. But once you made it, I just . . . I'm ashamed to say it, but I was really hoping you wouldn't make it through the first round or would quit. But I got word overseas that you kept excelling and doing better and better. And that scares the hell out of me because the last thing I want is for you to be on the Rescue/Take-down team, to be in immediate danger like that. I'd die if anything happened to you."

"Dad, nothing will happen to me," I begin to say but he cuts me off.

"You don't know that," he counters, his voice almost angry. He sucks in a noisy breath through his snot-filled nose and looks away, his eyes scanning the room before he turns them back to me. "It's a very, very dangerous world out there, Reagan. Getting more dangerous by the day. Being on the RT, you're on the front lines. The possibility of you getting injured or dying is very real. And I can't lose you, Reagan. I just can't."

Dad buries his face in his large hands, hiding his tears and breathing deep into his palms, trying to control his overflow of emotions. All this time, I had no idea his coldness, his betrayal, was a mask. And seeing him like this, watching him bat away each tear, I almost want to give up. I almost want to say I'll stop training. That I'll go to college. Be normal. But then I think of my mother . . . of Torres . . . and I can't. I cannot walk away from this. Not yet.

"Daddy," I whisper, standing up and facing him. He pulls his hands away from his face and the dark ocean he put between us, the wall he built around himself, disappears. We see each other for the first time since my mother died. His eyes shine, even through his crippling sadness, with love. Unmistakable, unconditional love. I put my arms around his shoulders and feel his wet tears on my face. He pulls me closer to him, hugging me for the first time since the barn in Colombia. "You guys used to tell me all the time that I was born to be a Black Angel. Remember?"

"Yes," my father answers, his voice muffled by my shoulder.

"I used to find that so annoying," I say and he chuckles, his tears slowing. "But you know what? I think it was true."

Dad slowly pulls away from our embrace, wiping his eyes with the backs of his hands. "I know it's true," he answers. "That's why I covered for you this morning. This could have been my key to keep you safe. To get you kicked out. But I saw the way you jumped into action. I saw on that video how you risked your life for someone you never even met. We always knew you had Black Angel in your blood. I guess now, I selfishly don't want it to be true."

"What would Mom want you to do?" I ask, leaning my body against the cold table next to him. "She wouldn't want you to put me in a box to keep me safe. She wouldn't want you to hold me back."

"No, she wouldn't," Dad says, a small laugh bubbling up his throat. He shakes his head and smiles. "She'd put me into one of her choke holds, I think."

"She totally would," I say and laugh. Dad grabs my hand and puts it to his cheek before kissing it twice. "Mom would want me to use my talent to help people. I couldn't save her. But I can save other people's mothers, daughters, brothers, sons. She told me once that's why she did this. Because those people meant something to somebody. And she didn't want them to die alone."

"Sounds like something she would say," Dad says with a smile, looking up at me.

"You have so much of your mother in you it's scary. Her strength, her courage. Her stubbornness and negotiating skills."

We both laugh and Dad kisses my hand again, holding it against his cheek for a long time. I feel the inside of his hands. They're still rough from all of his years on the RT squad, but they've softened a little, with less calluses, less wear and tear.

"I can't be selfish anymore," he says, looking down at our interwoven fingers and nodding his head. "If this is what you really want to do, I should be the last person standing in your way. Even when I was holding you back, I always believed in you. I hope you know that."

"Thank you, Dad," I say, kissing him on the cheek.

"I'm proud of you, Reagan," he says, patting me on the face before letting me go. "You're clearly here for all the right reasons. That video proved it to me. You're going to help make the world a better place."

A ragged lump unexpectedly gathers at the base of my throat, filled with an emotion I can't quite place.

"I won't let you down. I promise," I say and the emotional tumor thickens, making the words come out serrated. I clear my throat but the lump refuses to budge.

My body backs up toward the door, almost waiting for Dad to change his mind, grab me by my shoulders, and escort me to the exit. When I reach the massive doors, he gives me a small, sad smile. And that persistent lump hardens into an agonizing rock.

I grab on to the handle, push the door open, and escape into the dimly lit hallway. The overhead light above me buzzes, its irritating sound burrowing into my ear canals and curling around my brain. My legs suddenly take off running down the hall to get away from the sound, away from the Tribunal, away from whatever is causing this bulge to swell and restrict my air. Once I get around the intel center, I turn down the hallway and lean my warm body up against the cool cinder block.

Why do I feel like this?

I grab at my knees, trying to place the emotion rubbing my throat raw. And then I know. It isn't sadness or anger or fear. It's guilt.

Is my father right? Am I doing all of this because I care about saving people? Or am I only here for revenge? Am I only fighting for a spot in the training academy to end one life? Something that will undoubtedly kill my career. My father's belief in me, his parental pride, will be based on the lies of a manipulative girl with an ember at her core, a darkening heart and soot in her soul. He may not be the father he was before. But I'm certainly not the girl I was a year ago either. And I never will be.

Bury it, my mind instructs. *Play the pretender until Torres is dead.*

I place my scalding hands against the cold walls and take in a breath. I force the guilt away and allow the numbness to wrap around me like a blanket. The lump drops and disappears, my mind quiets with an emotionless fog, and I welcome back the feeling of being half dead. Something I always hated. But what other choice do I have?

TWENTY-FIVE

"GO, GO, GO," MICHAEL SCREAMS, HIS VOICE BOUNCING off the cement floors and concrete block walls in the training facility. I'm in full RT gear, from the bulletproof vest to the heavy black helmet, crawling my way through a timed obstacle course. I have one last obstacle: climb through a broken door frame to reach my target, a two-hundred-pound dummy lying in the corner of this makeshift hostage bunker. I push my body through, sweep my gun from side to side scanning the room for attackers, and then race toward the dummy, picking up the body and throwing it over my shoulders.

"Come on, Reagan," Michael hollers again, looking down at his stopwatch. "Thirty seconds and the bomb is going to go off."

My eyes search the room, looking for a better exit. I see a back window and decide to use that as my out instead of going back the way I came in. I carefully lower the body onto the ground outside the window and then jump through, somersaulting on the unforgiving floor.

Mother of Jesus, my mind and muscles are screaming as I pick up the two hundred pounds of deadweight and throw it over my shoulder again.

"Now get as far away as you can, Reagan," Michael screams, and I take off running. "Ten seconds."

I sprint toward the far side of the gym as Michael counts down. "Five, four, three, two, one." The alarm signal sounds with an obnoxious, high-pitched shrill that irritates my already throbbing spine.

I push the body off of my shoulders, dropping it down onto the floor. Beads of sweat drip down my forehead and I want to join the dummy facedown on the cool ground too. Lucky stiff.

"Fantastic job, Reagan," Michael hollers, jogging to my side of the gym and holding out his hand for a high five. I slap his hand and can't help but smile, despite being completely out of breath and kind of wishing for sweet death so this pain will cease. Running this obstacle course five times will knock out even the most in-shape trainee. He marks my final spot with a piece of blue tape and points to the others, several yards away. "Look at you. Best of the group. You're getting stronger and stronger."

"Thanks," I say, my voice thin, my lungs still fighting for air. "I had good trainers."

"Yeah," Michael answers, his mouth falling a bit. "Nobody better, right?"

I shake my head and begin walking back toward the course and the rest of our team. "Nobody."

Michael puts his hand on my back and squeezes my shoulder for a second before jogging toward the starting position where

Matthew DeVillers is waiting for his last timed run-through of the day.

My legs are wobbly as I make my way back toward the rest of the waiting group. My friends are smiling. Lex Morgan is scowling. But the annoying part about Lex is she's so gorgeous, even when her face is twisted with anger or annoyance, she's still obnoxiously pleasant-looking. If only her disgusting, rotting corpse of a personality could match her outside.

"So awesome, Hillis," Cam says, pounding his fist into mine.

"You just obliterate it every time," Luke says, holding out his hand for a high five.

"You two sure look cozy," Lex says, her head tipping toward Michael on the other side of the obstacle course, ready to count down Matthew. "Why don't you just suck his dick? Then you'll really be guaranteed a spot on the RT."

The start buzzer sounds and like a gunshot, Anusha shoots up from the steel bench, grabs Lex by the collar, and pushes her hard against the makeshift hostage bunker wall where Michael cannot see us.

"Go screw yourself, Lex," Anusha hisses, little droplets of spit hitting Lex's perfect face. Luke and I jump in between them, pulling them apart. I grab Anusha by the arms and hold her back but she still squirms under my grasp.

"Stop, stop, stop," I say calmly in Anusha's ear. "I love you for protecting me but please do not get yourself into trouble. She's trying to start a fight and get us kicked out of here."

"What is it, Reagan?" Lex exclaims, struggling against Luke's grip. "Too much of a pussy to fight your own battles?"

"Lex, shut up," Luke answers, pulling her to the other side of the wall. "You know Reagan would have you on the ground in two seconds."

"Yeah, right," Lex answers, spitting her words and lunging toward me. "I eat pieces of shit like you for breakfast."

"To quote *Happy Gilmore*," I begin. "You eat pieces of shit for breakfast?"

With that, Anusha bursts into laughter, her muscles finally relaxed enough for me to let go.

"Well played, Reagan," Anusha says, nudging me with her hip. "Well played."

"That was too easy," I answer, shaking my head.

"God, I really hate her," Anusha answers, glaring at Lex, who has been forced by Luke across the gym. He's let her go and I can tell he's trying to reason with her. Only Luke would have the heart to try to reason with someone like Lex.

"Yeah, me too," I answer.

"No, but I mean I *really* hate her," Anusha says, squinting her eyes and pinching her fingertips in the air for extra emphasis. "You probably have PG-level fantasies about filling her shampoo bottle with Nair or giving her Ex-Lax-laced brownies or something. But I lie in our bunk at night and dream of ways I could accidentally-on-purpose dislocate both her kneecaps."

"Don't even think about it," I say, waving her off. "She is just trying to start a big fight with me so that I'll hit her or something and they'll kick me out. All part of her strategy to nab one of the RT spots. I'm not stupid."

Lex Morgan has not let up on her efforts to get me cut from

Qualifiers. But so far, I've refused to give her the satisfaction of playing into her manipulative little games. I want my spot because of my talent, not because I play dirty. And she can just cry her pretty green eyes out and scream about how it's not fair when I get it and she doesn't.

The buzzer sounds and I turn around to see how far Matthew got. Not bad. About twenty yards away from my mark. "Nice going, Mattie," I yell across the cavernous space. He throws down his dummy and gives me a thumbs-up before doubling over and grabbing at his knees to regain his breath.

"You know, you guys all got your targets out of the hostage bunker," Michael says, marking Matthew's spot on the floor. "They'd be alive, so that's good. But you all just throw them down on the ground."

"Hey, what's a few shattered bones versus death?" Anusha questions, her hand out in the air and a smile on her face.

"True," Michael answers, pointing in her direction. "Okay, guys. Good job today. You've improved so much in the last few weeks. Another couple weeks of training at CORE, and then we'll be taking half the group to an RT camp in Indonesia, the other half to Russia."

"Awesome," Cam answers. He's the perfect tech intel operative, but he's been enjoying RT drills more than I think he thought he would.

"Okay, Reagan, Luke, and Matt," Michael says, pointing at each one of us. "I need you three to stay for a second. Rest of you can hit the showers. Lights-out in an hour."

Lex saunters past, her arms tight across her chest. She raises her eyebrows at me, a small, satisfied smile tickling the corners of her mouth, before turning toward the door.

The three of us move closer to Michael, anxiously waiting to hear why he wanted us to stay behind. Michael looks over his shoulder, waiting for the room to clear out before explaining. Cam is the last one to file out of the training room and the door slams shut behind him.

"Congratulations," Michael says, turning back to us, a wide smile spreading across his face. "The three of you have been selected to go on an overseas mission with the RT squad."

"Really?" I say, my voice soaring several octaves higher than its normal range.

"Yup," Michael answers and nods his head. "We think the three of you show the most promise out of all the trainees and we want to see what you can do on a real mission."

"That's awesome," Luke says, nodding his head, and I beam at him. He's trained so hard the last few weeks. He's mastered every take-down move I taught him, he's spent late nights working with Cam on hacking, and he's killing it in the gun range.

"The team leaves the compound at zero-six-hundred hours," Michael says, glancing at the clock over the double doors. "So take a shower, get some rest, and be dressed and ready to go then. You'll be escorted to the plane and receive your full assignment there. It's a real honor to be asked to go on a mission, but this is a dangerous one. Do not take either the honor or the danger lightly. You will be active participants on this, so don't blow it. All eyes will be on you."

"We won't," I answer, adrenaline and anxiety already surging through my body. This is my chance. My very best opportunity to show the Black Angels that I deserve to be in the training academy. That I deserve to be on the RT squad. Make a mistake on this mission, and I'll lose everything.

This mission is do or die. Not just for the people we're saving. But for Torres as well.

TWENTY-SIX

SALTY WIND WHIPS AT STRANDS OF MY HAIR AS OUR small boat silently approaches the *Agenia Princess*, a two-hundred-and-fifty-foot yacht owned by technology tycoon Mark Williams. Inside the luxury mega-boat are Mark; his wife, Cynthia; their two young children; and a small crew. Oh...and three pirates who stormed the ship a few miles away from the Philippines. The Gulf of Aden off the coast of Somalia used to be the most dangerous area in the world for piracy. But the pirates in the dark oceans around Indonesia have stolen their criminal crown.

Mark's two biggest clients? The US Department of Defense and the CIA. So this ransom and hostage situation has been kept out of the press, and the rescue mission went straight up the chain of command to the very best: us.

"All right, team, we're approaching the stern of the ship," Richard Turton, the RT mission leader, says quietly in my earpiece from a second small boat thirty yards ahead of us. We are approaching the yacht in the dead of night at a pace that's barely causing waves or making a sound, but still I push the small earpiece deeper in my ear. My stomach bubbles with a hasty rush of adrenaline and fear as I think about the family and crew trapped on that ship in the middle of an endless ocean. My job is to enter the ship with Luke and Matthew after the pirates are secure and bring the hostages to safety.

"Ropes ready?" Richard asks in my earpiece, addressing someone on the first team, but I grab at the yellow ropes in our tiny boat, ready to tie up once we reach the ship.

I can see the first boat reach a dark spot on the boat's stern and tie their rope around a shining metal post.

"Tied up," a member of team one says quietly in my ear. My skin suddenly spasms with nauseating familiarity, a million pins pricking at my spine, and I know something is wrong. I scan the back of the boat and in the shadow, I see a figure.

"Possible shooter, twelve o'clock, third-floor balcony," I say in my earpiece, lifting team one's heads and guns, but before their eyes can find him, the shadow fires the first shot.

A staccato spray of bullets from our team answers his first shot and I watch the figure retreat back into the darkness.

"He's not down," I say into my ear. "But he's gone."

"Go, go, go," I hear Richard say in my ear, ushering his team of six off the small dinghy and onto the yacht.

"Good eye," Luke remarks quietly next to me in the darkness. I'm still scanning the boat, looking for a second gunman or any sign of the hostages.

"I hate that we can't see what's happening in there," I remark, tightening the chin strap of my helmet. "We're so blind here."

"I know," Luke answers. "That's why we're not allowed to go in until they give us the all clear."

My skin bristles again, my body preparing for the maniacal chaos that is about to come. And as if on cue, the eerie silence of the night is shattered by round after round of bullets. I listen closely, trying to pick up the sound and speed of each weapon, identify who is shooting who. But the pirates are most likely armed with semi-automatic weapons too. All I can hear is the jackhammer of piercing metal.

"Sam, what's going on?" I demand in my earpiece, knowing Sam is watching this all unfold from team one's camera helmets back on our larger boat.

"Pirates attacked us first once we got inside," Sam yells over the gunfire that is ringing in all of our ears. Someone's mic is on. "One pirate down, two of our guys are down. Our final four are still fighting."

"Shit," I say and turn to Matthew, who is running the boat. "Come on, let's go."

"Absolutely not," Luke says, holding his hand out to stop Matthew. "They said to stay out of there until we got the all clear."

"Yeah, but our guys are down," I say, trying to reason with Luke but he shakes his head. "Orders are orders, Reagan."

"He's right," Sam says in my ear. "Stay back, Reagan. If you guys get in there and get hurt, there's no way we'll get these hostages off the ship alive. Follow. Orders."

Sam's tongue wraps around every single syllable of those last two words, verbally slapping me in the face. My spine curves, my body sinking into itself, my nails digging into the plastic seat of the boat, ashamed of how quickly I want to throw out the rule book on missions. I always just want to act. I don't think. And it's that impulsive rush of fearlessness that will get me in trouble, or even killed, every time.

The gunfire has fallen silent, and I pray that means good news for our team and the family on board. I grab for the M4 carbine on my lap, its steel slick with droplets of salt water and humidity.

"Sam..." I say in my ear.

"Looks like pirates are down," she answers, her voice calm. "Standby for the all clear from team one."

"Team one copies," I hear Richard say in my ear, his breath heavy. "Pirates down. Two dead. One secured. All clear. Team two, come aboard."

Matthew turns the motor on full speed and I ready myself to tie our line around the yacht to keep our boat in place. Once we reach the stern, Luke jumps on deck and quickly takes the yellow rope out of my hand, wrapping it in a perfect, secure knot (being a Boy Scout clearly paid off) before taking my hand and pulling me aboard.

"We're on," I say into my earpiece once Matthew is secure and standing on the back of the yacht with us. "Please state the hostage location."

"Second-floor bedroom suites. Come through the main salon and up the stairs," Richard says. "We untied the two little girls so they're ready for you. We're moving through the other bedrooms to untie the rest of the family and the crew now."

"Any injuries?" I ask as we walk toward the interior of the yacht.

"Just our guys," Richard answers. "Multiple shots, but luckily the bullets hit their vests. So they went down but will be fine."

Civilians think that bulletproof vests completely protect you from injury but that's not true. While it stops the bullet from piercing your body, being shot, even in a bulletproof vest, can feel like being hit with a baseball bat. So being shot multiple times will knock even the strongest person to their knees.

Matthew pushes a button and the salon doors slide open. I walk quickly across the plush carpeting, past enormous white couches, a dark mahogany wood bar with a blue marble top, and the biggest TV I've ever seen. The salon is nicer than any living room I've ever been in. And I've known some pretty wealthy people.

I race up the spiral staircase with Matthew and Luke close behind. Once I reach the second floor, I can hear a child crying somewhere toward the front of the ship and I follow the sound of her voice. When I arrive at the master cabin doorway, I see two little girls, probably no older than four and six, dressed in matching pink pj's and clinging to each other. The younger sister is sobbing, her dark hair being smoothed by her older blond sister. They are untied, but ropes and remnants of their days of terror are still at their feet.

"It's okay, girls," I say, and carefully put my gun down and out of sight next to the bed. I reach for them and at first they flinch. "It's okay. My name is Reagan and this is Luke and Matthew. We're here to bring you home. You're safe now."

"I want. To go. Home," the little one forces out through heaving sobs. I reach down and pick her up, carrying her in my arms while Luke picks up her older sister.

"I'm going to get you home," I say calmly in her ear, and her tiny arms clutch my neck so tightly, I lose my breath. "You're okay, sweetie. You're okay. I promise. You're safe with me."

"I'm going to go find the others," Matthew calls after us as Luke and I carry the girls out of the master bedroom and down the spiral stairs.

"Reagan and I have the two girls," Luke says in his earpiece as we make our way through the main salon and onto the back deck.

"Great. Get them on the boat and wait for Matthew to bring down their parents," Richard says, his voice losing breath as he quickly works to release everyone. "Then get them back to our main boat. They've had one hell of a trip."

"Copy," Luke answers in my ear and I tighten my grip on the little girl in my arms, her tears finding patches of my flesh and soaking into my skin.

"I want. My. Mommy," she cries, each word a struggle to push out of her still hysterical throat.

"Your mommy is right behind us," I answer, smoothing the back of her hair like her sister did. "She's okay. And so are you. You're going to be just fine. I promise. You're safe. Take a couple deep breaths. Okay?"

"Okay," the little girl says, sniffing back some of her tears. She's crying but starting to calm down.

Luke and I carefully climb on board our waiting boat and sit down next to each other so that the sisters can be close. The older sister is crying now too. Luke holds on to her and gently rubs her back. He looks over at me, a tiny smile creasing his dimples. Unanticipated tears well in my eyes and as I grab on tighter to the four-year-old in my arms, I suddenly understand. I bite down at my lip and stare up at the starless sky.

Now I get it, Mom. Now I get it.

————

My eyes slowly open from their forced rest. The cabin lights are off and everyone around me is sleeping. Just hours after the rescue, we're aboard one of the Black Angels' private jets on the long flight back to DC.

I've gotten maybe a total of four hours of sleep in the last two days, but I can't fall asleep. My mind is racing, the adrenaline still pumping through every part of me. To be able to rescue that entire boat, to hold that little girl (who I later found out was named Charlotte) in my arms and bring her to safety. I'll never forget it. Now I know, I am here for the right reasons. It's not just Torres that makes me want to be a Black Angel. It's Charlotte and the hundreds of others I could save after her.

By Black Angel mission standards, this was a very happy ending. But my mind still roils with the "what next" of it all. What's next for that crew? That family? Charlotte and her sister? The horrors they witnessed. Their father and mother being hit. Guns shoved in their young faces. The wounds on their wrists and feet where they were tied together will eventually fade, but the nightmares will not.

I pull my body up and slip past Sam sleeping on the reclined leather seat next to me. I follow the lower lights to the galley kitchen in the back, craving something sweet.

When I reach the kitchen, I see a shadow on the floor. I'd know that tall figure anywhere. I peer around the door frame and smile.

"Midnight snack?" I ask as Luke crunches down on an enormous handful of popcorn. "Hey, leave some for me."

I jokingly grab the bag out of his hand and he smiles sheepishly, his cheeks puffy with kernels. "Sorry," he says as soon as he's able to swallow half of it down. "I didn't know anyone was up. Can't sleep?"

"Can I ever really?" I say softly back and enter the galley that's just big enough for the two of us. A luxury for the largest of the Black Angel private jets. The other jets, you can barely fit one person inside.

"Want me to make you something?" Luke asks quietly and I rifle through the cupboards as silently as I can, careful not to wake everyone else up. Finally, I find a powder mix for hot chocolate in one of the bottom cupboards.

"Yes!" I hand it over to Luke and hop on the tiny granite countertop. "Hot chocolate, please."

"Oh, that sounds good," Luke says, looking in the miniature fridge. He pulls out milk and a can of whipped cream. "I'll have one too."

Luke opens cabinets, looking for mugs, but can't find any. He then reaches for the cabinet door behind me. I catch his scent as his body presses against me in the tiny space. Cinnamon and soap fill me, and suddenly, I'm flushed and dizzy.

"Found them," he says, tugging two mugs past my head, his body and heat pulling away from me. And as the pressure of his torso and chest leaves me, I have the overwhelming, irresponsible urge to pull him back.

Breathe, Reagan. Breathe. I have to coach myself into pulling air back in through my open mouth. My mind constantly lies to me. My body will betray me every time. The truth is, Luke still catches me. As much as I don't want him to, as much as I try to avoid it, Luke catches me in these breathless moments that blur the corners of my mind, the lines I've drawn, the strict rules the Black Angels have created.

I shake out my arms, trying to force that buzz out of my veins, grateful Luke is too busy heating the mugs of milk in the microwave to notice that my cheeks are painted cherry red. He opens the microwave door before the alarm can sound and stirs in two scoops of hot chocolate mix. He hands me a mug and the steam licks my face.

"Thank you," I say, blowing into the dark chocolate liquid. "It's perfect."

"Wait. Not yet." Luke shakes the can of whipped cream and squirts a perfect snowy peak into my mug before squirting one into his. "That summer I spent at the New Albany coffee shop really paid off."

"Cheers," I say, holding up my mug, and he clinks his against mine. I take a sip even though it's still a little bit too hot. The liquid coats my tongue and I swear I can feel the chocolate releasing endorphins. For a moment, I'm as blissful as I've been in over a year.

"I wonder how the girls are doing," Luke says, taking a sip of his hot chocolate.

"I know. I can't stop thinking about them either," I answer, swinging my legs slightly in the tiny, enclosed space.

"You did really good today," Luke says. "You saw that shooter. You warned the team. I didn't see him at all."

"You did great too." I take another sip. "You're sort of just what I need sometimes. You remind me what I need to do right when I want to just follow my instincts and sprint past all those rules."

"I know it's hard for you," he replies. "But rules are there to keep you safe."

My hands cradle the warm mug and I smile before quietly saying, "You keep me safe."

"Always," his hushed voice answers, his face folding into a smile.

I take a long sip of my hot chocolate, and when I pull my mug away, Luke's smile expands until he cannot contain himself.

"What?" I ask, unable to stop myself from mirroring his grin.

"You have whipped cream on your nose," he says and begins to laugh. I reach up, touch my nose, and feel the wet and sticky remnants of canned cream. I put down my mug, grab the can off the counter, and spray a large dollop on Luke's face.

"Well, now you do too," I say and bite down on my lips, not wanting to laugh and wake the others.

Luke sets his mug on the counter and shakes his head, still smiling, the whipped cream dripping down his cheeks. "Oh, it's on," he announces, trying to pry the whipped cream out of my hand. I squirm and squeal and try to hide the whipped cream behind my back. When Luke can't pry the can out of my hands, he takes a glob of whipped cream off his face and dollops me again on the nose.

"Luke," I say, faking my annoyance, and pulling the can from around my back, ready to attack.

"Oh, no you don't," Luke says, pressing his body against mine on the counter and grabbing me by both arms. And there it is again.

Our eyes lock and the heat surges. We stare at each other, our smiles falling. Our breath rises in unplanned unison. Before I can say a word or break our precarious embrace, his mouth has found mine. And just like that, all of my self-control, all of the emotions and feelings I've been holding back crash through my body like a broken dam. A rush of warmth fills every corner of me as I grab him by the neck and pull his body closer. His mouth, his hands, his chest, his stomach are pressed against mine but it's not quite close enough. I feel his lips part my unsteady mouth and I taste him. Cinnamon and chocolate and whipped cream and something so distinctively Luke, it has no other identity. His hands twist through my hair and my body goes limp, the world spinning me into a darkness that's exhilarating and terrifying all at once. And suddenly, two feelings enter my mind as one thought, impossible to untangle: *This has to stop.* And *I never want this to end.*

My hands push at Luke's chest even though my lips struggle to break free. "Wait, wait, wait," I whisper and shake my head. "We've got to stop. We're going to get caught."

Luke turns around and closes the galley door. "No, we won't," he says, his body pushing me against the cabinets, his lips back on mine, kissing me with an aching sweetness until I wrap my legs around his waist, giving him permission to kiss me harder and as hungry as I feel. My hands knot at his shirt as his fingertips gently trace the length of my jaw. My heart pounds in my ear, changing its beat from rejoice to warning. *Stop this. Stop this. Stop this*, it pulses. And I obey.

My lips reluctantly pull away from Luke's and I take a breath, looking down at the ground. "No. We can't, Luke. You know we can't."

My eyes finally find his two pools of pale blue, his face falling with frustration, but he quickly nods his head, backs up, and opens the kitchen door.

"I'm sorry," he says quietly, throwing his hands up in the air in surrender. "Won't happen again."

He backs out of the galley and disappears into the main cabin, leaving me still sitting on the countertop, my back against the cabinets, my lips blissfully stinging from our kiss, wondering if his words were a promise or a threat.

TWENTY-SEVEN

BANG. BANG. BANG.

I squeeze the trigger on my Glock 22, trying my hand at a difficult target. But the bullets hit exactly where they're supposed to.

We already had our ninety minutes of mandated shooting practice, but I went back to the range right after dinner. Yes, I could always get extra practice in, but the truth is I'm hiding. In the two days since our in-flight kitchen encounter, I've been a ball of awkwardness around Luke, stumbling over every word, not quite sure what to say. Because I'm not quite sure how I feel.

That kiss. The feeling I get when I'm with him, it's every cliché in the book. Shaking limbs, trembling lips, liquefied insides. But it's more than that. I'll never stop missing my mother. I'll never forgive myself. I'll never not feel the heat of revenge for Torres. But when I'm with Luke, there's hope for some type of life. Some type of happiness. I don't want to push him away, but it's too risky. If we get caught, we're out of here. And there go our chances for the training academy and RT squad. My chance to track down Torres.

And as much as I want to be with him, that's too great a penalty to pay.

"Reagan." I hear my muffled name from behind me through my bulky earphones. I turn around to see Sam standing behind me, dressed in black training gear, sweat from a workout still on her forehead.

"What's up?" I say as I remove my earphones.

"Can we chat?"

"Of course," I answer and walk to the nearby weapons shelf to return my empty gun and earphones. When I turn back around, Sam's lips are pressed into a purposeful, thin line, her hands planted squarely on her hips. "Everything okay?"

"Yeah, everything is fine," she answers, putting her hand on my back to reassure me, but I'm not quite sure if I believe her. "Just want to chat with you."

Sam leads me to one of the smaller, empty training rooms meant for private martial arts practice. She flips on the overhead lights and closes the door behind her.

"Take a seat," she says, pointing to the blue mat in the middle of the small room. My anxious nerves fire, my arms and legs suddenly heavy. A small, private room and a closed door mean this can't be good.

"What is it?" I ask as we settle in on the floor. Sam looks at me for a second, running her hand down her smooth, blond ponytail.

"Look, I could get in trouble talking to you about this," she answers quietly, looking around the room, as if there might be someone hiding in the corner, ready to catch a snippet of our conversation. "So you have to keep this between us, okay?"

"Of course," I answer. "It always is."

"I know," she says with a strained smile. She touches me lightly on my hand with her fingertips. "First, I'm really proud of you. You have really improved these last few months. You are strong and focused and determined. You have put your head down and worked hard, and we have all taken notice."

"But?" I ask, cocking my head to one side, sensing what's on the other side of this compliment.

"But," Sam repeats, lowering her head and lacing her fingers together. "The cracks in your talent are really starting to show."

Okay. I was expecting criticism, but I wasn't expecting that. I try to swallow but can't. I take a breath and choke out, "How so?"

"No one can deny that you see things others can't see," Sam says, glancing down at her threaded fingers. "On the mission, you saw the shooter before anyone else. Even those thirty yards in front of you. It's like you have a sixth sense or something. Your mom had it too. And you scored really high at the end of your assessment period. You're emerging as a superstar. But there has been talk among the leaders and trainers that you're not the best teammate."

My fingers dig into the dry piece of skin between my index finger and thumb. I've been meaning to lotion it for weeks but there's never any time. I push down harder, until I can feel little lightning bolts of pain.

"That RT mission was a test. And while you excelled in some areas, again you were ready to disobey orders."

"I thought our guys were getting shot," I answer, trying to curb the defensive stab in my voice. "I heard gunshots, I heard commotion. I wanted to help."

234

"Yes, but you didn't even want to check with us," Sam answers. "You always want to act first, ask questions later. You think your way is the right way. And I know why that is."

"Why?"

"You were trained solo your entire life," Sam answers, a layer of sadness in her tone. "Luke. Now he's a strong team player because he's actually been on a team. He was raised to be in the military. He's been trained his whole life to think like a group while your parents...I hate to say this...they brought you up to think you're special and that you should trust yourself first. And while you *are* special, they did you a disservice by keeping you in a bubble like that."

My chest walls feel like they're caving in, pushed closer and closer together by the fearful question on my tongue. Finally, it breaks free. "So does this mean I run the risk of not making the academy? Not making the RT squad?"

Sam looks down again at her hands, threading and rethreading them in different configurations. She tilts her head back up at me. "I know how badly you want this. That's why I'm telling you. So you can fix it. Before it's too late. Before they give the spot I know you deserve to someone like Lex Morgan."

"Lex is the worst team player of them all," I say, my body suddenly searing with the idea of Lex stealing my spot. "She's a total bitch, Sam."

"She may be," Sam says, shrugging. "But she knows how to play the game."

"You mean manipulate the system," I say, my voice punchy.

"You deserve to be in the academy. You deserve to be on the RT squad," Sam says. "But Lex has shown us she's a team player and that's what we have to go off of. So I'm not telling you to stop being you or be fake or anything like that. But you need to learn from Luke. Obey every command. Follow every single rule, no matter how stupid you think it is. Be a leader, but not so bossy. There is no room for selfishness on an elite Black Angel team, especially not the RT squad."

"I know," I say, slowly nodding. "I do know it."

"Good," Sam answers, her lips pursed to one side, examining my face. "You are brilliant on your own. On a solo mission, I'd trust you with my life. But you need to learn to trust other people. You need to learn that you don't always know best."

"Okay," I answer, my voice barely audible, emotion threatening at the base of my throat. "Thank you for telling me."

"I always want what's best for you," Sam says, reaching out and grabbing me by both hands. "And if this is what you want, this is what you've got to do to get in. You've still got some time left before the last round of cuts. So prove the doubters wrong. You hear me?"

My eyes close for a moment and I nod. I feel Sam squeeze my hands in hers, then feel her lips on my cheek. When I open my eyes again, she's standing up and walking toward the door.

I only have a few more months to prove I belong here. Or all of this will be for nothing. Without access to the RT's high-security clearance, I'll never find Torres. And that murderer will walk free forever, my mother's blood always on his hands.

TWENTY-EIGHT

"MY CALVES ARE SO SORE FROM THAT RUN, I'M HAVING serious problems moving."

"Who stole the latest *US Weekly* out of the library? You know that's my guilty pleasure and I cannot live without it."

"No, I haven't heard from them in weeks. They must be deep undercover on something."

"If we have to do one more hacking exercise, I'm going to die."

"I miss my grandma's banana bread. I wonder when I'll get to see her again."

I lean forward on the blue mat and grab at my toes, stretching my aching legs, surrounded by the seventeen remaining trainees. Their fragmented conversations swirl around me and I try to take them all in at once, like an insufferable poem that makes no sense.

I look up from my stretch just as her daunting shape fills in the doorway. Director Browning stands at the entrance to the large training room, dressed in a gray pantsuit, a sapphire scarf draped around her neck. She almost never shows up in the middle of our training sessions. I know she watches us. But probably on camera or at the end of the day on digital playback with the other senior leaders. They're always evaluating us, but rarely do they make their presence known.

Her thin lips press together as she scans the room, looking for someone. Looking for one of us. My warm skin chills, bristling with alarm. Because I know whatever words are waiting on the other side of her tiny mouth are not good.

Dad. My heart pulses wild beats against my chest. My father left on a new mission a few days ago. He wouldn't say where he was going or when he'd be back. Just kissed me on the forehead and instructed me to "Be good."

The sag in her posture and the uncharacteristic concern in her gray eyes makes every cell pulse. Someone is about to receive some very bad news.

Browning walks farther into the training room, her high heels echo against the polished cement floor, finally alerting the rest of the chattering trainees to her presence. Everyone quiets and swivels their head toward the sound we've all grown accustomed to fearing.

Browning scans the room again, her eyes finally fixing on the center of the pack. On me.

Please God. Please God. Please don't say Reagan.

"Cameron Conley," her voice booms against the high ceilings.

The tendons in my muscles relax and I'm immediately disgusted with my selfish sense of relief. My head turns to face my friend. Cam's dark eyes widen, his chest rises but refuses to fall, a fearful breath trapped in his lungs. I reach out and touch his hand, just inches away from my own. But he doesn't react, doesn't feel it. My touch glides off of his skin as he pushes himself off the ground and makes his way through the crowd of twisted, stretching bodies.

The other trainees turn toward one another, their lips forced together, their eyebrows raised, eyes wide and wild. Each face silently asking the same questions, expressing the same concerns. *What's going on? What happened? Poor Cam.*

Cam walks slowly across the gym, delaying whatever news is waiting for him, knowing his life will soon be divided by this moment in time. The life he knew before Browning said his name and the life that came after. I want to follow him. I want to hold his hand through whatever he's about to hear. As Cam finally reaches Director Browning, she gives him a tight, forced smile and makes a sweeping motion toward the door. As they walk together in silence, she gingerly reaches up and touches him on the shoulder. That all but confirms it. She never touches us. Someone is either hurt or dead.

———

"Where do you think they took him?" Anusha says, leaning across my body to look at one of the digital alarm clocks on a metal night-stand in the boys' dorm room. It's 12:32. The three of us are huddled on Cam's bed, skipping lunch to wait for any news. It's been over an hour since Director Browning escorted him out of the training room and with each passing minute, I grow more fearful about this news's degree of horror.

"I don't know," I answer and shake my head. "Probably a secure conference room or something."

"Do we even know where his parents are at right now?" Luke asks on the other side of me, his knees bouncing anxiously. "I know we don't know the mission, but do we even know where in the world they are? Does Cam even know?"

"They could be anywhere," I answer, pulling my arms closer to my body, suddenly cold. "They groom foreign targets into foreign agents and then meet with them periodically for briefings. They've got sources all over the world."

"Their agent could have turned on them. Been working for the other side all along," Luke surmises, leaning forward and resting his forearms on the tops of his bouncing knees. The weight does nothing to tether their restless pulses.

"Absolutely," I answer and nod my head. "There's always the danger of a double agent."

"Shit, I can't stand this," Anusha interjects and jumps off the bed. She rests her hands on the top of her head and paces in staggered lines in front of the row of bunk beds. "The not knowing is killing me. If something is wrong, I want us to be with him."

"Something is wrong," a voice says from the doorway. Cam stands frozen, his body slumped against the door frame, his eyes glassy and staring past us. Luke and I stand up so quickly, we almost hit our heads on the metal bar of the bunk bed.

"Cam, what's going on?" I ask, my body moving swiftly across the room. In just a few steps, I reach him and grab his arm.

"It's my parents," Cam says and shakes his head, still staring at nothing.

"What happened?" Luke asks calmly next to me, grabbing on to Cam's other arm, and together we shuffle him toward one of the beds.

"They were in Ecuador," Cam answers, his eyes still unfocused, his voice monotone and far away. "After they met their source, they were gunned down in an alley near their hotel."

"Are they alive?" Anusha asks quietly, kneeling at Cam's feet, carefully touching his left kneecap.

"Barely," Cam answers, his eyes filling with tears. "Mom's in an induced coma while they try to get some swelling down in her brain. We'll know more about her in twenty-four hours. They say the doctors are cautiously hopeful. But Dad . . . he . . . he . . ."

"What is it?" Luke asks, still holding on to Cam's forearm.

"He was shot in the back," Cam answers, sucking in his full bottom lip, a tear breaking free from his eye. "Severed spine. He'll never walk again. Never work again. Never be able to feed himself again. I know him. He'd rather be dead."

"I'm so sorry, Cam," I offer, my throat thickening with familiar grief. "Do they have any idea who did this? Have they told you?"

"They won't tell me," Cam says and shakes his head, his neck slowly swiveling toward me, his tears retreating and his eyes finally focused. "But I know who did this to them."

"Who?" I ask, the question escaping my lips in a thin whisper. That dark cloud of dread fills my body with my next breath, coiling around my lungs, because I already know the answer.

"Torres," Cam confirms through gritted teeth, anger burning behind his now tearless eyes. "I hacked into the files after they told me because I *knew* it was him. He has to be stopped, Reagan. That monster has to be stopped."

The ember at my core bursts into a series of tiny flames and my skin radiates heat.

He has to be stopped. He has to be stopped.

Cam's words rattle against my brain as that fire pulses through my veins, scalding me from the inside out.

This must end.

TWENTY-NINE

"YOU'VE GOT THIS," MICHAEL SAYS, LEANING OVER the treadmill and checking my time. "Keep that pace. And when you're ready to sprint, tell me."

Every week, we have a timed mile run, and this week, I want to break 5:30. And with a quarter mile left to go, I think I might just do it.

"Okay," I squeak out, my breath strained by my quick pace. I look at my time on the treadmill: 4:25. I look back at Michael and give him the thumbs-up, the signal to increase my speed to a sprint. He increases my speed and the treadmill whines beneath me, moving faster and faster and faster.

My tendons burn and want to tear apart but I keep sprinting. My heart is pumping so hard against my ribs I'm surprised Michael cannot hear it. My lungs struggle for breath as my feet pound and pound and pound. But I'm one of those lucky runners who gets a sick high from the pain. And as the endorphins in me surge, a smile crosses my face for the first time in days.

"You're gonna do it, Reagan." Michael's deep voice rises, bordering on giddy. "You're gonna do it!"

I pump my arms, careful to make sure they stay at my sides and don't waste energy by crossing in front of my chest. I cannot feel my legs anymore, but at the last hundred meters, I sprint faster than I've ever sprinted before, my body cutting through the training room's dense air, my lungs burning, my face scalding. I push my body through the last meter until I hit the one-mile mark. I glance at the time: 5:27.

"Holy shit," Michael exclaims, decreasing my speed before holding up his hand and giving me a high five. "You crushed it, Hillis!"

"Thanks," I say, my voice breathy, but my face still smiling. I take over the controls on the treadmill and lower the pace to a walking speed. "Thank you for cheering me on."

"Of course," Michael replies, putting his hand on my sweaty shoulder. "Wow, 5:27. I'm gonna mark it down. The other trainers will be super impressed. I think that's one of the lowest female trainee times ever. Now cool down and be sure to stretch."

"I will," I call after Michael as he walks toward the far side of the room to jot down my time in the log book.

"Nice job, Reagan." Cam appears at my side, holding out his elbow to give me an elbow bump, which I return.

"Thanks, man," I say, hitting the stop button on the treadmill. "I never thought I'd hit that time."

I glance up at the clock. It's already past ten p.m. and the training room is empty. I just want to sit and stretch and grab a shower before bed. But I can tell Cam wants to talk. He's been scary quiet the last few days. Understandably. So if he wants to talk, I'm more than happy to listen.

"So . . . how are you? What's the latest?" I ask, taking a seat on the mat in the corner. Cam has told me bits and pieces since the attack. He all but begged for the Black Angels to let him fly down to South America to be with his parents but they said it was too dangerous. That they needed time to recover. That he still needed this important time to train. So it's been business as usual for him. Through a fog of anger and helplessness, Cam's completed every test that is asked of him. He's showed up to every drill. He's kept his head down and so we've tried to do the same. But we can't help but keep an extra eye on him, handle our strong, ridiculously smart friend with kid gloves.

"Mom's awake and getting better," Cam answers, easing his body down next to me. He leans his back against the wall, his eyes cautiously scanning the empty room. "The swelling in her brain has gone down significantly. Thank God the swelling was just from her hitting her head and not from a bullet. They expect her to be fine."

"And your dad?" I ask, biting at the inside of my lip.

Cam takes a deep breath, processing all he's been told. "Same. Once a bullet severs the spinal cord, there's really not a whole hell of a lot that can be done. Browning told me they're already looking for a full-time caregiver for him. He's going to hate that."

Cam looks away from me, his fingers pinching at the insides of his palms, redirecting pain, swallowing the grief lodged in his throat. Over the last year, I've become more than a student in sadness. I've become an expert. I've come to know the subtleties and nuances of sorrow. The way a pair of caring eyes can sometimes make you feel worse. The way physical pain can momentarily relieve emotional pain. The old saying that time heals all wounds is bullshit. When you lose someone, or even lose a piece of them like Cam, your heart breaks and never truly heals. You carry the person you lost in those cracks. But in the other fractures, darkness can slip in, and sometimes, it refuses to let go.

"I'm so sorry," I say, which I know will do nothing to diminish the anguish he carries in his gut, a twin to my own. But sometimes, those three words are the only ones you can say.

"Thank you," he replies, a solid standard answer that I came to adopt myself from the pitying comments and questions about my mom.

"What's going on with Torres?" I ask, trying to redirect his angst. "Anything new in the files?"

"That's why I wanted to talk to you," Cam says, his eyes turning up toward me. "Alone."

My body winces, prepping for what can only be horrible news. I glance around the room, making certain we are truly alone. "Okay. What is it?" I ask, lowering my voice.

Cam pushes his lips together, staring down at the blue mat, like he hasn't already practiced what he's about to say to me in his head at least a dozen times. "I know you're trying so hard to follow the rules and stay in line. I've debated all day even telling you this."

"What is it?" I ask, my body heated, fresh sweat pricking at the glands under my arms.

"I accessed the Torres files last night," Cam confesses and closes his eyes for a moment. "And I found a folder I had never seen before. One that was hidden the last time we hacked in. Something the Black Angels really, really don't want anyone else to see."

My pulse pounds painfully against my neck, and my chest heaves, sucking in greedy breaths. My lips begin to tingle and go numb. I bite down on my bottom lip to stop them from becoming paralyzed.

"Do you want to know?" Cam asks quietly. "I almost don't want to tell you and get you involved or in trouble or anything, but I want to at least give you the option to say yes or no."

My heart constricts under the strain of conflicted emotions. I've been so obedient, so focused. Especially after my talk with Sam. I've been the perfect trainee. The ultimate team player. And I want to stay that way. I need that spot in the academy. Part of me wants to stand up, shake my head, tell Cam I don't want to know. But that rage has never died. It's been smothered out time and time again. I've held it down, pleaded for it to disappear. But still, its smoke rises. I have to know. Walking away feels like a betrayal. And I'd never betray my mother.

"Tell me," I finally say, moving my body closer to Cam's.

"Okay," Cam says, inhaling the deep breath needed to pull out the heavy information. "A rival drug lord of Torres and his entire family in Peru were killed two weeks ago. The files show that the Black Angels knew about it, thought it could be Torres, but wanted to get a small team on the ground to confirm their suspicions before sending a proper team down there to apprehend him. And of course, they got confirmation too late. By that time, he was long gone."

"Wait, you mean he was *actually* on the ground with his little army?" I ask, leaning in closer to Cam. "He wasn't in hiding. He was there and they let him get away?"

"It's not the first time it's happened either," Cam replies, his voice almost a whisper. His anxious eyes scan the room again. "Twice this year already, there have been rival killings that they suspected he was involved in. And each time, they reacted way too late and missed him."

"What the hell?" I say, throwing my hands up in the air. Cam puts his finger to his lips, trying to quiet me, and I lower my voice. "God, this is so typical. I *knew* something like this would happen. This happened last year when my parents were kidnapped. They're so concerned with following procedures and Directives, and they ignore their guts and their target gets away. This is bullshit."

My hands push my furious, shaking body off the ground and Cam's hand reaches cautiously for my wrist.

"Reagan, you cannot go to Sam or your father or any of the others," he says, his eyes now worried. "They cannot know we hacked into these files. Because then that will be the end. For both of us."

"I'd never, ever do that to you," I answer, my voice softening for a moment. "Never. I'm just sick of this garbage. Following the rules allows Torres to do whatever the hell he wants. How many Black Angels have to die or get injured before they actually do something about him? How many gallons of blood need to be spilled before they put an end to his lunacy?"

"I don't know," Cam answers, shaking his head. "I just . . . I don't want anyone else to go through what I'm going through right now.

What you've gone through. This has to end. I don't know how but we have to do something, Reagan."

Cam stares up at me, his dark eyes pleading. *Take him down. Take him down.*

"We will." As the promise leaves my mouth, my tongue feels cold because I fear the promise is an empty one. I'm desperate to find Torres. Desperate to put a gun to his skull and pull the trigger, watch the blood cascade down his face. Desperation can give you superhuman strength. But even so, I don't know how to properly track him, how to end this now. I'm tired of waiting to become an agent. I can't stand to watch another person die, to hear that someone else's mother or father has been paralyzed at Torres's hand. Cam is right. This must end.

The ember at my core flares, scorching my blackened lungs.

I can't breathe with him alive. I can't live with him alive.

The walls in the training room feel like they're closing in on me. I have to get out of here. I have to think somewhere alone. I start walking toward the door without saying good-bye to Cam.

"Don't do anything without me, Reagan," Cam says but I'm already out of the room, grabbing at clumps of my hair, my legs shaking beneath me as I walk down the nearly deserted hallway. I whip my body around the intel center, and hear someone call my name from the West Hall. I look up and see Luke's smiling face, the end of an ice cream cone in his hand. But I put my head down and keep walking.

"Reagan, where are you going?" he calls after me but I don't answer.

I head toward the South Hall and my dorm room, where I just want to scream into a pillow or punch a wall or something. A few seconds later, I hear Luke's feet running toward me.

"Hey, are you okay?" he says, grabbing at my arm, but I pull away. "Reagan, what's the matter?"

"Nothing," I answer quickly.

"Are you still upset with me about what happened on the plane last week?"

"Not everything has to do with you, okay?" I snap, my voice far meaner than I meant it to be.

"Jesus," Luke says under his breath but still tries to grab for me as I walk briskly down the hallway. "Then what is it? You're clearly upset."

"You think?" I reply with extra bite.

Luke grabs me by both of my shoulders and spins me around. "Talk to me, Reagan," he says, lowering his voice as we get closer to the senior leaders' rooms, knowing they could overhear our conversation.

"I'm fine," I say, trying to wiggle out of his grip. "I just want to go to bed."

"You need to talk to me," Luke answers, squeezing me gently. "I know you. You'll never sleep like this."

"You really want to know? Fine," I answer with a sigh. I grab him by the wrist and drag him in the opposite direction toward the secure and soundproofed conference rooms in the East Hall. We walk in silence until we reach one of the smaller conference rooms.

"Okay," Luke says, taking a seat as I close the door behind us. "Spill."

My body is feverish and I feel like I just can't cool it down. I take in a deep breath, hoping fresh oxygen will lower the temperature of my scalding blood, but it boils anyway, blistering my skin from the inside out.

"The Black Angels are royally screwing up with Torres, and good operatives like Cam's parents are paying the price," I say, throwing up my hands as I pace three steps to the left, then three steps to the right in the small area in front of him. "They've had chance after chance to take down Torres and they just let him walk away."

"How do you know?" Luke says, the skin between his brows cinching together.

"Cam hacked into the files on his own and told me," I answer, my hands digging deep into my hips. "Apparently there was a folder we didn't see last time. One they've kept hidden, probably because it shows what screwups they all are. Torres and his crew have been involved with the murder of rival drug lords all around South America. The Black Angels always think it's him but they do nothing about it until it's too late. I'm just so pissed off and sick of this shit, Luke. I'm sick of knowing he's still out in the world, living and breathing and killing people. I can't believe they've let him get away multiple times now. Do they not care about my mother? About the other agents who have died or gotten injured? Protocols are clouding their judgment and letting a dangerous man walk free."

"Don't jump to conclusions yet, Reagan. I'm sure they've had their reasons to wait," Luke answers, his voice irrationally cool, trying to calm me down.

"God, stop defending them," I snap.

"I'm not defending them," Luke says. "I'm just trying to explain that not everything is as simple or clear as it seems. Not everything can be done with the snap of someone's fingers. There are Directives and a chain of command for a reason."

"Oh, screw that," I huff, throwing my hair over my shoulder. "God, you really are just a rule-following, agency appeasing suck-up, aren't you? This is one of the worst serial killers on the planet—who happened to kill my mother. God forbid we don't cross every t and dot every i before trying to apprehend him."

The cinder at my center erupts into full-fledged flames, burning my organs, just as Sam had feared. But let them burn. I take in a deep breath, hoping to fan those flames even higher.

"Look, I'm just trying to be rational here," Luke replies, his voice steady.

"That's right, Luke. You have the luxury of being rational. Your parents are alive and living far away from all crap. So you go ahead and enjoy being rational."

"That's not fair, Reagan. My father may not be on the front lines anymore, but my family is not exactly safe," Luke says, his eyes flashing with frustration. He shakes his head, runs his hands along the lengths of his thighs, trying to regain his composure. "Look, I just think that you are not giving the team enough credit. They have been doing this for a long time. You don't always know what is best."

His words echo Sam's, and coming from him, they sting.

"Good. Now I can clearly see where you stand," I say, slowing my pace and turning my body directly in front of him, my arms crossing over my chest. "You're always trying to reason with me, and you mask it as calming me down. But really, I just think it's because you're never *really* on my side. You're always fighting against me."

Luke's face changes three times in three seconds. From shock, to horror, to anger.

"Are you kidding me?" Luke says, his voice rising and the cream of his cheeks streaking red. He jumps up from his chair, forcing me to take a step backward. "Reagan, how can you not see that I am *always* on your side? Even when I think you're wrong. Even when you hurt me and push me away. I'm always right here."

He stomps his feet and points to the ground next to me, emotion clouding his blue eyes. But it's not anger anymore. It's sadness. Betrayal.

"I would do anything for you," Luke continues, his voice beginning to shake. "But would you do the same for me?"

"Of course I'd do anything for you," I answer, my voice escalating. "How can you even say that?"

"Would you really?" Luke asks, his eyes narrowing and voice softening.

"Without question."

"You think that no one really knows you, but I do," Luke says quietly. "I know you want to kill Torres. I know that's why you're really here. For revenge."

Luke's words physically knock me back, forcing my body to sway. I've kept that secret so close to my darkening heart, how could he know? But then again, this is Luke. The only person who I sometimes think can truly see into my screwed-up soul. Even when I don't want him to.

"It's true, isn't it?" Luke continues.

"How could I not," I answer, my voice catching in my throat. "I've wanted to kill him since the moment he put a bullet in my mother's brain. And if the Black Angels aren't going to take care of him, I'm going to do it myself."

"It's way too dangerous," Luke says, shaking his head. "You'll get caught by the Black Angels before you make it out the door. And even if you do, it's a suicide mission."

"I don't care," I answer, my voice firm, my words true.

"You just said you'd do anything for me," Luke begins. "What if I asked you not to kill Torres? Would you give that up if I told you I was terrified and couldn't bear to lose you?"

Luke stares at me, waiting for my answer. My eyes stay locked on his, my mouth doesn't move. My chest heaves with heavy breaths.

"That's what I thought," Luke finally says, nodding his head. Like he has me completely pegged. "I've picked up on little things you say and do and put the pieces together. When you're not numb, when you're truly you, revenge is your only priority."

"If this had happened to you instead of me, you'd feel the exact same way, Luke."

"No, I don't think I would," he says and shakes his head. "I'd try to honor their legacy in some way. Do some good in the world instead of just perpetuating the bad."

"Well, aren't you just the good little Boy Scout," I reply swiftly, my voice cruel. "Sorry we all can't be self-righteous choirboys like you."

"Reagan, listen to yourself," Luke replies, pointing at me. "This insane desire to kill Torres has completely changed you. What kind of life is this? What type of impossible, rage-filled person have you become? Would your mother even recognize—let alone like—the girl that's in front of me? Because I don't think she would."

I stare at Luke, my mouth gaping open, tears stinging the corners of my eyes. His words are so excruciating, I want to knee him in the groin. Hurl my best insult into his chest. Slam the door in his face. But there are only three words, toxic and sour, on the tip of my tongue.

"Fuck you, Luke," I whisper, staring into his eyes for a moment so he knows I mean it. Before his face can change, I walk toward the door and heave my body into the dark hallway. Luke opens the door and calls after me. But I don't turn around. I just walk away, hot tears running down my cheeks. Not because of what Luke said. But because I wonder if his words are true.

THIRTY

THE ROAR OF THE PLANE'S ENGINE FILLS THE SILENCE in the cabin. We're in one of the Black Angel jets on our long journey toward the RT martial arts training camp in Indonesia. I look down at Mom's watch. We're several hours into our late-night flight and everyone around me is asleep. But I cannot rest. Not since my fight with Luke two days ago. I close my eyes, even slip into a half dream, but my mind is awake and annoyingly aware, taunting me the entire time. *You're still awake. You'll never fall asleep.* It's like I can only reach that first plateau, that hazy gray area between sleep and consciousness. All I want to do is spin into the black. I move my eyes in circles from behind my eyelids, nonsensically trying to pretend I'm being sucked into sleep's black hole. But it refuses to swallow me.

Luke chased after me that night. Showed up at my dorm before breakfast the next day. Waited for me after training and assessments. But I've refused to even acknowledge his presence. He says my name, stares at me with those big, sad eyes, but I won't look in his direction. I don't even flinch at the sound of my name.

Cam noticed our distance, cornered me in the weight room to ask about our fight. I told him the whole story and he frowned. When I asked why, he responded, "Luke loves you. He'd do anything for you. He didn't mean it."

But I think he did.

I rub my eyes with the back of my fists, fully awake now. I quietly pull open the window shade next to me, careful not to wake Anusha, who has fallen asleep on my shoulder. I stare out past the wing and look into the blackness. I wonder where we are, if we've flown past California and are now headed into the dark Pacific waters. The lack of gridded lights that make up subdivisions, shopping centers, and office buildings tell me we've left land and are now crossing the ocean.

I've been to this training camp in Indonesia before to study martial arts. It makes CORE look like the Ritz-Carlton. It's safe and secure, but without the luxuries of headquarters. The dorms are cramped, with lumpy mattresses, squeaky beds, and no air-conditioning. The meals are basic. No chefs cooking up lemon-roasted chicken or shrimp scampi. Outside of training, entertainment lies in a couple decks of cards or five-year-old wrinkled and water-spotted magazines left behind by trainees and operatives. But Indonesia is an important training ground when it comes to perfecting our martial arts and fighting skills. Black Angels come from all over to learn the Indonesian pencak silat, a martial art that focuses on the use of leverage and angles rather than size and power to take down an opponent. During my trip a few summers ago, I watched a 150-pound woman take down a 275-pound man with just a few elegant moves. Krav Maga and jujitsu are my specialties, but that's not enough. Being armed with several different forms of martial arts can be the difference between life and death on the RT squad.

"Come on, I don't want to miss the sunset," Anusha says, pulling me by the wrist down one of the sandy streets near our RT camp. That's the best part of this camp. It sits just a quarter mile from the beach and they actually let us leave the compound, albeit rarely, to see the island. Of course, we must always be heavily armed. Anusha and I have two guns hidden beneath our T-shirts. But having to feel cold metal on my warm skin is a small price to pay for a few moments of freedom.

"We've still got time," I answer with a laugh and point toward the sun still hovering high in the sky. "Look, it's not even close to the water."

"I know, I just haven't seen a sunset in forever," Anusha says, still pulling at my wrist like a willful child.

And she's right. It's been months since I watched a single sunset. I think back to the farmhouse and can't remember paying attention to the rise and fall of daily light. I should have. There are few wonders in the world like the moment the blue sky fades and the clouds streak pomegranate pink. You don't realize just how much you'll miss something until it's gone. Until the option is stripped away from you. I wish I'd watched more sunsets in my life. I wish I'd done a lot of things.

We reach the narrow stretch of white sand. With its crystal clear, aqua-blue water and green mountains in the distance, Indonesia is like nowhere else in the world. Towering palm trees stretch over the sand, casting shadows on the water and shading the last remaining beachgoers. But I'm not interested in their leafy canopy. I want light.

As we take a seat on the warm sand, I survey the beach, just to make sure we don't have anyone to worry about. We blend in well with the few remaining couples and young backpackers who have stayed on the beach to take in the day's fleeting luminous glow.

"God, it's beautiful here," Anusha says wistfully as tiny waves of turquoise water lap up on the beach, a few yards away from our feet. I take off my flip-flops and bury my toes in the powdery white sand.

"Did you go to the beach much growing up?" I ask as we stare out over the calm lagoon.

"The occasional family vacation," Anusha answers, leaning back and resting her hands behind her. "Hilton Head. Virginia Beach. Nothing like this. How about you?"

"We lived for a year in Miami when I was little," I reply. "We had this really cute bungalow a couple blocks from the beach. I was maybe four or five at the time. I didn't know what my parents did for a living then. I remember them being gone a lot. And Sam taking care of me. But the thing I remember most about living there was my blue bucket. It was always by the back door, and whenever I'd come home from preschool and see my parents were back, I knew that meant it was time for the blue bucket and sand castles. It was like our little bonding ritual."

"Whatever happened to the blue bucket?" Anusha asks, her eyes on me while mine stare out on the water.

"I don't know," I answer with a shrug. "I have vague memories of leaving Miami in the middle of the night. I remember my dad carrying me and putting me in the backseat in my pajamas. We'd played in the sand that day. I built this epic sand castle with Mom, complete with a moat. I guess that was the last time I ever saw the bucket. Or built a sand castle for that matter. I don't remember making another one."

"Do you ever wish you'd been born into a normal family?" Anusha asks, her voice quiet.

"Sometimes," I answer and think back to all the moments my parents missed. Plays and parent/teacher conferences and holidays. I think of all the things I missed. Sports, friendships, family trips. But if I had to choose between different normal parents and mine, I'd still choose them every time. Even with the agonizing aftermath of Colombia. My soul belonged to them.

"Do you ever feel her?" Anusha says, pulling me back to the moment.

"Feel who?"

"Your mom," Anusha states, her hands running along the smooth sand, creating tiny paths with her fingers. "I was really close with my grandma. She lived with us most of my life and after she died, I swore I sometimes felt like she was in the room with me. She loved butterflies and every year, almost without fail, I'd see a butterfly the week of my birthday. It was like she wanted me to know she was still there."

I lean forward, resting my chin on my kneecap, my toes digging farther into the soft sand. "It's a really nice idea," I finally say. "To think that we all live on in some way after we die. I just don't know if it's real or something we use to comfort ourselves."

"Do you believe in God?"

"I want to," I answer and chew at the inside of my lip. "I want to believe that there's something or someone looking out for us. But then I see all the violence and horror in the world and it makes me wonder if we're alone after all."

Anusha leans forward, creating tiny shapes in the sand with her fingertips. A sun. A smiley face. A heart.

"There's good in the world too, Reagan," she finally replies. "I know it's hard to see sometimes. Especially with what we're training to do. What you've lived through. But there is good out there. You just have to look for it."

I want to believe in everything Anusha says. That there is good in the world. A God. That I'll see my mother again. That she's still with me now. I wish I could say I feel her all the time. That I know she's watching over me or protecting me. I haven't asked her to come to me because I'm afraid she won't and that it will only confirm what I fear is on the other side. Blackness. Nothingness.

I've heard religious people say you feel no pain after you die. And while that comforts most people, it scares me. Because I wonder if that means you also feel no joy. Is being "at peace" just a nicer description for numbness? If that's the case, then perhaps I already know what it's like to be dead.

I pull my knees closer to my chest and we watch in silence as the glowing sun dips inch by inch into the water, tiny waves catching its light, like bobbing diamonds against the blue. And despite its beauty, that hollow spot inside me shrieks as the world spins closer to darkness.

THIRTY-ONE

"REAGAN, WAKE UP," I HEAR SOMEONE WHISPER, their hands on my shoulders, gently shaking me out of a REM cycle I haven't been able to achieve since Luke basically said my dead mother probably wouldn't like me.

My eyes flutter and are forced open by a quick rub of my palms. When my eyes adjust to the darkness of the room, I see the outline of a man. In the pale light, I recognize the shape of his head and his buzzed haircut: Cam.

"What is it?" I whisper, pushing myself up in bed by my elbow. "What's wrong?"

"Something is going on," he whispers back and grabs me by the arm. I slip on a pair of flip-flops at the edge of my bed. "Take those off. No noise."

My feet shimmy out of my shoes, dread stabbing at my skin, forcing tiny hairs to stand straight up. Whatever this is, a middle-of-the-night wake-up call that demands complete silence cannot be good.

I follow Cam down a dark hallway away from the dorms. On the other side of the compound, I can hear a flurry of activity. Boots running up and down the hallway. People speaking in low but panicked voices. I hear the crack of weapons being assembled and the calls for radios. Then the slam of a conference room door.

Cam and I carefully creep up to the edge of the dormitory hallway and peer down the East Wing of the compound where the control center, training facilities, and conference rooms are located. These rooms are secure-ish. You can still hear the murmur of conversations on the other side but cannot make out the words.

I walk close to the conference room door and hear very faint, muffled voices inside. The hallway is now silent and empty. All the trainers must be inside. I look at Cam and nod toward the door.

"I can't hear anything," I whisper. "What do you think is going on?"

"I don't know," he says, shaking his head. "I just heard a huge commotion and snuck into the hallway. I thought I heard Michael say something about drugs or a drug lord or something as he was going into the conference room. I was afraid maybe it was about Torres. That's why I came and got you."

"Shit, really?" I whisper with the sudden urge to burst inside the room. "We need to hear this."

"I know. Come on," Cam says, waving me down the hallway and back toward the dorms.

In less than two minutes, we're hunkered down in a pitch-black training room, our backs against the wall, hacking into the system on Cam's laptop. We scan the activity and see a conference call between the compound in Indonesia and CORE.

"There." I point at the screen and Cam clicks in, picking up the call mid-conversation.

"I say we get a larger team together," Michael's voice insists. "Really go after him this time. He's right in our backyard. What are the chances of that? We weren't expecting him to be in Indonesia and he has no idea we're so close. Let's finally take this guy down and be done with it."

"We can't," says a male voice on the other end. "We have no proof it's actually him."

"But it has to be Torres." Michael's confirmation of who is behind this flurry of activity causes a sharp and jagged breath to cut into my lungs. "It was his cousin who was just sentenced to death for drug trafficking here. And now, he's the one guy who is unaccounted for in that prison. Torres would not just send a team. This is his family. He'd want to oversee everything. Make sure things went right. We've got to get to him before he leaves the country. We cannot blow this, and sending only a surveillance team puts us at risk."

"No, Michael," the voice says gruffly. "We need to gather more intel before sending out an entire team. Minimize the blowback if something does go wrong."

No, no, no!

"I just think that—" Michael begins but is cut off.

"This is not a negotiation, that's an order," the voice interrupts. "We do not move an entire team on this until we know it's really Torres. We cannot insert the Black Angels into a drug conflict. The only reason I was even able to get Indonesian authorities to relinquish control is because they have so many dead guards at the prison and are overwhelmed trying to contain the remaining inmates. I only have approval for surveillance. That's it. So Michael, pick your second man and load up. We've got the vehicles on surveillance back here at CORE, so we'll be giving you coordinates as soon as you're ready."

"Fine," Michael answers with a heavy sigh. "We'll be suited up in five."

The call ends. I can hear the conference room door down the hallway open, followed by Michael saying, "Damn it!"

My sentiments exactly. I spring to my feet and head toward the door.

"Where are you going?" Cam calls after me but before I can answer him, I'm chasing Michael down the hallway.

"Michael," I yell after him, running toward him with my bare feet. He turns around and looks down at his watch, surprised to see me at this late hour.

"What are you doing awake?" he asks.

"Take me with you," I reply quietly once I reach him.

Michael's eyes narrow as he looks me up and down in my pajamas.

"What are you talking about?" he says, playing dumb.

"I know you're going after Torres right now," I answer. Michael starts to shake his head and walk away but I follow him down the hallway, two strides for his every large one just to keep up. "And I know you're right. You need a bigger team to take down someone like him. You know he's going to have a small army with him. It's unthinkable and irresponsible to send just two operatives."

"I'm not even going to ask how the hell you heard that call,"

Michael says, slipping into the weapons room at the end of the hallway. "I don't have time to write you up. But Reagan, I have my orders. You know how these things go. I have to follow protocol."

"Screw protocol," I answer as Michael picks a M4 carbine off the weapons shelf. "If you follow those orders, I promise you he's going to get away or worse, someone's going to get killed."

"You think I haven't already thought about that?" Michael answers, his voice annoyed as he slips a bulletproof vest over his black RT gear. "Look. These are the orders. Two people for surveillance. Besides, the team down here is small. We have to at least keep a couple people back here to protect all the trainees."

"Take me with you," I answer, jumping in front of Michael's path as he loads up his weapons. He looks me in the eye and shakes his head before moving me out of the way.

"Reagan, you know I can't do that," he says, opening up a black case and loading in pistols, ammunition, and zip ties.

"Please, Michael," I say and grab him by the shoulder. "Let me be your second man. Even if it's just for surveillance."

This is it. This may be my only chance to get close enough to Torres to kill him. He has to take me.

"Reagan, the answer is no," Michael answers sternly, slamming the black weapons case shut. "First of all, I'd be breaking every Black Angel Directive known to man and secondly, your mother would never want you to be in that kind of danger. I know her. If she was alive, she'd kill me if something happened to you."

"No she wouldn't—" I begin, but he cuts me off.

"Reagan, I'm your trainer," Michael says, finally stopping and looking me in the eye. "I know why you want to come with me. I get it. But I cannot let you get involved in this. I'm supposed to protect you and keep you safe."

"But I'm never safe," I answer, swallowing hard at the fear scratching at my throat. "I'll never be safe if he's still alive. So what does it matter?"

"Your life matters very much," Michael says, grabbing me by the shoulder and giving my arm a squeeze. "I'll do all I can to bring him down. To make you safe. I promise. You have to trust me."

Before I can respond, Michael grabs his weapons case off the counter and hurries out of the room.

"Let's go," I hear him yell down the hallway and I listen as two pairs of Black Angel boots stomp against the concrete until they disappear.

I want to believe him. I'm desperate to trust in his promise. But that black cloud of dread enters my body with my next breath, squeezing my lungs, whispering that I'm a fool.

———

"I can't take this much longer," I say as my legs carry me between the two cinder block walls of the small conference room. "Is there still no word back from the field?"

"We're trying, Reagan," Anusha announces, hovering over Cam's shoulder as he pounds away at his keyboard. He's hacked into the system but still cannot access every security level.

I glance at the digital clock above the door: 2:21 a.m. The team has been gone for over an hour, and so far we've only been able to access some of the satellite images of Torres's suspected vehicles traveling south. We haven't been able to listen in on radio contact yet, which is driving me insane. I need to hear what's going on.

A door swings open, making me jump. I turn around to see Luke balancing cups of very strong and very bad instant coffee. I didn't want to bring him into this. I know him. He's going to put up roadblocks. I told Cam as much but he insisted on waking them both up to help, with the reasoning that four heads are better than two, blah blah blah.

"Here," Luke says, handing me a cup of steaming black liquid. "I couldn't find any cream. But I put four sugars in."

"Thanks," I answer and foolishly swallow a large gulp. It scalds the back of my throat.

"What's the latest?" Luke asks, working his way around the conference room table and handing Cam his cup of coffee. Luke is wearing a white T-shirt and the red plaid pajama pants Harper and I bought him two Christmases ago. There's a friendly little snowman on the left pocket. We thought the sweet cartoon face looked like Luke.

"From the satellite photos and the notes in the files, it looks like Michael's right on them," Cam answers, still typing at the keyboard. "The photos are coming in to me a bit late though. And no radio interception yet but I'm working on it."

"What's our endgame here?" Luke asks, glancing up at me and then back down at the computer.

"What do you mean?" I ask, pausing my pacing and squaring my body toward him.

"I mean, we're sort of stuck in this compound," Luke says,

looking around the room. "What exactly are we trying to accomplish?"

"See, I told you not to wake him up." I glare at Cam and take another gulp of coffee.

"I'm just trying to understand our objectives here," Luke says, holding out his arms. "Reagan, you're a doer. You do, do, do without thinking about the reason behind it."

"We're not *doing* anything yet," I reply and cross my arms over my chest. "I just want to follow what's going on and make sure something actually happens. And that Torres doesn't get away this time."

"And what exactly are you going to do if he does?" Luke asks, cradling his paper cup, the steam rising around his face. "They can't know we've hacked into these files. We'll get kicked out."

"Luke, if you're so concerned then do me a favor and just go back to bed," I say and roll my eyes.

"I'm just trying to be helpful," he replies, throwing up his hands in surrender and taking a seat on the other side of Cam.

"Well, you're not," I answer, my voice hoarse and throat thick with piercing barbs of anxiety. I try to swallow, but can't. I take another swig of coffee, letting the hot liquid work its magic but the minute it coats my stomach, the pain returns.

"Wait, something new is coming through," Anusha says, pointing at the computer.

My legs quickly whip my body around the conference room table. I stand behind Cam as red letters in the Torres file flash *Alert, Alert, Alert* over and over again.

"What is it?" I ask, my pulse picking up speed, my breath immovable in my chest.

Cam clicks on the folder and it begins to download.

10%. 20%. 30%.

The little blue bar fills at an agonizingly slow speed.

40%. 50%. 60%.

I grip the back of Cam's steel chair so hard, I swear I can feel metallic splinters penetrate my skin.

70%. 80%. 90%.

My head feels dizzy, like I'm moments away from passing out. Fear scratches at my skin like fiberglass, needling my pale flesh.

Finally, the bar fills all the way up.

Download Complete flashes on the screen.

Cam clicks on the file again and it pops up. It's an email. There's no subject header. Just an attachment and one line written inside.

"What does that say?" Luke says and I lean in closer.

"*Dame lo que siempre he querido, y esto termina.*" I read it out loud.

"What does that translate to?" Luke asks, glancing back at me.

"Give me what I've always wanted and this ends," I say.

"What the hell does that mean?" Anusha asks, her fingertips running across the tiny words on the screen, as if human touch will unlock some kind of clue.

"I don't know," I answer, shaking my head. "Click on the attachment. Maybe that will tell us."

Cam clicks on the file and as the photo fills the screen, the room begins to spin, our collective breaths wrenched from our bodies.

"Oh my God," Anusha screams and even though I'm staring at the same image, I can't fully see it. It's like the horrific picture in front of me is still stuck in the cones of my eyes and hasn't registered in my brain. I shake my head, clearing it because that photo can't be real. I blink hard, expecting it to be gone the moment I open up my eyes, but it's still there in all its gory horror.

Michael's piercing blue eyes stare back at me from the computer screen, blank and clouding with death. His throat has been cut, his red tissue spilling from the thick line of a calculated strike. Blood pours down his skin, disappearing against the black of his collar.

"No," I whisper, tears ascending up my throat as my heart struggles to fully beat. "No, no, no, no! Not again. Not Michael."

My voice rises to a near scream and Luke wraps my raging body up in his arms, softly covering my mouth with his hand.

"Reagan, shhhh . . ." he whispers quietly in my ear. "You can't scream. We can't let the guards know we're in here. You have to calm down. Okay?"

I nod slightly in agreement, struggling to breathe into Luke's palm, trying frantically not to scream or throw up or crumple on the ground. Luke gently removes his fingers from my lips as Anusha and Cam hang their heads, casting their eyes away from the image on the screen.

"Get it off, get it off," I command and run away from the violent photograph. "Jesus Christ, help me. I knew they never should have sent that small of a team out. I was terrified something like this was going to happen. This is what happens when you follow protocols instead of listening to your gut."

"I can't believe it," Anusha interjects quietly, shaking her head. "I can't believe he's gone."

Not Michael. Not Michael. The words thread between the slimy coils of my brain.

He's been with us all since the beginning of Qualifiers. He's trained us, supported us, torn us down, built us back up. Everyone loves Michael. The trainees will be devastated. If they even tell us at all. Knowing the Black Angels, they'll make him disappear on some overseas assignment and never bring him up again. He'll be just like all the other silent heroes. Another black star on the white marble wall outside the intel center, no name, no label. Just a placeholder to be added to the body count this year.

"What do we do now?" Cam asks quietly from his seat at the computer.

"Well, what are they doing?" I counter, immediately turning my anguish into action to stop myself from falling apart. "They have to be sending another team after him, right?"

Cam taps at the computer, digging into the latest files. "Doesn't look like it," he answers. "Says the team down here is compromised and too small to send out."

"But what about all of us trainees?" I ask, holding my hands out. "Half our group is down here. That's an extra nine bodies who know how to shoot in addition to whatever guards and operatives they have left."

"I doubt they'll take the risk," Cam says, pointing at the computer screen. "This is a memo from Director Browning. Feels pretty final to me."

"They're going to let him get away again," I say softly as I return to my pacing, forcing motion just to stay upright. "If another team doesn't go right now, we're going to be having this exact same conversation again but with a different Black Angel dead next time.

He's right here on this island. He's so close. We can't just let him jet back to one of his mansions in South America."

The thought of Torres sitting on his private jet, sipping on Scotch and flying back home, causes the ember to flare, its black smoke spreading, filling every inch of my body with its poison. I dig my fingernails deep into the flesh of my hips until all I feel is heat and pain. I close my eyes, and even though I don't want to see her face, I do. Bloodied, swollen, and scared. A gun pressed to her temple, Torres's finger on the trigger.

Every vital organ within me feels heavy, like tiny metallic particles are cutting into my flesh. I can almost taste blood on my tongue. I open my eyes and they're all frozen, staring at me.

"What did that line in the email say again?" I ask, trying to remember. "Give me what I've always wanted and this ends?"

"Yes," Anusha answers, looking back at the computer. "What does that mean?"

And then it hits me. The bile in my stomach churns, violently sloshing from side to side, curling my body forward and forcing me to grab at my knees.

"What, Reagan?" Cam asks, registering my sudden terror.

"I think he means me," I say, looking up from my hunched-over stance but staring past them, my eyes fixed on the cream cinder block walls behind my friends.

"What are you talking about?" Luke says, his voice on edge, ready for a protest.

"Give me what I've always wanted and this ends," I repeat again, my mind flipping through memories. The panic room in Philadelphia, the janitor in the school parking lot, the secret room in his house in Colombia, his brother bleeding, dying at my feet. "I was a target back when his hit man entered my house when I was sixteen years old. I was the original target when my parents were kidnapped. I'm the one he's been after all year. I killed his brother. My parents killed his son. I am what he's always wanted. I am why he won't stop."

This is my fault. It's always been my fault.

My fists clench in my hands, my fingernails cutting into my flesh, as I trap the scream in my throat. I tuck my mother and Cam's father and Michael and the other fallen Black Angels into the dark corner of my heart. I could not save them. But I will save whoever could be next. This ends now, and whether it's my life or his, it truly makes no difference to me. Because death is far better than living like this.

"Reagan, please don't," Luke says, his voice weary and fearful, as if he can hear my thoughts, as if he knows what's next.

"I cannot stand by and read the same story in that file or see more dead photos of the people we love," I answer, pointing toward the computer. "I'm rewriting this ending."

"No, Reagan," Luke says and in a flash, he's standing in front of me, his body blocking the doorway as I turn around to leave. "Don't do this. In a few months, you'll be in the training academy. You'll be assigned to a team. You'll gain security clearance. You can take care of Torres then."

"I don't even know if I'll make it to the academy, let alone the RT squad," I answer. "Sam already talked to me about how I'm not a team player and my spot could go to Lex in the end."

"And you think this is going to prove that you deserve to be on the RT squad?" Luke scoffs, still blocking my path.

"No, but this might be my only shot to end this, Luke," I answer, trying to push past him. "Don't you understand? I could have a desk job or get cut and that will get me nowhere near Torres. And if I actually become an agent, you think the Black Angels are just going to let me go rogue? Hell no, I'll be kicked out either way. I have to do this. I can't let him just get on a plane and escape when he's so close."

"Reagan, this is beyond stupid and dangerous," Luke says, grabbing me by the shoulders. "Michael is already dead. You're not going to get yourself kicked out, you're going to get yourself killed."

"Well, that's a risk I'm more than willing to take," I answer and turn back toward Cam. "Can you track him from your laptop? Feed me intel so I can find them?"

"I can," Cam affirms and looks down at the computer. "Grab your earpiece and some radio equipment. I'll grab mine and talk you through where they're heading next and how to get there."

"Reagan, I won't let you do this," Luke says, spitting his words and then turning his sharp tongue toward Cam. "Why are you encouraging her? This is practically suicide."

"Because I think she needs to do this," Cam answers, his dark eyes gleaming with the agony he tries to bury. "My father may still be breathing, but he'll never be the same. And if anyone can stop Torres, you know it's Reagan."

"Please, Luke," I say and gently touch his forearm. "I have to do this. I can't live like this anymore. I'd rather be dead. I know you don't want to see me go, but I'm doing this with or without you. So move."

Luke stares at me hard, his eyes angry and pleading. But I won't break. I won't change my mind, even for him. He finally lowers his head and moves out of my way. I turn back toward Cam. "I'm grabbing my guns and radio stuff. Anusha, get me keys to one of the Jeeps and figure out how to get me outside that gate without anyone noticing."

I turn on my heel, my bare foot squeaking against the polished concrete floor. My body moves swiftly, without me telling it where to go, what to do. In a matter of minutes, I've silently dressed in my gear, run to the weapons room for my Glock 22, M4 carbine, bulletproof vest, and earpiece and run back to the conference room to grab the keys. When I walk back in the room, I'm breathless. My body feels bloodless and numb. It takes me a few seconds to realize Luke is no longer there.

Anusha hands me a set of keys. "It's the black Jeep. The one closest to the end. It's nearly three a.m. so there are no guards at the back gate, just security cameras."

"I've already spliced in and frozen all the cameras," Cam says from his computer "So unless they're staring at the time stamp, the remaining guards will have no idea that you've gone out the back or pulled out the gate."

"Genius. How do I even get out?" I ask, adrenaline rushing through my body.

"Just tell me when you're at the gate," Cam answers, sitting back down at his computer. "I've got access to that stuff. I'll open the gate for you. Once you get out of the gate, take a left and start driving south. I'll get you more details as they come in."

"Okay, thanks, Cam," I say and begin to turn around but his hand on my forearm stops me.

"Reagan, before you go, I just have to say one thing," Cam says, his voice soft. "I know how badly you want to do this. And if you do, I'm one hundred percent behind you. But Luke may be right. Who knows how many guards Torres will have with him? Michael's been on the RT for decades and now he's dead. This really could be a suicide mission."

"I know," I answer, my voice struggling to escape my throat.

"And you still want to do this?"

"Yes," I say, a touch stronger this time. I look into Cam's eyes, holding his gaze. He studies me and then nods before letting me go. I gather in the pieces that make him Cam. The way he smiles at me, the right side of his mouth before the left. The way his eyes flutter, a steady flapping of blinks when he's nervous. The way his glasses are almost always smudged. I take him in and wonder if it's the last time I'll ever see him.

"Go get him, Reagan," Cam finally says, his voice hushed. Determined, but scared.

"Be safe," Anusha whispers, pulling my body in for a quick hug, her curls soft on my cheek.

"Thank you," I respond, holding the keys up in the air. But really, it's for everything. I couldn't do this without them. And they know it. I take in their faces once more before racing out the door. I take the next hallway and quietly push through the back exit door.

The thick air immediately burns my aching lungs. I cough into the crook of my arm, trying not to make a sound, and I'm surprised that when I pull back, my shirt isn't speckled with blood. I spot the black Jeep in the dark gravel parking space and run toward it. I unlock the door, throw my gear in the backseat, and just as I'm about to climb in the driver's side, I hear my name.

My body tenses. But then I hear it again. I swing around and see Luke rushing across the parking lot toward me, dressed in his gear, weapons in his hands.

"What are you doing?" I whisper loudly as he reaches me.

"I won't let you do this alone," Luke answers, shaking his head.

"But you said it yourself," I answer, grabbing at his shirtsleeve as he throws his gear in the backseat. "It's a suicide mission. I'm willing to risk my life. I'm not willing to let you risk yours."

"No way. I'm coming," Luke answers, walking around to the other side of the Jeep and climbing into the passenger's seat.

"Luke, go back," I reply, my voice forceful as I climb into my side of the car. "I will not let you do this. Get out of the car and go back inside."

"No," Luke responds firmly before lacing his fingers through my open hand. "Either we both go or you don't go at all. I will not leave you. I promised I'd always run after you. Remember?"

I nod my head. "I do."

"Well, then what are you waiting for?" he answers, letting go of my hand and settling back into his seat. "Let's go get Torres."

I stare at Luke for a moment, trying to find the words to change his mind, force him back into the compound. But I know him. He followed me to Colombia. He followed me out of that truck and into the barn. He followed me into Torres's house. He followed me into Qualifiers. He has followed me into danger every single time while I kicked and screamed and begged him to reconsider. There's nothing I can say to get him out of this car. So I turn the keys of the Jeep and the engine revs to life.

"Okay, Cam," Luke says into his earpiece as I put the Jeep into drive and pull toward the gate. "Let us out."

"On it," Cam answers and the heavy metal gate shakes before opening. "Glad you decided to join us, Luke."

"Me too," Luke answers and stares out into the black, Indonesian night.

I switch on my headlights and turn left, toward the south. And toward Torres.

THIRTY-TWO

"OKAY, GUYS, STAY ON THIS ROUTE," CAM SAYS IN MY ear as I drive down a lightless two-lane road somewhere in South Sumatra, Indonesia. "I finally got radio transmissions working so I can actually listen in on some of their conversations. It looks like one of Torres's SUVs is heading west toward a river town about ten miles from where you are."

"Why do you think they'll go there?" I ask, pressing the talk button on my earpiece.

"Because it's the only thing around for miles," Cam answers. "I'm following CORE's intel, and they suspect he'll stop to change vehicles at a warehouse in town."

"Do we know how many cars or people are involved in all this?" Luke asks next to me.

A beat-up pickup truck with only one headlight passes us in the other lane. I glance at the clock: 3:13 a.m. I wonder where they're going.

"CORE is tracking two SUVs," Cam answers. "One is about

twenty minutes behind the other. Pulled out of the same area near the prison."

"And you have no idea which car Torres is in?" I ask.

"Nope," Cam answers and I imagine him sucking on his bottom lip as he shakes his head. One of his twitches I've come to learn over our many months together. "Just keep heading southwest. I'm tracking everything I can think of. I'll feed you more info as soon as I have it."

"Copy. Thanks, Cam," I answer and grab the steering wheel with both hands. It's then I realize I can't really feel my fingertips. I can't feel my hands either. My body is moving, grabbing on to things. It's functioning, but I feel transparent. I bite my teeth down into my lip, welcoming the sharp sting, just to make sure I'm still alive.

After many miles of silence, I can feel Luke staring at me. But my eyes stay focused on the road in front of me, my mouth growing drier by the second. I wish I'd remembered water. A few seconds more, he's still staring.

"What?" I say without bothering to look over to his side of the car.

"You don't have to do this, you know," Luke finally says. "You don't have to kill him. You could apprehend him. Bring him back to the compound."

"Not a chance," I answer.

"You'd be a hero," Luke continues.

"I'd be a hero if I killed him too," I answer, shaking my dark hair over my shoulder.

"No you won't," Luke replies softly. "I mean, perhaps in some eyes, yes. But you'll be back to being a combative rule breaker again. This could very well mean the end for you."

"I don't care," I say. "I don't need to be someone's hero. In fact, I don't want to be someone's hero."

"You're that little girl's hero," Luke answers and my body seizes. "You could be a lot of people's heroes."

Tears rise to the base of my throat at the thought of Charlotte. The way she clung to me, crying so hard she could barely form a complete sentence. The overwhelming emotion of her parents when they saw their daughters alive. She is one of the reasons I wanted to become a Black Angel. But it all takes second place to Torres. Always has. And always will.

My head throbs as I try to swallow the tears, clawing their way up my raw throat, their threatening sting in my ragged eyes. "Look, if you didn't want to help me, you shouldn't have come," I say sharply, gripping the steering wheel so hard now, I fear my knuckles will break through my skin.

"I do want you help you," Luke replies. "I just want you to really think about this."

"I already have. For a god damn year I've been thinking about this, Luke."

"Look, I know this is what you want. But at least consider apprehending him," Luke says. "I've got handcuffs and zip ties in the back. You could take one of our most wanted men off the list. Continue with training. Become the Black Angel your mom wanted you to be."

I grip the steering wheel tighter, the tendons in my arm twisting until they throb. Since the moment Torres killed her, every mile

I've run, every bullet I've shot, every skill I've mastered has been for her. But I haven't stopped once to think about what *she* would want me to do. Would she want me to kill Torres? Or would she want me to arrest him? Bring him to justice. Confine him to an eight-by-eight-foot cell for the rest of his life.

Before I can answer Luke, the radio crackles in my ear and I ready myself for an update. "They were right. Their SUV is slowing down up ahead. Looks like they're stopping in the river town. I'll keep tracking them to see where they go. In about two miles, you guys are going to come up on an unmarked road on your right. Take it. That will take you into town. But hurry. We don't know how long they'll be there. Because after they switch cars, they'll head to an airport and be gone."

"On it," I answer, pressing my earpiece deeper into my ear.

My feet slam on the accelerator, pushing the SUV to over a hundred miles an hour, Luke's plea still floating in the air. But that ember burns, hotter and higher, until all I can smell is smoke.

THIRTY-THREE

"CAM, WE'RE PARKING TWO BLOCKS AWAY FROM THE warehouse," I say as I quietly roll the car up to an empty block, my headlights off for the last quarter mile. I put the car in park next to what looks like an abandoned apartment building. But the dirty tricycle on the sidewalk and the playpen on the front porch tell me no, people actually live here.

"Good, all signs point to them still being in the warehouse," Cam replies in our ears. "They entered two minutes and forty-seven seconds ago but they will not be there for long. You've got to move it, Reagan."

"Copy," I reply, leaving the keys in the ignition for what I hope will be a quick getaway. My lungs tighten at the thought of not making it back to the car. Or even worse, making it back here without Luke.

"Ready?" Luke says, reaching for his bulletproof vest in the backseat.

My right hand reaches out, grabbing his wrist before his hands can touch his vest. "Luke, stay here. I don't want you to come. Please. Stay in the car."

"No way," Luke says, shaking me free and grabbing his vest. He pulls it over his body, quickly tightening the Velcro straps. "I wouldn't let you go in alone in Colombia. I'm sure as hell not going to let you go in alone now."

"It's too dangerous," I reply, shaking my head. "Please. You could die. I'm not willing to risk that."

"Well, without me," Luke says, handing me my M4 carbine, "you *will* die. So either we go and do this together or we drive back to the compound right now. Your decision. What will it be?"

My veins expand with my racing blood, pellets of fear throbbing, as round and real as my red blood cells. We could just turn around. Make it back to the compound before anyone even knows we were gone. Resume training. Let the Black Angels take care of Torres. Live the life that was planned for me before I was even born.

My eyes tear away from Luke and look down the block at the lit warehouse where Torres may be changing clothes, changing cars, and getting away with another horrific set of murders. Two blocks away. The monster is only two blocks away. And I didn't come within two blocks of my mother and Michael's killer to turn around now.

"No," I say, my head firmly shaking from side to side as I turn my eyes back to Luke. "Let's go."

Luke slowly nods his head as he takes in a deep breath that matches the anxious rise of my own chest. Our eyes trace each other's faces, not blinking, not wanting to forget a single curve or hue, in case these are our last few minutes together alive.

I break our gaze first, popping open the door and leaving it ajar so as not to alert Torres or his guards to our presence. One slam of a car door in this sleeping town and their guns would be in their hands.

Luke and I silently run down the two blocks, keeping our bodies in the shadows and away from any post light (although in this desolate part of Indonesia, those are few and far between). The night air is dense, almost suffocating, but despite its temperature, it chills me all the same.

As we reach the warehouse, I signal for Luke to stop. Our heads pivot around the building, searching for a low window. Luke spots one first and points to the west side of the warehouse where light penetrates through a small window in a metal door. We push our bodies along the wall, clinging to the darkness, the coarse brick rubbing against our clothing. Fifty yards away, forty yards away, thirty yards away, twenty, ten, five. Once we're just feet away, I push my hand to the center of Luke's chest, stopping him from peering inside. If anyone should look and get caught, it's me.

My arms begin to tingle and the gun feels heavier in my hands by the second. I breathe in, trying to quell the shaking that I know will follow the tiny pinpricks to my skin. I take a step closer to the window, peering through its corner. And then I see him. Torres stands in the center of the warehouse, his clothing drenched in blood. I study him for a second more, just to be sure, but there's no mistaking that black hair with sparks of silver, that salt-and-pepper goatee. His strong jaw and dark, empty eyes.

My heartbeat pounds out distress signals like Morse code as I pull my body back to the safety of the shadows. "It's him," I whisper.

"Are you sure?" Luke whispers back.

"I'd know that face anywhere," I answer, my heart now pounding grotesquely against my sternum as his face in that dark basement comes back to me. Pistol in his hand, arm around my mother's throat. I shake my head, wiping the image away.

Focus. Focus. Focus.

"How many guards?" Luke asks.

"I counted four," I answer, stepping carefully to look back through the window. I quickly count them again, assessing the situation. I pull myself back. "Yes, four. They're all still in their bloody clothes but they are pulling bags out of another SUV. They're getting ready to change. We'll move in when they're getting undressed. Their weapons will be down. They'll be at their most vulnerable."

"Copy," Luke answers, slightly out of breath, adrenaline gripping his lungs. "Just wait a few before looking back."

"Got it," I answer, my eyes staring into the darkness. My pulse throbs anxious beats against my throat. *Swish. Swish. Swish.* The blood hisses in my ears. My calf muscles sting, my arms begin to twitch, and all I want to do is open that door, pepper the room with bullets and spray their blood on the walls. I lean my head back, the coarse brick pulling at strands of my hair. I take in another breath, trying to focus on something to calm me down. I close my eyes, trying to imagine something peaceful, a sunrise, an ocean. But all I see is my mother, her cream robe cinched around her waist the night before that final, failed mission. That moment comes back to me in slow motion. Mom looking up from the bed, a trace of sadness in her normally fierce green eyes I couldn't quite pinpoint at the time. Her smile, slight and fragile. I had never seen my mother look like that before. She was always strong, always a commanding presence, but in that moment she looked like someone who needed to be saved.

Mom, help me. Please help me, my mind whispers to her image. And then she's gone.

I open my eyes, stare back out into the black night, and start a silent countdown.

10, 9, 8, 7, 6, 5, 4, 3, 2, 1.

I creep closer to the door, my eyes peeking again through the corner of the small square window. This time, the bags are open, pants and shirts and underwear strewn over the hoods of the SUVs, their bloody clothing thrown into a heap on the floor.

I turn back to Luke and nod. He ducks below the window, out of sight from Torres and the guards, pointing to the door's handle.

Please be unlocked. Please be unlocked, my mind silently begs.

Luke puts his hand on the metal handle, pulling it down just far enough, and it gives. It's open.

His eyes spark as they lock with mine. He quietly releases it back into its fully closed position. I taste blood on my teeth and realize I've been biting down hard on my bottom lip. I wipe the blood off with my thumb and peer through the window. Their guns are all down as they stand in various states of undress. It's now or never.

I duck down below the window, standing next to Luke, my gun ready to fire. I know as soon as that door swings open, guns will be back in their hands, so I have no choice but to shoot to kill or in a matter of seconds, Luke and I will be dying in a pool of our own blood.

The gravity of the next sixty seconds of our lives hits me across my face. And I am numb.

I look up at Luke and nod. He holds up his hand and silently counts down. And with each finger that falls, my lungs collapse one centimeter at a time.

5, 4, 3, 2, 1.

Luke swings the door wide and I open fire.

Boom. Boom. Boom.

Three guards immediately drop to the floor with bullets through their skulls.

The last remaining and stunned guard lunges for his weapon on the floor, but I shoot him before he can even reach the shining metal.

Boom.

The power of the shot ricochets off my chest as it pierces the young guard's brain and he drops to the floor, his blood pooling and tarnishing the shine of his weapon that's just out of reach.

Torres stands in the middle of the warehouse, his boxers and white undershirt now speckled with elongated red splatter, the bodies of his guards losing blood and warmth by the second at his feet.

He stares at me, his stunned faced changing with the recognition of just who I am, why I've come. Torres's head slowly looks down at the ground, the guns of his fallen guards just feet away; his fingers quiver, eager to grab his last chance of protection.

"Don't even think about it, Torres," I hiss, my weapon pointed directly at his head. His dark eyes return to mine, a small smile tightening at the corners of his mouth, flipping my stomach inside out.

"Reagan Elizabeth Hillis," he says, his voice almost singsong, like I've just arrived for afternoon tea. "I've been looking for you. Must you always be pointing a weapon at my head every time we meet?"

"Hands up, Torres," I answer, my body moving closer to him, Luke and his weapon pointed at Torres just a few feet behind me. "Luke, keep your weapon on him."

I lower my gun and turn over the body of one of his guards, unbuckling his belt and yanking it from around his waist. I grab another belt that's been thrown on the ground and then point my M4 carbine back up at Torres. He stares at me, his hands weakly raised in the air.

"Let's go," I say, stepping closer to him and motioning toward the corner of the warehouse. Torres doesn't move, just stares at me, waiting for me to balk, to shake and lose my nerve like last time. I raise my weapon.

Boom.

I fire a shot just inches above his shoulder and scream, "I said let's go!"

Torres doesn't even flinch. Just raises his eyebrows. After another moment in our stare-down standoff, I ready my gun to shoot again, this time in his shoulder for real. Finally, his body moves, his rough and calloused feet scrape against the cement as he slowly drags himself across the warehouse to where a metal pipe runs from the floor to the ceiling. Once we reach the pipe, I yank on it, checking its stability.

"Stand here," I demand, pointing at the ground next to the pipe with my gun. Torres just stares at me, standing still. "I said move, Torres."

Finally, I push the barrel of my gun against his back and this time he moves closer to the pipe.

"You ever get déjà vu?" I ask, my voice gravelly, strained by fury, as I roughly loop Torres's hands together with the belt, then tie it tightly to the pipe. "You should be feeling some serious déjà vu right now. I know I am."

As I tie him tighter against the pipe, my forearm brushes against his hand, and even that minimal contact makes the acid in my stomach roil like a god damned ocean.

"Feet, too," I demand, breaking contact and pointing down at his bare feet.

Torres obeys, shuffling along the dirty cement floors until they are next to the pipe. I tie the second belt around his ankles before anchoring it to the rusting metal. I pull on the leather strap to make sure he's completely secure. It doesn't budge. When I stand up, Torres is full-out grinning at me.

"What are you smiling at, you fool?" I snap, pointing my gun back at his skull.

"Just how much you've learned," Torres says, sounding almost wistful. "A year ago, you were a trembling child. And now look at you. I've killed lesser agents. In fact, I killed two just today. You are not like them. You are smart and strong and quick and confident. Elizabeth would be proud of her handiwork."

"Take her name out of your mouth," I reply, my voice aching in my throat. "You don't deserve to say my mother's name out loud."

"I didn't want to kill her," Torres says, his dark eyes narrowing. "But you gave me no choice."

"Liar," I reply, steadying my weapon. "You were going to kill her anyway."

Torres stares at me, a sinister smile separating his lips. "Well, I guess you'll never know. Will you?"

His words pull at the center of my chest, where my lingering doubt has always been buried. Had I not come to Colombia, had I not entered that house, would my mother still be alive?

"Reagan, let's call for backup," Luke's voice says calmly behind me. "Let's take him into custody. Bring him to justice."

"No," I answer firmly over my shoulder, then turn back to Torres. "He doesn't deserve the luxury of three meals a day and a warm bed in federal prison. Visits. Yard time. Ramen noodles from the commissary. What kind of justice is that?"

"Reagan, I think you should really . . ." Luke continues to push but I cut him off.

"I said no!" I yell curtly without bothering to look back at Luke.

"You know, you remind me of myself, Reagan," Torres says, his accent thinned from years in the United States; years with the Black Angels. "When I was an agent, I was the best. But I was a rule breaker too. Always getting into trouble. But always for good reasons."

"I am *nothing* like you," I reply, that ember burning hot and high. I'm shocked that when I speak, fire doesn't leap off of my tongue. "I could never spend years with the Black Angels, fight alongside them, save their lives only to turn around and stab them in their backs."

"You think you know me, don't you?" Torres says, shaking his head. "But you don't know the half of it. You don't know everything about your beloved Black Angels. There cannot be good without evil."

Stop, stop, stop, my mind screams as his words rattle against my brain, poisoning my willpower, my clarity. I roll back my shoulders, standing up straighter, not ready to fall for his line of bullshit.

"You're just trying to get inside my head so I'll lower my weapon," I continue. "Let you go free. How stupid do you think I am?"

"Not stupid at all," Torres says, shaking his head. "In fact, I think you're smart enough to know that even if I'm dead, this will not end."

Pins prick at the back of my spine and it takes all the strength I have to suppress a shiver lingering below my skin's surface.

"You will always be a target," Torres continues. "The people you love will always be in danger. Because of you."

Because of you, my brain repeats. *It's your fault. It's always your fault.*

I shake my head, clearing the taunt in my mind, and press my lips hard between my teeth until they ache.

"Save your breath, Torres," I finally say, my weapon still pointed at the center of his face. "You can't manipulate your way out of this. Your mind games don't work on me."

"Tell me something," Torres says, almost in a whisper. "Does Cameron Conley know I have the power to cripple him the way I crippled his father?"

A foul smile spreads across Torres's face as shock registers on my own. I feel my eyes expanding from their narrowed slits, my jaw slack and dropping out of its scowl.

"Does Anusha know she was much safer flying her little airplanes? That she wasn't at risk until she got involved with you?"

My hands begin to tremble, my finger just centimeters away from the curved trigger of my M4 carbine, my mind resisting the itch to pull it.

How does he know this? How does he know their names?

"Sam Levick. Your father. Harper," Torres says, his voice punchy, every syllable deliberate as he delivers his final blow. My best friend's name on his tongue physically knocks me back and I have to stop my knees from buckling. "No one is safe. Especially if you kill me."

Torres's dark eyes scan my body and penetrate my skin, their chill stealing what little breath I have left in my chest.

"How do you know Harper?" I finally whisper. Sam, my father, even the trainees he could have figured out. But Harper?

"I know everything," Torres whispers back, his eyebrows rising almost as punctuation, an exclamation point at the end of his cryptic declaration. "You don't even know where she is. But I do."

My throat clenches and I try to swallow the piercing lump wedged in my throat as I imagine Harper walking across Washington Square Park on her way back to her dorm at NYU. Her books in her hand, the wind whipping her wavy hair off her face, a man fifteen paces behind, watching her every move.

"The headline practically writes itself, doesn't it?" Torres says with a sickening glint in his eye. "Poor little midwestern girl moves to the big city only to be raped and murdered outside her dorm."

I turn my gun around, striking Torres across the face with the hard, wide handle. His lip splits open, blood dripping down his chin.

"*Jesucristo*," Torres cries out, his face recoiling in pain. He instinctively pulls his hands toward his lips, trying to comfort himself, but the leather strap pulls his arms back into place.

"Don't you touch her!" I scream, pointing my gun back at his face.

"I will do what I please," Torres responds, blood spitting from his mouth with every word.

"He's lying, Reagan," Luke says behind me. "Don't let him get in your head. He has no idea where she is."

"Oh yeah?" Torres counters, glancing at Luke before turning back toward me with a slow smile, blood smeared across his white teeth. "She should have thought twice about those evening film classes. The dark streets of Lower Manhattan aren't safe for a beautiful blond like Harper."

With that, I point my gun at Torres's kneecap and squeeze the trigger.

Boom.

Torres's knees buckle and he screams in pain. His wrists pull violently against the metal pipe, the belt scraping but not budging.

"I don't believe you!" I scream over his groans. "You are a liar and a manipulator and a traitor. You'll say anything to get your way."

"Believe this," Torres cries out in pain, his head slumping as he looks at me through the slits of his distressed eyes. "Your family destroyed my life. Your parents killed my son. You killed my brother. So I will destroy you, Reagan Hillis."

"I won't let you hurt them," I yell over his grunts. "This ends now."

My finger is wrapped around the trigger, ready to fire the final shot.

"Reagan, stop . . ." Luke protests from behind me but I drown him out.

"You think you can protect them?" Torres squeezes the words out as he gasps for air, his body failing him. "You obliterate everything you touch. You think you're helping but all you do is hurt. It won't matter if I'm dead or alive. You can't save them. You couldn't even save your own mother. You killed her by coming to Colombia. By coming into my home. You might as well have pulled the trigger yourself."

"No, no, no!" I shriek, shaking my head, and everything around me begins to blur; the gray walls of the warehouse, the blood, Torres's wincing, excruciating face. I feel like I'm about to spin into blackness, disappear through a hole, swallowed to the center of the earth.

Suddenly, the warehouse falls silent. Torres's lips are moving, but I don't hear his words. All I hear is my shaking breath, my heart pounding in my ears, shouting its commands.

Do it. Do it. Do it.

I point my gun at Torres, close my eyes, and scream. I can feel my finger squeezing the trigger, knocking me back.

My screaming ceases, the bullet's shattering echo disappears. When I open my eyes, Torres's body slumps to the floor, a bullet at his left temple, blood running down his cheek.

Blazing red. His blood is brighter than any blood I've ever seen. Just as I imagined it. I shake my head, wondering if I'm trapped inside one of my vengeful daydreams. I bite down hard on my lip, taste my own blood, and know that this time, it's very real.

"Oh my God," Luke says from behind me, his voice a reedy whisper. "Reagan, what have you done?"

THIRTY-FOUR

REAGAN. REAGAN. REAGAN.

I hear my name being called out, but it sounds hollow and far away. Like someone trying to wake me out of a nightmare. The warehouse, its walls, its floors, the dead guards on the floor start to lose their color and fade. The only thing I see is Torres, with a bullet in his brain and bright blood dripping off of his chin, hitting the dirty concrete floor like a tiny drumbeat.

Drip. Drip. Drip.

"Reagan, we've got to go." Luke's voice is panicked as he grabs me by the arm, pulling me away from Torres.

"You guys have got to get the hell out of there." Cam's voice intensifies in my ear. "Torres's second team knows something is going on. They'll be there any minute."

"Shit," Luke answers, still pulling at me, practically dragging my feet across the warehouse floor. "Reagan, what is wrong with you? Let's go."

"I want to make sure he's dead," I say, pulling back toward

Torres, wanting to feel for a pulse, make sure the bastard is really gone.

"Reagan, no!" Luke barks. "He's dead. We've got to go now or we'll be dead too. Come on." He grips my arm tighter, pulling me away from Torres's body, past the dead guards and finally, the spell is broken. The sounds and smells and colors inside the warehouse come back to me and I begin running toward the door, away from the scent of death.

"Cam, they're all dead," I say into my earpiece as we run out the warehouse door and toward our waiting SUV two blocks away. "Where do we go now? Do we come back to the compound?"

"Absolutely not," Cam answers. "They'll find you here. And then we'll all be in danger. You guys have to get out of the country!"

"What? Out of the country?" I say as we reach the waiting Jeep.

"Yes, go back toward that same route and keep driving south," Cam says, his voice almost breathless on the other end. "The Black Angel plane is still at the private airport. Look. I have to tell CORE what's going on."

"No, don't you dare," I reply as I turn the car on and slam the gearshift into drive.

"Reagan, I have to," Cam answers, his voice firm. "Torres's second team could look at the security cameras in the warehouse or on their vehicles and know it was the two of you. Do you even know who you're dealing with? If we don't get you off this island right now, you'll be dead before sunrise. I *have* to tell them."

"Shit," I answer and slam the steering wheel with my left hand as I turn the car back onto a desolate stretch of highway that leads toward one of Sumatra's largest towns. "Okay, do it."

As we pull away from the infrequent, dim lights of the river town, we're swallowed back into darkness. I push my foot against the gas pedal, picking up speed, racing toward so many unknowns. My eyes glance sideways at Luke. He sits, stone-faced, his jaw tight and eyes staring straight ahead, his hands wrapped around the gun on his lap.

"I didn't have a choice, Luke," I say, my voice more forceful than I meant for it to be. I want him to look at me. But when I glance at him again, he's still staring straight ahead.

"There's always a choice, Reagan," he finally replies, his voice strained, like he's trying to control an underlying fury. "There's always another way. But your mind was made up over a year ago. There's nothing anyone could have done to change it . . . to change you."

We drive in silence for the next mile and a half. With one bullet, I've shattered my life forever. But as I look over at Luke, I realize I've shattered his too. Despite his pleading. And without his permission.

"Are you angry with me?" I ask, my voice wobbly, struggling to get out each syllable.

"I don't know what I am right now," Luke says with a long, low breath. "All I know is I'm not nearly as angry as the other voice that will soon be in our heads."

I glance over as Luke points to his earpiece. And he's absolutely right. Not more than thirty seconds later, I hear the voice of my father.

"Reagan Elizabeth Hillis," his voice booms into my ear. "What the hell were you thinking?"

"I was thinking about killing the man who destroyed our family," I answer back, trying to find some defiance, but afraid I sound more like a willful teenager being berated for sneaking out after curfew.

"We were on him!" my father screams. "We were monitoring the situation back here."

"Nothing was happening! He's killed or injured at least half a dozen Black Angels all because he wanted me," I answer, gripping the steering wheel. "I had to go after him, Dad. Even if it meant I died, maybe then the violence would have ended. I couldn't let him target any more Black Angels. I couldn't live with myself if someone else ended up dead."

I leave out the fact that Torres somehow knew the names of everyone in my life who mattered. His promise to destroy us all, even after he was gone.

He was lying. He was lying. He was lying.

I rock my body back and forth in my seat as my mind whispers these words over and over again. But they do little to untie the noose wrapped around my chest. Because what if his threat wasn't the last desperate manipulation of a psychopath? What if every word he said was true?

"There are procedures for a reason, Reagan." My father's voice soars in my ears. "Now you've got one of the most dangerous men on the planet heading right for you."

"Reagan, listen to me for a second." Sam's voice comes through my earpiece and I can almost see her pushing my father away from the microphone. "Torres's brother and second in command, Fernando, was in that second car. I'm sure all they did was take a quick look at the security cameras on their vehicles to find out it was you and Luke. We have the pilot up and at the airport now. He's fueling the plane and will be ready to go when you get there. The airport is still ten miles away. You better speed up or you're not going to make it. Fernando will find a way to catch up with you."

"I can do it," I answer and step on the gas, watching the needle rise from 100 miles per hour to 125 miles per hour.

"Okay, good," Sam answers, her voice calming my rattling nerves. "Now, do you remember where the airport is?"

"Yes, it's down that hidden dirt road on the right-hand side," I answer as I dig through my memory. "Right after the billboard for some type of beer. Bali Hai, I think."

"That's right," Sam says into my ear.

"Sam, where are we going?" I ask, pushing the earpiece farther into my ear. "Once we get on the plane, where are we going?"

My question is answered with a few seconds of silence. I assume Sam is checking with the rest of CORE before relaying the information to me. "I can't tell you that, Reagan," she finally says after several beats. "We just need to get you guys out of the country. Get you somewhere safe."

"When can we come back home?" I ask, my voice squeaking on the very last word.

Several more seconds of silence follows and I can feel Luke's body tense next to me. "I don't know," she finally answers, her voice soft. "I don't know when you can come back."

Out of my peripheral vision, I can see Luke's head fall, hit by the reality of what's being taken away from him. What I've single-handedly done to him.

That ember that flamed at my stomach is gone. Snuffed out, just like I knew it would be, the moment I saw the blood fall from the hole in Torres's skull. But what's replaced it is something far worse. A bubbling acid ripples against my aching stomach lining, causing sores and rips and tears; a toxic mixture of guilt and fear and something I didn't expect: remorse. Sam was right. My body feels like it's been burned from the inside out. I move my tongue around the inside of my mouth, expecting it to be filled with ash.

"I'm sorry, Sam," I say weakly, even though I'm not quite sure she hears me. But a moment later, she sighs on the other end. And I know what she's thinking.

I warned you.

"There's no time for apologies," she finally answers. "Just get to that airport, Reagan. We're monitoring you both on the satellites and Fernando is gaining on you. You've got to go faster."

I push the pedal to the floor, racing toward the shadow of Sumatra's volcanic mountains, the car shaking against the uneven pavement of the highway. I stare down at my speed and watch the needle push from 125 to 140 miles per hour.

The car hits a big bump and I pray our tire doesn't go flat. Luke grabs at the armrests to steady himself. But the wheels keep turning, moving closer to the airport.

"Hang on, Luke," I reply as his hands settle back to the gun on his lap. His body turns around in his seat, his eyes searching out the back window for Fernando's headlights.

"How far are they now, Sam?" he says into his earpiece.

"They're still gaining," she replies, her voice heavy back in DC. I hear the *click, click, click* of her biting her thumbnail as she checks the satellites. "They are less than a mile from you now."

"Shit," I say, staring down at my speed. "I don't think I can go much faster. How far away are we?"

"Two miles," Sam answers. "Just keep it steady. You're almost there."

"Make sure that pilot is ready to take off the second we get there," I say, my voice rising as I push the accelerator down as far as it will go.

"He knows," Sam answers and I can hear her typing on the other end. "He's fueled up. He's sitting on the runway. The second you guys get on, he'll take off."

"Okay," I say, taking in a shaky breath as we zip past a lone big-wheeled truck, probably carrying his load to the next, tiny populated town. The car is flying down the highway, but everything around me seems to be happening in slow motion. My movements, my breaths, Luke turning around to watch for Fernando out our back window. It's like I'm outside my body, watching this all happen to someone else.

"I think I see them," Luke says and I look up in my rearview mirror to see two tiny headlights, like pinpricks against the black, in the distance.

"Yeah, that's them," Sam answers. "They're just over half a mile behind now. But you're almost there. Turn coming up, Reagan. Do. Not. Miss. It."

"Copy," I say, my eyes spotting the billboard in the distance. Just to the right of the billboard, the faint lights of the tiny private airport.

My foot pushes down on the accelerator as we race closer to

our waiting plane, our only escape from certain kidnapping, torture, and death.

"You've got this, Reagan," Luke says quietly next to me, anxiety and adrenaline causing both of his knees to bounce.

I ease up for a moment on the accelerator as we approach the turn, scared I'll tip the Jeep over and kill us both. The tires squeal against the road as I make a wild, right turn onto the dirt-covered, rocky street of the airport. The gravel goes flying beneath our tires and a cloud of dust surrounds our Jeep as I race down the bumpy road.

"We're here," I say, scanning the airport for the plane. "I don't see the plane."

"It's at the other end of the runway," Sam answers.

"Damn it," I spit and look into my rearview mirror for Fernando. "They'll try to cut us off on the runway."

"We didn't exactly have much time to fuel up and get out of here," Sam yells back. "Just get to the plane."

I turn left onto the runway and hit the gas, reaching almost 150 miles per hour as I race toward our waiting plane.

We pull the Jeep beside the plane and jump out. Just as my feet hit the pavement, I see headlights pulling off the highway.

"Shit," I say and race up the plane's steps with Luke right on my heels.

"Go, go, go!" Luke screams at the pilot as he pulls up the private plane's steps, locking them into place. "They're right behind us."

The pilot pulls down on the throttle and the wheels begin to move, picking up speed with every passing second. Luke and I lean down, looking out the pilot's window, silently hoping the sight of our plane in motion will slow down Fernando and his team. But it doesn't.

Luke grabs on to my arm as the SUV races down the bumpy road then turns onto the runway. Just as I feared.

"They're going to try to cut us off," I scream at the pilot. "We've got to get airborne."

"I'm trying," he yells back, pulling down harder on the throttle, the plane racing down the runway as the headlights head directly for us.

"Oh my god," Luke whispers next to me as both the plane and SUV race toward each other in a deadly game of chicken.

Fifty yards away. Forty yards away. Thirty yards away.

I grab on to Luke's arm, my mind begging, pleading, screaming. *Please God. Please God. Please God.*

"Oh god," I whisper, my grip tightening. "They're gonna hit us. They're gonna kill us."

When we are fifteen yards away from the SUV, I feel the nose of the plane point toward the air and lift off. A second more and we're completely off the ground. Luke and I fall backward and grab on to the seats behind us. We strap ourselves in and I look out the oval plane window in time to see the SUV stopped on the runway, a group of men illuminated by twin beams of light. They point up to the sky, shouting, and I can only imagine the irate words on their lips, the promise of revenge.

EPILOGUE

LUKE STIRS IN THE SEAT ACROSS FROM ME. HIS EYES
are closed but he's not asleep. His breaths are too deep and angry.
Too far under his conscious control. He's avoiding me. But I'll take it.
I don't know what to say. How to apologize for ruining his life. Making him a wanted man. Putting a price on his head.

The pilot still won't tell us where we're going. Just that we're
being taken to a safe house somewhere outside of Indonesia.
We've been crossing a dark ocean for an hour, so I can only assume
we're heading west. Toward Europe, perhaps? Africa, maybe? Russia?
Either way, we're not going home. And at this point, I don't know if
we'll ever go home.

I trace the lines of Luke's face in the dim light and bite down
hard on my lip as the corners of my eyes sting with tears. What have
I done to him? He was months away from making the training academy. Months away from fulfilling a lifelong dream of serving his
country, helping others. And I stole that from him. I stole him from

his family and friends. With one bullet, I took away several lives. Torres's. Luke's. My own.

My fingers dig deep into my hip bones until the tears retreat. I don't deserve to cry. I don't deserve to cleanse myself in any way. I will always be dirty. There's no amount of tears, no amount of holy water that can take away my sins. I've killed others. But that was because I had to. They were trying to kill me. Kill or be killed. But Torres. I dreamed about it. I planned it. For over a year. I stare down at my hands, hold them up to my face. Torres's blood freckles my skin. A shiver runs through my body as I realize these are no longer the hands of a Black Angel. They're the hands of a cold-blooded killer.

I choke down the bile rising up my throat, shove my blood-covered hands under my legs, and press my forehead against the plane window. The sun is rising from a black, bottomless ocean, its light reaching out for me, like a long, accusing finger.

What have you done, Reagan? What will you do?

ACKNOWLEDGMENTS

TO JEAN FEIWEL, KAT BRZOZOWSKI, LAUREN SCOBELL, Kelsey Marrujo, Ashley Woodfolk, Brittany Pearlman, Emily Settle, Holly West, Rich Deas, Starr Baer, Raymond Colón, and the entire rock-star team at Macmillan: You've changed my life. My love and gratitude for all of you is boundless. Thank you, thank you, thank you. I am one lucky author.

To Merrilee Heifetz: I couldn't ask for a more encouraging, compassionate, and loving person to call my agent. I won the lottery with you. To Allie Levick: I will always be grateful. Thank you for believing in my writing and all the stories I want to tell.

To the amazing authors I'm now lucky enough to call friends: I'm so happy to have you on this journey with me. Thank you for the constant love and support. To Kayla Olson: Thank you so much for your friendship and for the daily motivation with this book. To Sara Shepard: Thank you for your kindness, words of wisdom, and guidance.

To my friends: I'm so fortunate to have such special people in my life. Whether you were at signings, sending me enthusiastic messages, or helping me patch plot holes, your endless encouragement means the world.

To my readers: It's a total dream come true to create stories for you. The privilege to write books you want to read is not lost on me. I'm so grateful for each and every one of you.

To my family: You guys are my biggest cheerleaders. I feel your love and pride in everything I do. Thank you for shaping me into the person I am today.

To Samantha Rose: Sweet girl, you make me so happy. Your smile is the best part of my day. I love you so much.

To Michael: Thank you for being the most supportive husband a girl could ever ask for. There's no one I'd rather have by my side in life than you. You have given me everything and I'm so grateful. My love for you has no end.

Check out more books chosen for publication by readers like you.

DID YOU KNOW...

READER **Swoon READS** APPROVED

this book was picked by readers like you?

Join our book-obsessed community and help us discover awesome new writing talent.

1

Write it.
Share your original YA manuscript.

2

Read it.
Discover bright new bookish talent.

3

Share it.
Discuss, rate, and share your faves.

4

Love it.
Help us publish the books you love.

Share your own manuscript or dive between the pages at **swoonreads.com**